# COSEGA SWITCH

## BRANDT LEGG

LAUGHING RAIN

**Cosega Switch** (Book Eight of the Cosega Sequence)

Published in the United States of America by Laughing Rain

Cataloging-in-Publication data for this book is available from
the Library of Congress.
ISBN-13: 978-1-935070-84-9
ISBN-10: 1-935070-84-3

Cover design by Eleni Karoumpali

PUBLISHER'S NOTE
This book is a work of fiction. Names, characters, places and
incidents are products of the author's imagination or are used
fictitiously. Any resemblance to actual persons, living or dead,
businesses, events or locales is entirely coincidental.

BrandtLegg.com

*As always, this book is dedicated to*
*Teakki and Ro*

# ONE

*Cosegan Time - Trynn's Eysen Lab Barge, open ocean, parts unknown.*

The Switch gleamed gold, its slender toggle handle, nearly a foot long, bathed in swirling photons, giving it the appearance of the mystical sword in the stone, glowing in an eerie, fantastical mist. The shimmering light around the Switch constantly shifted from violet to amethyst, azure to cobalt blue, with frequent electric pulses of yellow and green, as if one should be afraid to touch it, to even be near it.

"There should be no doubt the Switch is indeed fraught with danger," Trynn had said once to his daughter, Mairis. "It is the most threatening apparatus devised by man."

Trynn, the famous Eysen maker, had been the man who'd constructed it. Few knew of its existence. Mairis, Shanoah, Nassar, Cardd, and Anjee were the only living people other than himself with any awareness of the device, and that came simply because it could not be hidden from them. Yet none of them knew how to operate it, when to push the lever, what the full consequences of such an action would be, and if it might alter eternity.

Pushing it, thereby flipping the Switch, would instantly set all humanity onto its *proper* course, but as a result, much more would happen. As Trynn often said, *The Switch will do so many good and awful things.*

His floating lab and home these past months found itself in heavy seas. As the barge rose and fell with the swells, Trynn stood on deck, watching the stormy skies. His short, dark hair, close beard, and smooth, tanned skin gave him the look of a hard-working young sailor on the Mediterranean. The Cosegans' youthful appearance belied their great wisdom and experience. Staring out to sea, his exceptional mind considered the Switch, easily *the most* precious piece of equipment onboard a vessel that contained countless precious items: Eysens and Odeons, projected views captured and stored, digital blueprints for weapons, a vast array of fascinating marvels, engineering devices, and thousands of varied plans for bending and manipulating light, touching the universe, altering time, and tools for prying into existence itself. Yet it was the Switch that captured and dominated his mind.

*I must teach Mairis how to operate the Switch,* he thought, knowing there was a decent chance he would be dead when it needed to be pushed, and hoping his daughter would still be alive when the time came.

His thoughts drifted to Shanoah, the way they always did when he thought of pressing the Switch. Her stunning beauty took his breath even in memory; her brown hair, so dark it could be black, cut short and whimsical, as if to only frame a flawless face, and those eyes, an undefinable color between blue and green. *They change with the light, with the passion and power of any given moment.* Yet, more than anything, it was her splendid mind that drew him to her most.

*I must find a way to get Shanoah safely home before the Switch is pushed, otherwise she will be trapped in the Far Future forever.*

A distant clap of thunder sounded above the noisy, churning ocean.

*A bad omen,* he thought, if he believed in such things. He didn't, really, but so many of the Etherens he knew did, so a mental note was made, the warning heeded.

*Saving the world is more difficult than one might imagine.*

---

"We are closer," Nassar said, finding Trynn later in the Room of a Million Futures. His apprentice's statement could have been taken several ways; in referring to the barge's ultimate destination, or in timing for pressing the Switch. Because Nassar did not know where the barge would end up, and sometimes wondered if Trynn even knew, since they were no longer welcome in any port controlled by the two great powers, the Cosegans and the Havloses, and were, in fact, being actively hunted by both, he most probably meant the Switch.

"We seek Finality," Trynn said defiantly, clearly knowing what Nassar meant.

"Is that even possible?" Nassar asked, watching the endless stream of changing Far Future views. "Can this ever be perfect?"

"Perfection is not the goal."

"Then what is?" he asked, his surprise evident in his tone, a pinched expression on his face.

"Something closer to normalcy. A kind of correctness."

"What does that look like?"

Trynn shook his head. "I'll know it when I see it."

"But it's close?"

"Dangerously close."

"Can we stay afloat long enough to get there? It's amazing they haven't found us yet."

"We won't have to, we're going to Solas."

"What? In the middle of a war, you want to go to the capitol city of Cosega, where you are wanted for the murder of almost four million Cosegans?"

"Maybe."

"*Maybe?*" Nassar echoed, staring at Trynn, who was staring into a scattering of futures. "It sounds like suicide to me."

"It can't be helped."

"Why?" Nassar tried to see what future Trynn was looking at, as if it might contain an answer to this crazy plan. "Why would you need to go to Solas?"

Trynn turned and met his eyes. "I'm going to Solas to die."

# TWO

Welhey checked his seat belt for the third time. His normally jovial and persistent smile was unusually absent. He'd been nervous all along, having never flown on anything other than a goeze, and the noisy analog Havlos plane vibrated so much, it seemed impossible that such a mechanical contraption could even fly. He cursed the ban he had renewed several years earlier, as a high Cosegan official and Circle member, which prohibited selling the goeze flying technology to Havloses, which left them with only a limited number of goeze vehicles that were much more basic in design and features than what Cosegans used.

"Don't worry," Mudd, a former Havlos scrounger, said. "I've been on hundreds of these planes. They always land safely. Well, most of the time." He paused, realizing his assurances might not be helping. "It's definitely the safest way to travel." He paused again. "You know, not counting a Cosegan goeze." Another pause. "We'll be fine."

"Unless Jarvo shoots us down," Julae said. As an Etheren and former GlobeRunner, she understood the risks perhaps best of all. She glanced out the window, as if looking for incoming missiles, suspicious that they were the only three passengers on the large plane, a military jet about the size of a Far Future 737. Her robin's egg blue eyes held an electric intensity found in many Etherens. They missed nothing.

"If that was the game, we'd already be a debris field on the ground." Mudd had figured the plane was also carrying supplies for some front-line troops, and that the three of them were simply a way to guarantee the flight went unmolested.

"Can we just think positively?" Welhey said, his trademark smile still absent. The former Circle member couldn't help dwelling on the fact that they were flying through a war zone, that it didn't need to be Jarvo who shot them down, it could be some hotshot Havlos commander with something to prove, it could be the Red Guardians, or any number of other furious scenarios that occur during a world war.

"Besides, this pilot has probably been flying for *decades*. Did you see how old he looks?" Mudd said. "And most Havlos pilots have extensive military experience—bombing missions, supply runs, this guy may have even been in real combat with other planes before."

"Dog fights," Welhey said, not feeling any better.

"What?" Mudd asked. His dirty, almost greasy hair could have been the reason for his name, but it might have been his muddy complexion, or more likely the puddled brown color of his eyes.

"That's what plane battles are called in the Far Future, where the people seem to have inherited the Havlos' lust for fighting amongst themselves."

"Dogs can't fly," Mudd said, brow scrunching. "Makes no sense."

"Neither does killing your neighbors."

"Do you think Trynn got out?" Julae asked, hoping to change the subject.

Welhey nodded. "Trynn's too smart for any of this."

"That's for sure," Julae agreed, thinking she had a soft spot for Welhey because his short, dark beard and olive skin made him look as if he could have been Trynn's brother, only with shaggier hair. "No one's smarter than Trynn."

Mudd wasn't going to argue. He wanted to believe Trynn was still a free man because that meant a high probability of Mairis being safe. "But what did he give up for our freedom?"

"It might have been the Arc who made a deal," Welhey ventured. "We were in Havlos at her behest."

"What if Jarvo traded us to Shank?" Julae asked, thinking of the brutal dictator who now ruled the Cosegans. "From one nightmare to another."

"Why would Shank want us?" Mudd asked, not nearly as familiar with the current Cosegan leader as the two of them were.

"Shank hates one thing on earth more than anything else," Welhey said. "Trynn."

"Oh," Mudd said, sounding discouraged. "We'd be leverage."

"Or bait," Julae said, tying her brown hair back in a ponytail.

"Trynn would never give himself up for us," Welhey said. "Not because he's selfish, but because Trynn is painfully aware that he's the best chance we have to save all of humanity."

"I'm willing to be sacrificed," Julae said. "If it comes down to Trynn or us, I want him to live, to finish his work, to stop the Doom."

Mudd thought of Mairis. "It'll never come to that. Like you said, Trynn's too smart." He leaned forward and looked up the long aisles to the cockpit. The door was closed. "Besides, it's very possible that it *was* the Arc, and we're heading to freedom in Cosega."

"Yes, let's think positively," Welhey said again, but he couldn't help but focus on the fact that even though the Arc still had some connections, the last he knew, she was hiding in the woods, in no position to negotiate a prisoner exchange.

"Where do you think Abstract is?" Mudd asked.

"I'd like to think he's safe," Welhey said. They had all been working together to incite a revolution against Jarvo from within his own population.

"Hopefully he's still spreading the word, growing the League," Julae added. The League, made up of mostly young people from across the seven Havlos sections, was an illegal organization trying to force change, stop the war, and form an alliance with Cosega. They sought enlightenment, and wished to benefit from Cosegan technology and their vast knowledge. The League ultimately believed the only way to achieve their goals was to start a revolution.

"He could have been caught," Mudd said. "Any time since we were captured. He may have already been executed." Mudd's voice broke a little when he said it. The three of them had been sentenced to death. It was as likely a guess as any that Abstract had been as well. "Maybe nobody saved him."

"He's not easy to catch," Julae said. "Seems like a wizard to me. I think he's Eastwood."

"Mairis thought so, too," Mudd said. Eastwood, a legendary Etheren who'd disappeared in Havlos lands, was said to possess amazing shaman-like powers. He hadn't been seen or heard of for many years. Most believed him dead.

"We'll find out everything when we get home," Welhey said, but they all knew it wasn't that simple.

"Home?" Julae said. "What's that?"

An explosion blew a hole in the back of the plane. Immediately, the jet plunged more than ten thousand feet, dropping and rolling, then nose diving toward the ground.

The pilot's voice crackled over the radio, barely audible above the straining engines, rushing wind, and a suddenly raging fire.

"*Brace, brace, brace!*"

# THREE

**_Present Day – Somewhere in Ohio_**

Alik, nicknamed the Black Russian, Booker's top hacker, stared into a one-hundred-twenty inch computer monitor. Six of the giant screens filled the wall in front of him, set up to form a long running curve so that he sat inside a digital cave. Alik relished his current amount of screen real estate since he didn't always have the luxury of his preferred configuration. Two of the monitors were dedicated to Eysen data, streaming in directly from Rip and Gale on a near constant basis.

"How's the lag today?" he said out loud. Skinny and lean like a basketball player, his mind faster than his hands and feet, Alik thought sports a time-waster. In fact, anything that didn't build code and solve problems he considered trivial. "The off lag."

"Twenty-three hours," came the monotone computer voice response.

"Give me real time," Alik said, finding a stick of caffeine-infused coffee-flavored chewing gum.

A third monitor shifted from a long flowing matrix feed of longitudes, latitudes, times, and dates and began flashing wildly.

"Slow," Alik said, unable to even make out anything clearly enough to recognize it.

"Slower will not be real time."

"How slow to make it recognizable?" He pushed the stick of coffee-gum into his mouth, letting the wrapper fall to the carpeted floor.

"Recognizable to you?"

"Yes, to me." Alik looked around the dimly lit office suite, wondering if the AI had seen someone else in the room, but knew the machine learning program was only trying to determine if Alik wanted the computer to interpret the images and data.

"Sixteen-hour delay, although visual fatigue would degrade that during an increasing ratio. Within one hour, the delay will be increased to twenty-hours. Would you like me to continue the calculations?"

"No. Track and slice based on the slick program, and I'll follow the twenty-three hour delay."

Frustrated, he stared into the slowed Eysen feeds, then glanced at another monitor showing summary results from the slick program. He'd written "slick" to instruct the AI how to look for anomalies. This wasn't for making discoveries about the universe or gleaning additional Cosegan secrets, though. Booker had large teams working on those things, people who'd been parsing data for years. No, slick was about one thing: Kalor Locke, the man determined to uncover the Cosegans' longevity and technology secrets to extend his life by centuries and use that time to shape humanity's future into something vastly different from its current course—a new order and direction he had decided to be "a better way."

Booker had charged Alik with the Kalor Locke project. He'd simply said, "Find him, don't let him find us."

Many times, Alik had brought the clues together to put Blaxers within hours of Kalor. On several occasions they'd been only minutes behind. Yet somehow Kalor always made the move, always knew.

"Call Rip," he voice-commanded the encrypted phone he'd custom built from two iPhones and an Android.

"Alik, did you see the colors?" Rip asked, picking up the call, a lot of gray creeping into his unkempt, dusty brown hair. Even so, the ruggedly handsome archaeologist still looked younger than his years.

"I'm not current." Alik spit the gum into a waste basket and reached for his coffee cup. Cold, but still half full. He sipped it gratefully.

"It's an Eysen flare!"

Alik slid his fingers across a pad and opened the stream from Rip's workstation, then linked in the Eysen he'd been using. "What's the frequency?"

Rip shouted a series of alphanumeric sequences.

"Got it."

"Where's it coming from?"

"Western United States . . . could be southwestern Canada."

"It's a big flare. Has there ever been a larger one?" Rip asked.

Flares were a byproduct of an Eysen using huge amounts of the equivalent of bandwidth on the internet, except Eysens ran in the ethers. Massive enough usage could trigger widespread power outages, and even EMP-like results, creating crushing failures of electronics and computer-based equipment in areas near the epicenter of the drain. It allowed them to trace the locations of Eysens when someone pushed the limits of Eysen power.

"It's about as big as Iceland in August, but it doesn't surpass Thailand in October," Alik said. "Still, what's he doing?"

"Shaking EAMI," Rip said, referring to Eysen Anomaly Matter Interference. They had been able to develop the ability to use Eysens to create anomalies and interfere in scientific measurement and technologically based equipment—in effect changing reality, or at least making it appear to have been changed. "He must be making a play in the past."

Alik shifted to another screen. "Not if we get him first."

"Blaxers scrambling," Booker said, coming on the call after Rip had pushed an alert to his phone. "Where are they going?"

"Trying," Alik said, preoccupied with thousands of points of data.

"What is Kalor doing this time?" Booker asked.

"He must know we'll see him," Rip said.

"Something that's worth the risk," Gale, Rip's wife, said. "He might be going for a time grab."

Booker, standing in his own command center, paced the middle of the dimly lit circular room. He was surrounded by floor-to-ceiling screens projecting satellite images from multiple points across the globe. Inside the round bunker, he pulled metaphoric levers of power that world leaders could only dream of. "Kalor Locke." Booker said it like a profanity. A time grab did require awesome amounts of Eysen power, and Locke certainly possessed more Eysens than Booker. "He hasn't attempted one since Egypt."

"That we know of," Rip interjected.

"I heard that," Alik said, sensitive to the possibility that Kalor Locke had developed something like Alik's cloak, a shield using Cosegan specs that rendered Eysens invisible to other Eysens. "This proves he doesn't have a shield, 'cause he ain't got an Alik!"

"All it does is tell us that if he *has* a shield, it has limits," Rip said. "This is a *huge* flare. It *has* to be a time grab!"

Booker's jaw tensed. "He knows we'd see this. Why is he letting us? How close are we to landing his location?"

"Still eight or nine minutes, but we're definitely in the fifth quadrant of North America," Alik reported.

"Too much real estate," Booker said, checking another screen. "But the teams out of Chicago and Seattle are launching." They all knew every second counted, but it wasn't just *finding* Kalor Locke and his horde of Eysens, they needed to know what he was *doing*. "Everyone ready?" Booker asked. "He could be on top of us in seconds."

# FOUR

Trynn needed a new Eysen, or at least a portion of it. He had to leave *something* behind. Not just an ordinary Eysen like the others he'd inserted into the Far Future, this would be for the Missing Time, and this Eysen would be different.

It would be him.

Unfortunately, manufacturing was not possible on the barge. Initial components could be assembled and structured, but the precision necessary for the internals and the fine finish work needed a full Eysen factory with stability and controls—a place that didn't rock to and fro with the tides.

He'd tried installing the lasers, but found alignment could not gain seating, meaning he couldn't achieve the precise placements within the Eysen of so many nano lasers. Still, he arrayed and processed the hundreds of rare earth, rare air, and rare space minerals. Typically, in spite of exact measurements and content analysis, there would be natural differences between each Eysen. The minerals, obtained from asteroid mining, were strangely always the most inconsistent. Globotite was the most important ingredient, and the most stable, yet even its consistency levels had minute variations which, over time, were magnified to be significant.

Trynn, working in secret, added the Globotite, altering the amount to less than he'd used with his previous Eysens. "This one will not need to get through the eleven million years of the Missing Time," he muttered to himself. The Missing Time had been shortened, therefore Globotite energy yield needed to be reduced.

Still, he wasn't sure.

"It all depends on when I push the Switch . . . *if* I push the Switch."

This sphere would be an insurance policy against the Switch *not* being pushed. Perhaps even more important, in the event of his untimely death—which could come very soon—there would be something for his followers to work with.

"I'd better put in more Globotite," he decided, although the precious mineral was in desperately short supply. "This must *not* fail. I cannot predict what happens during the Missing Time, and with those in the Far Past working against us, it could expand again before I get to the Switch."

The notion disturbed him. His life's work, to use the Eysens to benefit humanity and then to save humanity, would come down to a single moment, and so many forces were opposing his attempts.

"The Far Past . . . " Anjee began, interrupting him in a somber tone.

"Yes?" he replied irritably.

"Complications. They seem to be preparing for Kalor Locke obtaining a Super- Eysen."

"Why does Locke exist?"

"Apparently only to annoy you."

"Not funny."

"I know. The report is in your crystal," she said as she was leaving. "Figure out a way to stop that lunatic from powering his

Super-Eysen, or you'll never reach Finality, never push the Switch."

The interruption over, now back to work, he tried to forget Kalor's Super-Eysen. *This insertion will be different . . . I can't track it like the others.* Each Eysen contained unique differences, much like a human fingerprint, or a specific strand of DNA. Knowing the origin point and the exact ingredients that went into the manufacturing of an Eysen made tracing them through time possible and added to the security. In this case, he wanted to avoid that. The risks of letting it loose in the wild with no digital leash were major, but the possibility of someone other than the intended recipients discovering it, locating it, *using* it, was too horrible to contemplate.

He would need to use the special AI controlled pressing machines, which worked similarly to how coal compressed into diamonds, to seal and complete the sphere. That would also mean another imprint from that process, something else to erase from the records. The hard, crystal, unibody sphere was produced by the pressing machines, which then spun the spheres using the same formula as the formation of stars. The final, and most dangerous aspect of the machining process, was setting the never-ending power supply, which relied on two things: Globotite *and* solar manipulations. This created the core of the Eysen, a spinning vortex, and required a large, costly, and complex operation that extended hundreds of feet into the air and rapidly descended hundreds of feet into the earth. In that stage, the Eysen core would be fused, activated, and engaged, the final sealing done internally. Dismantling Eysens was even *more* dangerous, as the active core would already be fused upon opening.

Trynn would be doing both while in the Cosegan capitol, Solas, a war zone, as the world's most wanted fugitive.

*A hundred ways to die . . .*

# FIVE

*Present Day – Somewhere in Ohio*

Alik continued narrowing in on Kalor Locke. At the same time, Booker braced for an attack from the Vans. Gale ran to get their teenage daughter, Cira, who, growing up in the Eysen labs, had become a gifted researcher and Cosegan scholar in her own right. Lately, she'd been working on Globotite originations, acquisitions, and prevention, essentially finding out where it came from and accumulating as much as possible—which had proven nearly impossible—and attempting to stop Kalor Locke from getting any. Her best success had come with understanding how it formed. She had a long way to go, but had already become the leading expert on the rare air mineral in the modern world. Although Rip, Gale, and Cira had no idea Shanoah was in their time, the Imaze's knowledge of Globotite did not surpass Cira's.

Booker had kept the secret of Shanoah for many reasons, not the least of which was her request. He also knew the consequences of allowing the three most important people to the future of humanity to cross paths too soon: Shanoah, Rip, and Cira.

"He's gone," Alik said, deflated.

"Damn," Booker said, calling back the Blaxers. He stole a

quick sip of an herbal smoothie and checked the bank of monitors for the next crisis.

"What did he get?" Rip asked as Gale and Cira entered the room.

"He's dark?" Gale asked, her keen blue eyes flashing over the monitors.

"Yeah," Rip said, discouraged. "What was it for?"

"Analyzing," Alik said. "Something's coming in. Looks like he was going after Clastier."

"Oh my— Did he—" Rip started checking Eysens.

"We wouldn't still be here," Gale said. "And if we somehow were, there wouldn't be these Eysens."

"But remember, we *don't* have Clastier's. It was the eighth insertion."

"What happens if Clastier never gets an Eysen?" Alik asked.

"Without Clastier, it all falls apart," Rip explained. "You don't know that part of the story, but I came from that. I was the last descendant of the church builders. They were the group who preserved Clastier's writings, what he gleaned from his Eysen. His words began my interest in discovering more. I'm standing here because of him. Without Clastier, Cira doesn't exist, because I never meet Gale."

"Kalor Locke is trying to take Cosega out of our time," Gale said. "If Rip doesn't make the discovery, then only Kalor Locke knows about Eysens. He gets the Florida sphere and builds from there." She hugged Cira after seeing the horrified look on her daughter's face at hearing her father say she wouldn't exist, terrified that Kalor Locke could now do more than simply kill her and her whole family. He could actually erase her from eternity.

"He didn't get it, but I don't think he was trying. That would take too much," Alik said.

"Then what?" Gale asked.

"He was hiring people in Clastier's time," Booker guessed. "Planting poison within the church."

"Exactly," Alik said. "I may be able to track his connections, but it will take some time."

"Good information to have," Rip said, "but we don't have enough power to get there."

"We can ask Trynn," Gale said.

"If we can ever speak with him again."

"If Clastier hasn't been inserted yet, Trynn could add something, warn Clastier, give him something to defend himself with."

"That's a lot of ifs," Rip said.

"But all possible," Alik said. "We can beat him. Never forget that."

Rip nodded, then noticed Cira's teary eyes for the first time. "Don't worry, honey. You're here. That isn't going to change."

"How do you know?"

"Because I won't let it," he said, pulling her into a hug.

"But Kalor Locke took Savina. He's done *so much* damage. And now he's building a Super-Eysen . . . he can do anything—"

"So can I," Booker said across the video call. His dark eyes, intense and determined, gave the African American an angry appearance right then. However, Booker, the world's wealthiest man, simply had dozens of grave matters on his mind. He knew humanity was never assured existence beyond today.

"That's right," Gale assured her daughter. "Don't worry."

"Okay," Cira said, but she was frightened.

"Turn it around," Alik said. He and Cira had worked together a lot on the Globotite project because of Alik's abilities to access and process data. He had helped test her theories and mesh Eysen data with modern scientific research.

"What do you mean?" Cira asked.

"Take that fear you're feeling and turn it around. Focus it on getting the bastard. Then *you* own the power, not him."

"But he could get there first," Cira said in a shaky voice. "I don't want to die." The tears fell again.

Alik stopped looking at his screens and stared into the

camera so Cira could see into his eyes. "Cira, you are made of courage. You were born on the run, at the center of a storm. Every moment of your life has hung in the rebounds of an epic history to decide the fate of humanity. You are no accident, you are the purpose. Do you understand that?"

Something in his accented English, his deep voice, the objectiveness of his place in her life and the wisdom of his words got to her. A short laugh escaped her mouth and ended the tears. "Yes. I have the power. It's in my hands."

"Exactly."

"He can't hurt me if I don't let him."

"Yes," Gale said softly, not wanting to interrupt the moment between Alik and Cira, but unable to help herself.

"I can do it," Cira said defiantly. "I can stop him."

"You *will*," Alik said. "I study this man all day. I follow everything in this whole situation, every waking moment. These Eysen wars are my whole life. I'm an expert, and I believe you are the one who will unlock this Kalor Locke. You will win it."

"Me?" she said, surprised.

"You are the one."

Cira smiled. "Thank you, Alik."

He touched his heart and pointed at her. "Thank *you*, Cira."

# SIX

Trynn looked at the images of the clandestine field operations. *Dangerous* was too simple a word to use when describing what had to be done. The operatives, volunteers from a pool of Eysen loyalists he'd known for decades and yet was not entirely sure they could be trusted, went behind enemy lines. The insertion spot had once been Cosegan lands, but now they were occupied by Havloses.

"This is the final one," Trynn told Nassar.

"You will not insert another Eysen?" his apprentice asked, surprised.

"That's not what I meant. This is the last recipient chosen by Ovan."

Nassar nodded. "I miss him."

"Yes. These chores are empty without him, something like an affliction."

"This is the one that leads the archaeologist to search for proof of us," Nassar said. "In some ways, one might call this the most important Eysen."

"Clastier turned out to be an excellent choice. He led a good life, a wise man who gave us a running start into the Far Future."

The floating images continued to stream in. "So far, so good," Nassar said. "No Havlos Enforcers."

"It's the Coils I'm worried about," Trynn said, referring to Jarvo's elite and lethal unit of Enforcers. "Even more concerning is the potential for some unified group of armed gangs working for an alliance between Shank and Kalor Locke."

"Does that exist?"

"I don't know yet, but they're trying to put it together."

"Look," Nassar said, pointing to the main image, now carrying out in 3D. "They did it."

"It's done," Trynn sighed, thanking the stars for a flawless insert, then watching as the team exited the area safely. "Clastier, we're waiting for you now."

Trynn thought of the next Eysen he already knew needed to be inserted. Ovan had died before choosing the recipient, therefore, it fell to Trynn to decide. Although he'd narrowed his selection to four potential candidates, the process was nearly making him crazy as he tested and challenged each scenario, playing out the possibilities for millions of years in every direction.

*I'll need more Revon . . .*

The barge moved across the great ocean on a journey that would end near enough to Solas that Trynn could take a goeze into the city. "Perilously simple," Trynn said when Mairis asked how he would get into the most fortified urban area in all of Cosega. "The war will be there by then."

"Will Solas fall?" she asked suspiciously, as if her father might play a part in it.

"Everything will fall," he'd said, then, softening his tone, added, "But it will not be something I could cause or prevent. We are beyond the Room."

Mairis knew he meant this was out of the reach of changes

he could make in the Room of a Million Futures. *This* was already set. More and more events were slipping into that category now. No more control could be taken.

"Does it go to the right side?" Mairis asked, wondering if it at least worked them closer to the Switch. She still looked so young and innocent to him; a slender, lovely young woman now, Mairis had the fair looks of her late mother, tousled blonde hair, light gray eyes, pale complexion—she could be easily mistaken for an Etheren, where she'd been raised.

Trynn had explained to her just the day before that every single event, no matter how small, weighed toward the balance needed to be able to push the Switch. The gravity of the event didn't necessarily mean it moved them closer than something trivial did, and the formula's complexities were impossible to understand even with Revon. The mind crystals and Eysens were all needed to track the routes and connections to the outcomes, like a crisscrossing roadmap with trillions and trillions of intersecting streets and highways.

"It does."

"Will you make it out alive?" she asked.

"Beyond the Room," he repeated, but she had a feeling he already knew.

---

Anjee found Trynn and gave him a report he'd been waiting for. "They're still involved," she said, speaking of Veeshal and Kenner, the inventor of the Eysen and her son, still interfering with Trynn from a million years in the Far Past.

"Why?" Trynn asked.

"They still see you as a threat."

"How? What am I doing, what are they seeing?"

"We should ask them."

"Aren't they still blocking communications?"

"Yes, but there may be another way."

"I'm listening," he said, already trying to figure out her solution, possibly a double Eysen transfer—something he'd been working on for a while, but he still couldn't overcome the time dilemma.

"Shank."

"*What?*" This was a shock. He couldn't imagine how *Shank* could help them talk to Veeshal. Other than the fact that both of them wanted him dead, it was difficult to find a common thread.

Although, he had to admit that sharing an enemy was certainly a fairly big thread.

"The Imazes he sent back to the Far Past," she explained.

"They made it?" He thought of Sweed, her attempts to kill Shanoah, to sabotage everything he'd been trying to do. She must have also stolen Shanoah's way of getting through the Belt. It could go both ways. The idea of Shank having a direct connection to Veeshal now through Sweed was terrifying. "Catastrophic."

"If we can get a signal through to one of the Imazes, we can ask them to carry a message to Veeshal."

"Which Imazes are on the mission?"

She read him a list of eight names, including Sweed.

"I know two of them quite well," Trynn said. "Lusa and Drifson. They were close to Shanoah. I'm sure they do not know of Sweed's treachery."

"Let's hope not," Anjee said. "Cardd has a way to slice into the Imaze ISS comms. He developed it—"

"I know, when Shanoah was lost in the Belt, the time Stave and the others didn't make it back," he said, referring to Shanoah's husband, Stave, and the disastrous mission inside the Spectrum Belt that had cost his life.

She nodded. "Shanoah and the others . . . would you want to contact Drifson and Lusa?"

"We have to try." He looked out to sea. "The only question is, what is the message going to be?"

# SEVEN

***Present Day – Grand Canyon, Arizona***

The vastness of the Grand Canyon opened behind Rip and Gale, the early morning sun highlighting the colors of the canyon in bright vermilion, alizarin crimson, aquamarine, coral, burnt sienna, maroon, emerald, indigo, and a hundred more shades that would overwhelm any artist. However, they weren't there to sightsee. They were there on a secret mission to win the Eysen wars.

Gale had spent weeks in and around the Canyon years earlier doing pieces for *National Geographic* magazine, but she'd never been to this particular location.

*The Canyon is so big . . .*

This outlying side of the gorge leading off the main section, like many places in the vast Colorado Plateau, hid its secrets in plain sight. During the past decade, on a rotating basis, the National Park Service had closed small areas for archeological surveys in an attempt to complete a research mandate by 2050.

"You made it down the chimney," a thirty-something red-headed man called Rusty said, referring to the narrow crack just wide enough to accommodate the body of a climber.

"Yeah," Rip said. "I haven't rappelled in years."

"My first time," Gale said.

"Oh, sorry," Rip said, introducing her, "Rusty, this is my wife, Gale." He went on to tell Gale what she already knew, that Rusty had been a grad student who had worked on at least a dozen digs with Rip over the years. What Rip didn't say, but she also knew, was that Rusty had not been on the dig that day in Virginia when they pulled out the first Eysen.

All those students were dead now. Only Gale and Rip remained.

Rip explained that the four men behind them were part of a security detail. The people within the small circle who knew Rip and Gale were still alive certainly understood their need for protection. Rusty nodded, but said nothing, even after he glanced up above and saw another dozen Blaxers on the rim.

"They'll be staying up there?" Gale asked, seeing where Rusty had been looking.

"The ramp's a little tight," Rusty said, pointing to the ledge they'd walked down, which narrowed to twenty-one inches in places.

"Terrifying," Gale said. "It must be two thousand feet straight down!" Her heart was still pumping from the adrenaline rush of rappelling.

"Actually, almost three thousand feet," Rusty corrected, rubbing his red and gray beard as if deciding whether she'd want the exact measurement. "You can go back the long way if you want." He pointed to some long steel ladders bolted into a cliff about half a mile away on the other end of the jagged mesa where they stood. "We bring the equipment down that way on account of the chockstones in the chimney."

The ladders, some of which were more like horizontal bridges across equally sheer chasms, didn't look much safer to Gale. "I'll stick to the route we know," she said, smiling, even though she dreaded going back up the *ramps*.

"So you really think you have an Eysen here?" Rip asked, getting back to business.

"You saw the photos," Rusty said. The day before he had texted Rip photos of a spherical object embedded in orange limestone. The images had convinced Rip to come immediately. For years, Booker had been bankrolling trusted archeologists under Rip's supervision. They were looking for more Eysens, Odeon Chips, any evidence of Imaze visits or Cosegan civilization. After millions of dollars, and out of more than one hundred fifty dig sites on four continents, this was their first potential find.

"It reminded me of Virginia," Rip said, looking down at a layer of siltstone. "We found the first one in limestone."

"I know," Rusty said. "I read about it."

Rip nodded somberly, recalling the names of each student who'd been there that day and, of course, his best friend Larson, and Gale's photographer Josh, and all the others along the way.

The Eysens had brought so much death . . .

"This way," Rusty said, leading them over to a section of the wall cordoned off from the rest of the dig.

They navigated another narrow walkway until they reached a couple of heavy brown tarps suspended from a makeshift rod. Rip looked at Rusty, then separated the tarps like curtains. He couldn't help but flash back to Virginia again as he stared at a sphere protruding from the limestone. "It's a smaller casing," he said.

"But is it Cosegan?" Gale asked.

"From what I can see, it could be nothing else. Black polished casing, different from any of the others, yet there are at least a few Cosegan markings."

The circles and dashes used by Cosegans to convey words and numbers had been on every Cosegan find.

Rip wasted no time chiseling the rest of the sphere out. Less than half an hour later, he turned the smooth black casing in his hands, working to decipher the symbols, when he suddenly saw something he'd never expected.

"Is that English?" Gale said from over his shoulder.

Rip used the magnifier on his phone to inspect the tiny inscription found below two long dashes. "It says, *For Ripley Gaines*, and it has today's date."

"Then we need to get down into the Canyon," Gale whispered. "The Imazes have been here!"

# EIGHT

***Cosegan Time - High Peak Eysen Facility***

Shank, the stocky Cosegan leader, stood next to Markol in the elaborate underwater Eysen facility at High Peak. The location had previously housed the great Eysen Maker, Trynn's, operations. Shank, who the Arc often said looked like a smart thug, cut his thinning hair into short bangs instead of fixing the cells which controlled it, as if making a statement he was too important to bother with vanity, yet everyone knew how deeply vanity ran in his veins.

"I have done all that you asked. Let them go!" Markol pleaded. A monitor floating above him showed live images of his parents and two sisters in a large prison cell. He recognized the location, not far from High Peak, where a crane dangled the entire room above the choppy ocean waters.

Shank stared at Markol for a moment. He'd always looked a lot like an Etheren to him; fair and skinny, lanky even, but perhaps it was the elfish face that sold it.

The dictator smirked before responding. "One word from me, and their prison cell will be dropped into the sea." Shank, who constantly wore an expression that implied he might at any moment punch someone in the face, had calmly completed the scene for Markol. "Trapped, your loved ones will drown within minutes—a rather *unpleasant* final few minutes for them, and you as well, I'd imagine, since you'll have to watch."

"Please, I've answered your questions," Markol tried again.

"We have only begun," Shank said. Recently, the dictator, faced with a brutal war and diminishing prospects, had realized his only path to victory might be in the Far Future. He needed information, strategy, a way to find Trynn, and to destroy the Havloses. "Tell me all that you know about the archaeologist, about each of Trynn's insertions, and show me how it is connected to Trynn. Show me *everything*."

During the next several days, Markol took Shank through an intensive course on Ripley Gaines, Booker Lipton, and Kalor Locke.

"I will know the Far Future better than the pathetic participants in that miserable time," Shank told Markol.

"But why do these people matter?" Markol asked, although he already knew the answer. There was value in understanding Shank's motivations and, more importantly, how much the Cosegan dictator knew.

"They are living in what is a direct result of the Havloses winning this war. How can you not understand this?"

"I have some sense, but—"

"If we can change the Far Future, we change now."

"Isn't that what you have been attempting to *prevent* Trynn from doing all these years?"

"Trynn is doing it through subtle manipulations. You know what he does in the Room of a Million Futures, touching this or that, tweaking . . . he literally tweaks *one* moment and watches the ramifications of that slight change stretching out forever. What a waste of time. He has run down the Terminus Clock while playing god to a pack of numb and primitive people who should never have been born."

"They are our descendants," Markol protested.

"*Yours* maybe, not mine!"

"Don't you think they deserve a chance?"

"To do *what?*" Shank sneered. "Foul up our time, ravage our great achievements?"

"There is some validity to the fact that our errors led to Havlos domination."

"You fool. It is *Trynn's* errors, and his alone, that handed the world and the future to the Havloses."

"I thought you blamed the Arc."

"*Former* Arc," Shank snapped. "And she blundered often, but all of her mistakes trace back to Trynn. I mean, do you realize what he *did* with these insertions? Giving the primitives extreme power and infinite knowledge? These animals were not ready for any of it, yet he thrust a continuing stream of Eysens into the Far Future knowing its effects on our time, our very existence, would be disastrous."

"We have contributed."

Shank shot him an incredulous look. "Do you *want* your family to die?"

"What happened to you?" Markol asked. "You used to be rational, reasonable, fair, a man who could be relied upon."

Shank's eyes narrowed. "I'll tell you what happened. I did not change, the world around me changed, and it requires a different approach to avoid being swallowed by those changes. I am responsible for saving my people from the darkness. The farthest place in the Far Future demands my attention because without my swift actions, Trynn will destroy us all, or Jarvo will do it, or the Arc, or Kalor Locke . . . Oh, and let the stars help us, what if the *Etherens* grow in power? We'll all be worshiping trees and eating twigs, grass, and dirt."

Markol looked at the screen that for days had been streaming constant images of his sisters and parents. "Please let them go. You only need me. My life alone should be threat enough."

Shank huffed in amusement. "Don't be ridiculous. We all know your life is not worth much."

# NINE

***Present Day – Grand Canyon, Arizona***

Years earlier, Gale, Rip, and Cira had made a pact to never again be separated. Their vow came after they had been ripped apart while hiding and living in Fiji. Each of them had almost died, and almost done so alone. Since that traumatic experience, they'd been involved in numerous other life-threatening situations. This, the first time they'd left their daughter for any substantial amount of time, had been at Cira's insistence.

"I'm too close to the Globotite," she'd told them, having spent months on efforts to locate veins of the powerful air mineral in the modern world. "I can't go. And anyway, I'm older now. I'm protected by an army. I'll be fine."

Rip would have preferred to leave Gale behind to make sure Cira remained safe, but she had other reasons for going. As soon as they received word there was a potential Eysen located near the Grand Canyon, she told Rip and Cira about an incredible experience during her time working for *National Geographic*.

"It's a strange story," Gale began, then she laughed, adding, "Although, I guess no stranger than the one we're living through. Anyway, back in 1909, The Arizona Gazette, which later became the Arizona Republic, published an account of a seasoned explorer named G.E. Kincaid, and an anthropologist named S.A. Jordan, who were part of a Smithsonian expedition, working in the Grand Canyon. Kincaid claimed to have discovered a massive cavern inside the Canyon."

"What do you mean *claimed?*" Cira had asked. "That was more than a hundred years ago. If he discovered it, wouldn't we know for sure?"

"One would think so, but almost immediately after the newspaper article appeared, access to that part of the Canyon was restricted, and the Smithsonian quickly denied the story."

"Why? With all the geological activity in and around that area, what's the big deal about a giant cavern? Aren't there lots of caves around there?"

"Yes, but what Kincaid talked about was something very different. He said the cavern entrance was almost completely inaccessible, but after much effort, he made his way inside. Apparently the caves were so enormous they could have comfortably housed fifty thousand people."

"Wow! That is huge."

"He described a center cavern with other caves branching off of it like spokes on a wheel, and they contained countless artifacts, but the crazy part of this is that it wasn't what you'd expect. These weren't Hopi or Navajo, but were said to be clearly of Tibetan or Egyptian origin."

"What?" Rip asked. "How have I never heard about this in any archeological journals?"

"Because they buried the story, denied either of the two men worked for the Smithsonian. They completely covered it up. Some people said the men were silenced."

"Killed?" Cira asked.

Gale nodded.

"What kind of artifacts?" Rip pressed.

"Granaries full of seeds. Copper weapons and other implements said to be hard as steel. There were urns, gold and copper cups, enameled and glazed pottery, engraved yellow stones, platinum-like gray metal."

"Incredible," Rip said. "*If* this is true, those are definitely OOParts." An out of place artifact, or OOPart, was an artifact found in an unusual context that did not fit the accepted historical or archeological timeline. Eysens were perhaps the best example of an OOPart.

"Rip, it's beyond that. Kincaid reported that there were hieroglyphics and mummies."

"We know the Imazes were in Egypt," Cira said. "Maybe they gave some of them a ride to Arizona." She laughed.

"It may sound funny, but what if they were here to hide?' Rip theorized.

"Or here to protect people," Gale said.

"What people?"

She shrugged. "I don't know. Other Imazes or Cosegans . . . or their descendants."

"Like how I'm a descendant of the Clastier church builders," Rip said. "People wanted me out of the way."

"But is it possible that there was once fifty thousand Egyptians living in caves within the Grand Canyon?" Cira asked.

"And are you suggesting the Imazes moved them there somehow?" Rip asked. "Why would they do that? To keep them safe from attack, cataclysm, to seed the new world . . . were they somehow special, different from the other Egyptians? Did they take them to other locations around the globe?"

"I'm not suggesting anything," Gale said. "Just that with all we know now, it warrants further investigation."

"Did you, or the people you were with, look for Kincaid's cavern?" Rip asked.

"We did, as best we could. I'm a journalist. We kept it objective, asked questions, interviewed Park officials, locals, oldtimers, rangers, members and elders of the Havasupai and Hopi tribes, elders of the Navajo Nation, even people within the Arizona state government. I asked everyone."

"And?" Rip asked, not at all surprised by her thoroughness.

"The native Americans all had stories that could fit into Kincaid's accounts. Everyone else pretty much laughed at me."

"How come you never told me about this before?"

"There are lots of stories I've done through the years that we've never discussed."

"But this is *archaeology*."

She shrugged. "They'd mostly convinced me it wasn't. And, I don't know, I never really put it together until now that there could be a Cosegan link."

"But there really could be," Cira said. "You and Dad need to find that cave."

Gale nodded. "You know, the government and the Park Service did a number on me back then. They hit me with hard suppression, fringe whack job labeling, calling me a conspiracy theorist. At the time, I was worried about my reputation, my career, and thought maybe I had been caught up in a sensational-ized story. That's what they said. It had been made up to sell newspapers in 1909. The Smithsonian and my own superiors at National Geographic were calling it pure bunk." She looked at the Eysens. "I mean, really. How *could* it be real? That was way before the day in Virginia with you and the Eysen, long before I knew about Cosega, the Imazes."

"We need to know how much impact the Imazes have had on our history," Rip said. "And the bigger question is, are there any Imazes *still* here?"

# TEN

***Present Day – Somewhere in England***

Kalor Locke paced the worn floor. The old oak planks dated to the time of the American Revolution. *Fitting,* he thought. *We're living in a kind of rolling, as of yet undeclared revolution. However, in this one, there are many sides.* He listed them in his mind. "It's a lot to contain," he said out loud.

"What is?" Lorne asked.

"I didn't know you were there," he said, not admitting she'd startled him.

"I'm not actually here," she replied, her image appearing on a monitor in the corner. "I'm in Washington."

"DC?" he asked. Always immaculately dressed in casual business attire, he looked like a successful, fit billionaire—which he was. Yet, it might have been his piercing eyes, hardened stare, politician's charm, and movie star looks that gave some indication of his ambitions to run the world. His wanting to live forever, though, came from something concealed, something deep in his molecular make up.

Ever since he first saw inside an Eysen, Locke had believed he was a descendant from the Cosegans, and was destined to lead his people back to the light.

"Yes, the nation's capital."

"Because?" Locke asked.

"There's some noise."

"Eysens?"

"No, on Booker. FBI launching another covert probe into his empire."

"That'll go nowhere."

"It's not just that," Lorne said. "Langley's picking up a trail on Ripley Gaines."

"What kind of trail?"

"That's what I'm here to find out."

"Good. Keep me posted. I'm leaving here in the morning." He looked around the old house. Nothing about it appealed to him. It was drafty, had subpar plumbing, in a little village too far from London, with *lousy* wi-fi—fortunately he had his satellites —but worst of all was the awful weather; nothing but rain, fog, and cold.

"Are you certain?" she asked.

After Booker's raid on the hockey arena a few months earlier, Kalor had laid low for a several days to be certain he'd shaken the Blaxers. Savina had been sent ahead to the Ranch, an eighty-eight thousand acre spread in Montana that made his facility outside Toronto look like a coffee shop full of laptops and smart phones.

Multiple outbuildings housed incredibly sophisticated super computers, technology centers, futuristic weapons development plants, and at the center of it all was the Super-Eysen factory. He'd joined her there briefly to make sure she was set up, and then went on the road again. While his brother was looking for Rip, Gale, Cira, and Booker, Kalor had a bigger target: Shanoah.

"Shanoah is not in England," Kalor said. "I've missed her again."

"If she really *is* in this time and alive to talk about it."

"She arrived in 1974 to retrieve Markol's inserted sphere before I could get to it."

"We don't know that for sure."

"I do."

"You *think* you do," Lorne challenged. "Circumstantial evidence, hunches, and leaps of faith are not facts."

"They are if they're *my* hunches. She's here."

"Even if she did come to intercept the sphere—"

"We have her ship."

"It is *too small* to make a journey across time, especially that distance of time. Even if the Cosegans discovered a navigable worm hole and they sent Imazes, the ship that HITE uncovered could *not* have done it."

"You are applying laws of physics as known to us, in our current narrow understanding of such things," Locke countered. "The Cosegans were far beyond. Just listen to what you just said —they discovered a *navigable worm hole*. Can you imagine? And that ship did not just *materialize*. It's Cosegan."

"It is *possibly* Cosegan."

"It was found in the immediate vicinity and timeframe of Markol's sphere. Why are you arguing this?"

"I seek conclusive evidence."

"I have that," Kalor said, exasperated. They'd had this argument before.

"No reason for further discussion on that point, then?"

"No."

"As you wish. Then let's revisit the premise that she *is* still here and *is* still alive."

"We have her ship," he snapped. "She could not return."

"We don't know that," Lorne said. "As you just stated, applying our current narrow understanding of such things is not reasonable. She might have many ways to return. Perhaps the ship HITE has—which is too small to have made the journey in the first place—was simply a pod, or a shuttle to a much larger craft. She could be long gone."

"Parson and I visited her when we were teenagers. Back then, we had no idea she was an Imaze, but now I know. It was Shanoah, and she is still here."

"That was *decades* ago. She could be dead now by any number of ways, one of which is by her own hand."

"She is not leaving, and is not going to let herself die until she gets the sphere back."

"How are you so *sure?*" Lorne asked.

"Because the sphere is the mission. The sphere is the key to everything. I have it, and they cannot allow me to keep it."

"You have laid many traps, we have followed many leads, and yet she has never been seen," Lorne tried again.

"I saw her."

"You were a *teenager*."

"She is still here!" he repeated, this time yelling.

"Why are you so obsessed?"

"Because if I don't find her, she will find me. She's the only one who can stop me."

"What about Booker Lipton?"

"No! It is only her."

# ELEVEN

***Present Day – Grand Canyon, Arizona***

Rip held the sphere in his hands and immediately felt the difference. "It's not an Eysen," he said to Gale.

"It sure *looks* like an Eysen. Nothing else quite has that, you know, *radiant* appearance," she replied, her curly blond hair blowing in the wind. "Let me see it?"

He shook his head.

She saw something beyond disappointment in his expression; confusion, suspicion . . . and fear. "What?"

"Maybe it's a bomb or something." He looked at Gale, making sure she was a safe distance away. "Kalor Locke."

Gale froze, recalling Cira, Rip, and she had once discussed planting a fake Eysen for Kalor to find. "A trap?"

"I don't know, but I'm telling you this is *not* a real Eysen."

Rip and Gale exchanged a glance. In it, they questioned every decision they'd made since Cira had been born. They both might die and Cira would be alone in the world. Rip knew Booker would always take care of her, but Booker wore a target on his back as well. How long would he live? And worse, the same people would want Cira dead, too. Some would want her dead even *more* than the trillionaire.

"Each one has been a little different," Gale said. "Maybe it's a Markol Sphere."

"This one is a *lot* different. It weighs a fraction of what the others do."

"It was embedded in the limestone," Rusty said. "I don't know who this Kalor Markol is, but there's no way this was placed here anytime in the last ten million years, if that's what you're suggesting."

Rip knew he was right, but something didn't add up. He just didn't know what it was.

*The Eysen wars have made me jumpy*, he thought. *And maybe somebody back there needs me dead, needs a bunch of us dead.*

They were planning to try to find the Kincaid cavern as soon as they were done here.

*Maybe we'll find an answer there, but this damn thing has my name on it.*

Rip took a deep breath and inspected it further. Slipping it from its strange micro-casing, a projection cast from the sphere. An old man appeared in the light stream. His thick white hair moving in a breeze, his rugged bearded face expressive, wise, he began to speak.

"Hello, Rip. You don't know me, but I am a Cosegan, an old friend of Trynn's. I have watched you and this conceptual epic from the beginning. My name is Ovan."

Rip gazed upon the sphere as if he'd never seen anything project from an Eysen before, as if the concept of Cosegans was new to him.

Rusty, too, appeared as if he had just seen fairies fly out of the Canyon carrying champagne bottles. "Wha-aa," was all he could muster.

"Are you . . . like Crying Man?" Gale asked, dazed herself, but perhaps her experience as a journalist made her more able to cut through the shock. "I mean like Trynn?"

"Hello, Gale. If you're asking if I am contacting you from

eleven million years past, from a place where I am still alive, that is a complicated matter, but I'll do my best to explain."

Rip continued to stare in silence as they stood there on the edge of the earth, the sun shifting on the Canyon, making it suddenly appear bigger, different, like a magical realm, and this man from millions of years ago was speaking to them in English.

"Are you the one who left this here?" Rip asked.

"Yes, I went to quite a lot of trouble so that you and I could speak directly."

The sound of machine gun fire echoed off the canyon walls. Rip shoved Gale to the ground, then, an instant later, landed on top of her. The barrage of incoming rounds made it impossible to orientate their source. Ricochets and fresh shots commingled with dust and chipping rocks, leaving them huddling for cover under a slab of granite that rested on the basalt shelf.

"Are you okay?" Rip asked.

"I will be once you get *off* me," Gale groaned.

"Sorry." He shifted so she could get loose.

"We're pinned down," she yelled as the shooting continued.

Rip slipped the sphere in his backpack, having another flashback to Virginia.

"Oh no, look!"

Rip saw what she'd seen. Rusty's bloody, shot-up body sprawled on the stone ground where he'd been standing. It would be crazy to crawl to him, and Rip had witnessed enough death to know it wouldn't matter anyway. Rusty was gone.

"There!" Gale said, pointing at the two Blaxers who'd escorted them down. They, too, were dead.

Rip crawled toward the closest of their bodies. An upward rock jutting from the Canyon wall provided enough cover that he was able to get there and strip the man of his guns. He slid a submachine gun back to Gale and kept two handguns for himself. The other body was too exposed to chance it. He could hear more Blaxers above on the rim engaged with whoever was trying to kill them.

*Or are they trying to get this Sphere?*

Rip suddenly had a frightening thought that the Sphere was more important than their lives, and someone else already knew that. Someone who had sent an army to retrieve it.

# TWELVE

*Cosegan Time - Unknown Location, possibly near Cosegan/Havlos border.*

The plane carrying Welhey, Julae, and Mudd plummeted like a smoking, fiery hunk of metal, losing altitude at a dizzying rate. Other than Mudd cussing, no one said anything, there was no time. Impact was coming fast and hard, and bringing death with it.

No one would have heard anything anyway. The muffled sound of everything distorted all normalcy. There only seemed to be pressure, the plunge, the disaster of hope. A wing cracked and tore away like a branch snapping off a falling tree. The screeching of rending metal broke through the muted terror.

Like a rocket going the wrong way, a soaring bird shot from the sky, they were overtaken. This brutal sense of loss, of trapped air, of energy closing in was too much, too much.

Pieces ripped off the fuselage as they careened toward an evil moment of terror waiting to mangle the plane and everything inside of it, including their mortal bodies. Julae tried to look out the window, but the g-forces would not allow it. She managed only to catch a glimpse of trees, mountainous terrain, water . . .

*Yes, water, maybe . . . a big river cutting through the wilderness. Could the river save us? Is it deep enough?*

*Isn't hitting water like hitting stone?*

No answers came, only a loud, crunching crash.

Then water. Water everywhere. Consumed.

Julae couldn't find the seatbelt buckle. It cost her a critical three seconds.

*Where is—? What?*

She wanted to scream for the others, to see them to orientate herself, but whatever was left of the plane was tumbling in the churning river and the water was *cold*. Icy liquid frozen cold, and everything was dark, a gray silvery confusing awful darkness. Visibility was not definable. Nothing was anything she could make sense of, but she got the buckle open, and she was free, except for her foot.

*No, why?*

Her brain wanted to find the surface, a source of oxygen, but now it had to figure out why her foot wouldn't follow.

*What is trapping my foot? Something caught . . .*

Julae kicked. She couldn't think what it could be, but it could be anything. Everything had moved in the descent, in the crash, and the river was big and moving swiftly in a canyon or somewhere going down, like toward a fall . . .

*A waterfall . . .*

*What has my foot?*

She kicked, hit something. Then a moment of clarity, a visual, actually came from a pocket of air. It was Welhey's face. She'd been kicking him, his hands grasping, flailing. His seat shouldn't be there, but the belt had caught them both, trapped like animals caught in a hunter's snare.

*Dizzy . . .*

She fought the confusion as the scene shifted every second in the raging waters. Julae had underwater skills that surpassed even the Cosegan's incredible abilities, which exceeded Far Future humans by more than three times. Continuing to hold her breath, she twisted and contorted her body until she could reach him. There was blood. It was hard to tell if he was conscious, or even alive, but then she lost visibility again. The churn never stopped.

Working her hands up his belt, she finally found the buckle. His hand found hers and fought her, pushing fingers away. *He's alive, but he's going to kill us both.* Julae, stronger, with more presence of mind, forced his hand away, and deftly flipped the buckle. She unfolded her body and pulled his arms up. They both floated to some disoriented direction that seemed opposite of where they wanted to be, but everything kept moving, rolling, tossing.

Then she saw the thing Cosegans loved most. *Light*! Still towing Welhey, she swam to it. The closing coffin that had carried them in the air and nearly drowned them in the water took another swipe as it flipped and spun in some deep water eddy. Pushing them back down, in the bitter chill of the gray depths, her grip slipped, and Welhey was gone. As she righted herself, once again seeing the sun invading the river, Julae tried to find him, but everything was white now. Nothing remained still for even an instant. Even with her record-breaking breath-holding, she needed air or her lungs would fail, then fill.

*Seconds. I only have seconds, six, seven at the most.*

She swam toward the light.

Julae broke the surface five seconds later, gulping in oxygen until she could spare another sense and she spun, searching for Welhey. *If he's not out already, he's dead.* She breathed in, still gasping, trying to slow her breath, to regain control, scanning wildly for any sign of life.

*Welhey? Mudd? What of poor Mudd?* she wondered.

All the while the river carried her, sweeping her downstream toward the source of the madness, the reason the water flowed so violently on its angry, chaotic way to its end. The falls. She heard them now, thundering, taunting. She gauged the banks blurring by, the river so wide. There was no way to stop. She was too close to the edge and too far from the banks. The fury of the tumultuous white water screamed at her, *No escape, no escape!*

*I'm going over.* She wondered how big the falls were. *How far is the drop, what's the bottom like? A pool? Or all rocks?* Then she spotted Welhey, his dark hair bobbing in the frothy foam like a drowned cat. She might be able to get to him, maybe twenty meters away. *I might have that much strength left,* but then they'd both go soaring off the edge of the earth to a watery grave, dying together . . .

*Or I could try for the bank. Even then, I could easily die trying, but maybe . . .*

*Welhey or me?*

Already the river was stealing her options as it sucked her toward the falls, every second growing closer.

# THIRTEEN

*Cosegan Time - Trynn's Eysen Lab Barge, open ocean, parts unknown.*

Trynn sent a message into the Far Past the only way he knew how; he gave it to a trusted ally of Shanoah's who worked in the communications zone of the ISS. The Imazes were in regular contact with all missions, including the ill-advised Sweed-led exhibition to the time of the first Eysens.

Moments after he returned to the lower level of the barge, Nassar ran in, breathlessly telling him to look at a specific date and place in the Far Future.

Inside the Room of a Million Futures, Trynn found the view, then stood stunned, looking at the scene unfolding at the Grand Canyon. He frantically began shifting views, dashing in and out of the projected events as if changing reality. "Why would Ovan have done this?" Trynn shouted above the whir of transferring episodes.

"You didn't know anything about it?" Nassar asked, surprised.

Trynn shook his head. "Beyond why Ovan did this, two additional questions arise from this murky news: Why didn't he tell me, and why the archaeologist?"

"There is perhaps an even more important question," Nassar said. "What is in that sphere?"

"Ovan is inside the sphere," Trynn said, preoccupied in the amazement of what his mentor had done.

"But Ovan is dead," Nassar said.

"His body is dead, yet the energy of his soul soars in the ethers of eternity," Trynn said, adding absently, "but his mind is contained inside the shell of an Eysen sphere, which is now in the possession of Ripley Gaines, who is currently being hunted by Kalor Locke."

"Fate of the world," Nassar said. "Again."

"I didn't need this, with the Solas operation pending."

"Ovan would not have taken this radical step if he thought it would make things worse."

"Then why didn't he tell me?"

"I know how you can find out. Ask the archaeologist to ask Ovan."

"No."

"Why not? You already have to talk to him about the Far Future Eysens."

Trynn nodded, but he wasn't agreeing. The Ovan development was a distraction, but his mind was filled with thousands of distractions and the prioritized lists of all that needed to be done at the Eysen factory in Solas.

*Can I even get there?*

If Trynn made it in, first he had to strip eighty research Eysens of their materials, especially Globotite. He planned to give the rare air-mineral to the Arc to help fortify the shields and dome at the protectorate, a city-state island called Lantis, a Cosegan word meaning 'new beginning'.

"I'm also going to need to bring the archaeologist to the factory," he said to Nassar as they continued monitoring the Canyon. "*If* he survives this Ovan debacle."

"Why the archaeologist?"

"If we can reach Finality and get to the point when I can

push the Switch, imagine what the Far Future will be like, with somewhere between fifty-six and one hundred twenty-nine Eysens remaining there, many unattended, some we won't have any way to trace. They could wind up in anyone's hands."

"But they will be unlinked, so—"

"The potential damage that could be done in the Far Future, to that time and their future, is incalculable, but catastrophic, even apocalyptic, is not out of the realm of possibilities."

Nassar nodded. "Unlimited knowledge in the hands of an unevolved person . . . It's easy to see that going very badly."

"Yes." Trynn stifled a nervous laugh. "Very badly indeed." His impatience with those in the Far Future had once neared contempt. Yet since Shanoah had been trapped among those *children,* as he sometimes referred to them, he'd adopted a gentler approach. Still, Trynn knew better than anyone the limitations of those in the time of the archaeologist.

"You have a plan?"

"Ripley Gaines will have to lead a relentless mission to locate and secure all surviving Eysens."

"What about after his death? The Eysens will never be safe. Kalor Locke and others will always be hunting them.

"Once the archaeologist locates an Eysen, he will disassemble them. Some will be cannibalized for parts and minerals, others can be modified and reassembled so that the Cosegan descendants in the Far Future can use Eysens to assist their efforts to overtake the Havloses."

"The Eysen wars continue?"

"No," Trynn said, still shuffling views. "Eysens will only be in the hands of Cosegan descendants who will use them for good, to advance the people of the Far Future to create the utopian society we had."

"That didn't necessarily work out for us," Nassar said.

"They will learn from our mistakes. They'll make sure the Havloses are fully integrated."

"You're convinced the current hierarchy of elites, all Havlos descendants, who totally control the world in the time they call the twenty-first century, is going to willingly cede their power to an ancient ancestral enemy?"

"There is always a way."

# FOURTEEN

***Present Day – Grand Canyon, Arizona***

Rip made it back to Gale. From their vantage point, it was clear the other two Blaxers who'd been with them were dead, and by the sound of it, there weren't many Blaxers left up top either. They'd find out soon enough, assuming they made it up there.

Rip tapped her leg. "Let's run for the ladders."

"Crazy," Gale said.

"Crazier to stay here and wait until all sixteen Blaxers are dead."

Gale had been in enough situations like this to know they were sitting ducks. Within minutes their options would fade, and what came rapidly next would be either capture or execution. "Okay, let's do it."

"We've got to shoot as we go," Rip said, already crawling under the line of fire. The dusty stone ground was still cool where the morning sun had not yet penetrated.

The first ladder was laid nearly horizontal across a gap chasm. The drop went more than eight hundred feet down to the top of the next shelf, which cut thin out of a longer pinnacle rock that hardly had enough space for a single person, much less two. Of course, anyone falling that far couldn't survive, but if one happened to wind up on the lower ledge, it would only be a brief stop before sliding off and plummeting another two thousand feet. Gale led the way, getting off quick bursts of the Uzi submachine gun Rip had pulled off the dead Blaxer. She had fired one before, and was not an expert, but as Rip liked to say, "It's harder to miss with a machine gun, but even if you do, you're going to slow someone down," and that was their main objective, to slow down their attackers.

When they reached the first ladder, Gale saw the flimsy plank of plywood that had been laid across the rungs had not been fastened down, and there were some fairly wide gaps. It was less than four feet wide, but it looked a lot narrower, with nothing but endless air below.

"Go!" Rip yelled at her hesitation, continuing to fire at unknown targets in the distance. "I'll be out of ammo soon!"

Gale, not knowing whether to run across or crawl, thought the safest thing to do might be to just stay and fight.

"Go, now!" Rip yelled again.

She crawled at first, seeing the bottomless pit below her. It took more courage and strength than she'd have thought possible. The other side, actually a distance of thirty feet, seemed a thousand miles away. Trying not to hyperventilate as the plywood creaked and buckled, she screamed, "This hurts!"

"Are you hit?" he shouted, moving toward her and the gap.

"No! This, this whole . . . " She couldn't speak anymore. All her concentration was required to physically force herself farther out over the abyss. Several bullets hit the plywood just behind her. She screamed and went flat as chunks of splintered wood fell beneath her and disappeared into forever.

"Run!" Rip yelled as more bullets ricocheted all around him.

Gale moaned, forced herself up, and muttered, "Die either way!" Wobbling at first, fighting dizziness, she got six or seven feet before another bullet hit, as if meaning to spur her on, and she broke into a jog.

When she was halfway, Rip ran onto the ladder, causing a vibration and bounce that made her lose her balance. She fell. One foot slipped off. Rip stopped, deciding the best way to help her was to keep firing cover rounds behind them.

Gale recovered, in as much as she got back to the middle of the plywood, and crouched, still unsure what to do.

"Keep going!" Rip yelled. "Get to the other side."

"What about you?"

"I'm fine, I'm shooting them. Go!"

She thought of Cira and started moving, keeping her head as low as possible, trying to focus on the center of the ladder and the ledge on the other side. *Getting closer . . .*

The gunfire behind her, the screams from Blaxers going down in what now clearly had been a planned massacre, distracted her as her journalist's curiosity wondered how they'd found them.

*Where is the leak?* The puzzle scared her, and also helped her edge out the fear from the fall.

*Almost there . . .*

# FIFTEEN

***Present Day – Unknown location, Rocky Mountains, Western United States.***

The sun had risen fifty minutes earlier, yet its light had only turned the lake a shimmering gold a few minutes ago. A dominant eastern ridge and dense forest robbed the water of at least an hour of direct sunlight each day. Shanoah didn't mind. She preferred it that way. Solitude, nature, and stars. If she had to name the thing she missed most about Cosega other than Trynn, it would have to be the stars. She'd confessed it to her audio journal many times, most recently saying, "If I have to spend more than two days in a place without visible stars at night, I believe I shall go mad."

Shanoah had never grown accustomed to the muted views of the stars in places where they were visible, and often sought out remote locations around the planet in order to soak in the starlight. She traveled for other reasons as well—many, actually—but most of her time on the road entailed seeking trustworthy descendants, mostly Etherens. The Eysen wars still raged, but a new conflict had risen to the forefront: the Globotite-time war. Factions from the Far Future, Trynn's era, and the Far Past fought over the dwindling Globotite supplies and for control of time itself. Every single day, every day was on the line.

With no communications between Shanoah and Trynn during her first half century in the Far Future, she'd taken matters into her own hands decades earlier. Shanoah, head of the Imazes, a brilliant thinker and versed in all fields of science and technology that could have easily earned her a pile of degrees from MIT, or any other top university, also knew Far Future history, some of which had yet to occur. Her perfected mind had kept her alive and allowed her to amass fortunes, and she'd created a strategy to change the world—assuming the world survived. Her accumulated wealth funded the strategy and other efforts to make sure the world survived *first*, and then to make sure it changed.

As the morning sun warmed the area, Shanoah prepared to leave. This had been a wonderful spot, and one she would return to, but not for several years. Those that were hunting her could not be given such an easy trail to follow. Carefully reviewing the latest list containing names and addresses for several dozen descendant candidates, she memorized all the details, including profiles and photos for each of them, and then deleted the complete list.

There were people to meet, stories to tell, lives to change, and she would see to all of that. However, this list had been special. It contained two names that weren't just ordinary Cosegans, or even Etherens. These were Imaze descendants, people who, if given the proper guidance to remember and understand their true ancestry, could help her.

*Help me rebuild my ship . . . help me go home . . .*

Trynn's face flashed in her mind, as it did so often. The thought of flying through the stars again invigorated her, but her mood quickly darkened with questions as to what would be left of Cosega when she returned, and that just as swiftly transformed to anxiety and stress, wondering if she could schedule her arrival to just after she and Trynn had met, before the Havlos war, before the Eysen bans, before the Arc's exile, before so many things, and if so, could she convince Trynn to choose another course.

*Much to think about, but first, I must find the Imazes, and then retrieve my ship from its impound by the US government. And these things have to be done in the shadow of Kalor Locke's search for me.*

Shanoah took one last look at the golden lake.

*He grows closer by the day.*

---

### Cosegan Time – Command Center at Imaze Space Summit, Cosega

Shank waited at the ISS, wanting to personally oversee the mission to the Far Past that he hoped could eliminate Trynn and the former Arc.

"They should come into a communication frequency lane soon," the technician explained.

"You told me that when we first arrived," Shank said impatiently. There were several ongoing missions into the Far Past. However, his specific interest was in the one led by Sweed. She had the orders and the capacity to change Cosega and everything *after*, yet the *before* meant the most, and Shank believed Sweed had a real chance at making it happen—or not happen, as the case may be.

Markol, under duress, had consulted on the project, as had other top Cosegan scientists from the Predictive League who Shank had held under house arrest to ensure their silence and cooperation. When necessary, he also had their families imprisoned and threatened with torturous deaths.

All the scientists had unanimously cautioned that such a radical undertaking to alter time from the Far Past could result in the absence of origin. The term referred to an anomaly caused by manipulations in past time periods.

"You seek to eliminate Trynn's existence," Markol said. "The ramifications of this are difficult to track, and absolute certainty of new outcomes is impossible to reach since it takes place in our time. You could inadvertently erase yourself, or me, or someone else who could alter an entirely different time thread."

"We could live without you, Markol," Shank said. "If we do this surgically, we will only remove the two of them."

"The two most important Cosegans in the period of mad reckoning," another scientist said. "Because of their lofty positions and crucial roles in the fight against the Terminus Doom, Trynn and the former Arc affect every instant going forward."

"You overestimate their importance!" Shank snapped.

"How can that be? They are the two central figures of Cosegan leadership, science, and technology over the past several centuries at least."

"Highly debatable."

"You may not like them," Markol said, "but you must see their impact and understand that removing them would make even minute happenings veer into places we cannot model or anticipate."

Shank gave them a disgusted look. "You can tell what's going to occur or change eleven million years into the Far Future, but not what would change tomorrow if Trynn had never been born?"

"We can tell the future because we have the past and the present as a base from which to project," the other scientist said. "If you remove our fixed knowledge base of the present, the world will potentially begin unravelling, and there will be no way to correct or reverse the process once it begins."

# SIXTEEN

***Present Day – Grand Canyon, Arizona***

After momentarily looking down into oblivion, Gale almost froze at the last step. Then she heard Rip running across the ladder behind her. The plywood buckled and snapped against the steel rungs as he sprinted across like it was nothing. The whole ladder shook. Worried it might come loose, she was about to tell him to slow down, but he was suddenly next to her. They hurried around the side of a granite column, huddling inside a tight area crammed with supplies for the dig, but out of the line of fire.

"How did you do that?"

"Do what?"

"Run across that razor blade!"

"People were *shooting* at us! I'd run across hot coals, jump through rings of fire, whatever it takes to avoid getting shot. I hate bullets!"

Gale shook her head. "Me too, but—"

"Another ladder," Rip said, pointing up.

"At least it's bolted to the cliff and the drop isn't so bad."

"As long as we don't get shot," Rip said. "We'll be exposed once we get about halfway up."

Gale's eyes went wide. "They'll shoot us off the ladder."

"That's when we'll need to start shooting. I have a pretty good idea where they'll be. This time, I'll take the machine gun. One of the handguns is empty, so go easy."

Gale looked up at the ladder, ascending straight up the sheer cliff, and wondered if Rip seriously believed she was going to be shooting at the same time as she climbed. "Maybe we should wait until the Blaxers thin out the attackers. Less people to shoot at us."

"I think it's going to go the other way." Rip looked back over to where they'd come from, then back up to the rim. "We better go right now, or there isn't going to be anyone left up there to defend us."

"We should call Booker."

Rip shook his head. "Whoever this is, and I'm betting it's Kalor's Vans, they knew. They knew we would be here. I'm not calling Booker until we know *how* they knew."

"You're not saying Booker compromised us?" Gale said, starting up the ladder.

"No way. But somehow they've gotten into our communications." He shook his head in frustration. "We need to disappear for a while to figure this out."

"What about Cira?"

"Booker has her, she's safe. We just can't call."

"I'm almost halfway," Gale said.

"I'm ready."

Rip, right behind her, held the ladder with one hand, holding the submachine gun in the other, ready to spray cover fire and hoping there wasn't a sniper in this group—at least not one left alive. He silently thanked the Blaxers, gave a quick plea to whatever power in the universe could protect him, knowing full well that power might be a Cosegan living eleven million years earlier, and somehow maintained his balance climbing up the ladder one rung at a time with that single hand preventing him from falling back down. Three feet later, he had to fire. The action threw off his balance. He slipped two rungs down before finding his footing. He would have lost his weapon if it wasn't strapped over his shoulder.

Gale screamed when he slipped, but kept climbing. Shots hit all around them, but distance and angles were on their side. Half a minute later, Gale was on top, crawling behind a rock for cover.

Rip made it soon after. The two of them scampered to a small stand of trees about a hundred feet away. From there, they surveyed the scene.

"Three Blaxers left," Rip said, pointing. "We need to move fast."

"Rip, they're going to die," Gale said. "Look at all the Vans."

There were at least fifteen that they could see. What worried Rip was how many they *couldn't*.

"I'm sorry, but . . . we can't save them."

"I'm so tired of people dying for us."

He pulled at her arm. "Come on."

She followed, cussing, mumbling, wishing she was an action hero that could defend herself against this kind of invasion, but she kept running with Rip, as fast as she was capable, past Park Service sheds, through a parking area, around some stone building. Soon they couldn't hear gunfire anymore. The acoustics of the Canyon were baffling, somehow swallowing the sound.

*Unless all the Blaxers are now dead . . .*

# SEVENTEEN

***Present Day – United States***

Shanoah reached the first Imaze descendent too late. Kalor Locke's death squads, the Vans, had already found him. She did not yet know the cause of death, but he'd likely been strangled, his home burned to the ground after. This next step was to be certain there would be nothing left for her to find.

The second Imaze descendent was still alive. However, she'd had a difficult life, and was now in her late seventies. Still, Shanoah convinced her to visit *the center*, a place where experts would work with her. Shanoah had created an organization which ran a center dedicated to rehabilitating Etheren descendants.

First they would work on slowing her aging process, and then to actually begin to reverse it. Eventually they would get her to a point of controlling her own cells, and in that stage they would teach her about her ancestors, open her mind, then show her what was possible.

*All that will take a year, or two, possibly three or more,* Shanoah thought. *It is doubtful we have that much time left.* Her only hope of returning home was to find Imaze descendants who could help her. She knew there were others. She just had to find them.

Shanoah had thousands of profiles, names, and addresses floating in her head. The project to identify people as either Havlos, Cosegan, Etheren, or Imaze had yielded all kinds of fascinating data. Havlos descendants were definitely running the world. They especially dominated the areas of politics, business, finance, pharmaceuticals, military, and law enforcement. Surprisingly, the former Cosegan rivals also controlled medical, education, journalism, and most of the media. Etheren descendants had the highest numbers in the alternative health fields. Most creatives turned out to be Etherens, although a fair number of regular Cosegans, and even a few Havloses, were part of this group as well. Etherens made up the largest percentage of those institutionalized for mental issues. Prisons also had high numbers of Etherens, but there were Cosegans, and a few Imazes there, too. Havloses, however, represented the biggest part of the inmate population, as well as most all of the guards that worked there.

Imazes were difficult to find, perhaps because so many had left the planet in the initial days after the Terminus Doom had been discovered.

The Center—founded by Shanoah in the early 1980s to identify and help the descendants of Cosegans and particularly the Cosegan subsets of Etherens and Imazes—had grown to an international network of what she called *Knowns*: descendants who knew who they were and were known to the center.

Like any large organization, the Center had nine different department heads who Shanoah spoke with regularly, but reported to the Center's director, Slate, who in turn kept her abreast of the nine major operations. Multiple times a day, she received nine new reports that churned in her busy mind.

1. Descendent Recovery
2. Globotite Locating and Concealment
3. Cosegan Technology
4. HITE
5. Government Affairs (non-HITE)

6. Kalor Locke

7. Eysens

8. The Center – Rehab and Awareness

9. Security

With others handling the day-to-day details, and a handful of assistants bringing in steady income to fund the Center based on advanced knowledge of events, it freed Shanoah to concentrate on the big picture. Sifting through all the information coming in, she constantly searched for answers; how to get Markol's sphere back, stopping Kalor Locke, finding a way home. However, with the scale of the Center's operations growing, and its annual budget in the billions of dollars, Slate accused Shanoah of intentionally securing the means to start a war.

"You wish," Shanoah responded to his charge.

"I do," he admitted.

"We must be prepared for anything," she said. "If stopping Kalor Locke leads to war, we will be ready. If the road home travels through a revolution, then we will take it."

---

### Present Day – The Ranch, somewhere in Montana

Kalor Locke listened to his brother Parson, and then ended the call without saying goodbye. "Rip has escaped *again*!" he yelled.

Lorne heard him. "Parson sent me the data. I'm reviewing all the possible routes he could have taken, and there's a high probability we will catch him."

"I doubt it." Kalor stomped across the wooden floor. "We *had* to get him there at the Canyon. We had him trapped! We had him hanging on a cliff! The guy has some kind of magic on his side."

"The government had a theory about Gaines and the Eysen."

"I know the theory, and I don't believe it."

"Yet he always escapes," Lorne said.

"You said we may still get him."

"You said you don't believe it."

Locke snorted. "So, you're smarter than me."

"True."

"So who's right?"

"I'll tell you when we know."

"*Thanks!*" Kalor said sarcastically. "Maybe we'll get lucky and Booker will show his cards."

"That may not be a lucky thing."

# EIGHTEEN

*Cosegan Time – Unknown location near disputed border of Cosega and Havlos lands.*

Welhey and Julae shivered in the trees, desperately looking for some way to keep warm. They'd stripped off their soaking wet clothes and huddled together, but Welhey was barely hanging on. There were surprisingly no visible injuries, but she feared he might go into shock any minute, and worried she would only be a few minutes behind him.

Julae found a thin, wedge-shaped stone and began cutting sod. Soon she had dug out a big enough section that Welhey could crawl under the earthen blanket. On top of the three or four inches of dirt, she quickly piled pine needles and leaves. She didn't have the strength left to do as good for herself, yet she managed to get her whole body under the dirt and pull a few handfuls of leaves with her.

Many hours later, they woke up as sunlight found its way through the foliage, warm dappled light kissing their faces. After a couple minutes of silence, adjusting to being buried in a shallow grave, yet alive, Welhey finally spoke.

"You have saved my life three times, maybe more."

"I couldn't save Mudd."

Welhey knew she might have been able to get to Mudd, but could not have saved them both. "He could be okay."

"He went over," she said, shaking her head as she climbed out of the dirt.

"We survived the fall. Maybe he did, too."

She squinted her eyes. "You and I didn't go *over* the falls."

"We didn't?"

"You don't remember?"

He shook his head.

"We were still at the top, or almost. I thought we were done. The current sucked us down, straight to the edge, but then I spotted a tree wedged against the shore. A *big* tree. I went for it and caught it at the last second. I almost lost you, but you hung on. You don't recall any of this?"

He shook his head again, more slowly. "I don't think so."

"We worked our way to the rocks where the roots were still stuck. Just as we got to the shore, I swear we took one step and the ground gave out. We slid down all this scree and stuff maybe twenty meters. Steep, steep. Right next to the falls."

"How'd we get *here?*"

"As soon as we stopped sliding, I pulled us away from the cliff and lost footing again. We rolled down into the trees, down another hill, landed here. Or . . . over there. I'm fuzzy from then until now."

"Should we look for Mudd?" Welhey asked.

"We can't do much. We have no food, nothing to carry water, and I'm not sure if we're still in Havlos lands or Cosega. Even if I did know, we don't have a clue as to which side controls where now."

"We'll be lucky to make it out."

She nodded.

They put their still wet clothes in the sun and scavenged around naked, looking for any sign of Mudd, but when they reached the cliff and saw the size of the falls, well more than a five hundred meter drop to the pool below, they knew Mudd was dead.

---

**Cosegan Time – Etheren Territories**

Deep in the woods, outside the Etheren settlement of Teason, Kavid dispatched a group of scouts to the front lines of a nearby land battle between the Havloses and Cosegans.

"It's not wise," Prayta said after the group departed.

"Necessary, though, to protect from spillover into our territory.

"That's not why you sent them."

He looked at her, near anger, then softened, knowing he had to be honest with her, not only because she could see his concealment, but because she served honestly. "Not entirely. They will also survey the battle and alter the situation if need be."

"By *alter* you mean manipulate the minds of Havloses so that they lose the battle."

"We have an agreement with Shank."

"This goes well beyond that." She picked up a short, thick stick and aimed it like a gun into the distance, then threw it back down. "Just think what Grayswa would have said about this. Did you even consult with Adjoa?"

"I don't need to."

"It is customary."

"Yet not compulsory. And these are unusual times, Prayta. We cannot be bound to tradition and softness."

She stared at him. "You are a strong leader, Kavid, but don't lose yourself in the role. It is the goodness you possess as a person that gives you the strength to lead people."

"The Etherens will wind up ruling the world when this is done. Almost anything is worth that."

"It's not worth your soul."

He shook his head, as if that was crazy talk. "Can you imagine the kind of world we will create?"

She looked at him with something near pity. "It won't be how you think."

# NINETEEN

*Cosegan Time - Protectorate*

Inside the Protectorate, under the defensive energy dome, the Arc stood on a tower constructed of stone, accented with wood. The traditional Cosegan building methods of light and sound were no longer practical since the necessary materials and minerals were in short supply. Beyond that, Globotite had to be rationed for the dome.

"We must prepare," she told a group of eight Cosegan leaders standing with her, looking over the island and the constant construction projects. "This land must stay hidden and endure tens of thousands of years." Although the Arc had a good guess as to the future and the longevity of the protectorate, she never publicly shared that information with anyone. Her assumptions were based on dated materials from Trynn, data from the Predictive League, and words from Grayswa.

"How is that possible?" one of them asked. "There is not enough Globotite to last beyond a few years, the island has such limited space, and once the Havloses fully occupy the rest of the planet, they will search the world over for surviving Cosegan resisters. How can we remain hidden?"

The Arc, whose exact age was unknown, but was certainly

near one thousand, looked at the man and smiled. "We are Cosegans. There is always a way."

"Most of our people have perished or become prisoners to the Havlos way of life,"

They argued. "It doesn't seem like there *was* a way."

"You are standing on the way. Survival doesn't come with assurances that things will be just as they always were," the Arc said, the luster of her smooth umber skin, the awareness and vibrancy in her large dark eyes, and the focus of her stare, gave off an impression of youthful power. "The alternative to this way is not surviving at all, succumbing fully to the will of those who seek our destruction. Instead, we preserve the Cosegan culture."

"Is this really us?" another asked, motioning out toward what still appeared as a primitive island.

"It is now," the Arc said, also staring into the center of the new city, a spinning fountain of light flowing into a pool of colors and sound. "We will evolve as we always have. It may just appear more evident now as our people first regroup, and then rebuild. Soon, when we have stabilized our immediate needs and security, we will propel ahead with new technologies and discoveries."

"But to what end?" yet another asked. "Will we gain enough strength to challenge the Havloses and retake our former lands?"

The Arc shook her head sadly. "We are beyond that. Perhaps far off in the future, another Arc will see a different opportunity that I cannot envision. Maybe the Havloses will stumble twenty thousand years from now, beyond what I can predict." She paused for several moments. The breeze, gentle and reassuring, carried floral scents, salt, and the fragrance of freshly turned organic earth. "However, I don't think so. The Havloses will also be growing in strength. They will benefit from the expansion of their lands and the assimilation of Cosegans and Etherens into their own population. Each generation will make them more powerful, and their size will ensure their growth is exponential to that of our own."

"Then is it only to survive and hide that is our goal?"

"We fade into the background, a forgotten people. The Cosegans will slip into legend, myth," the Arc said, descending the open-air stairs. "Until one day, when we will return to the fore and show a broken Havlos world how to save humanity and find the true future."

"In the Far Future?" one asked.

"Yes," the Arc said. "If our people can survive the Missing Time, our destiny lies well beyond this era, and many to come. So we must build a great civilization on this island to preserve Cosegan culture. One day, we will show the world what is possible."

# TWENTY

***Present Day – New York City***

Shanoah followed the man closely, but not too close. Even after five decades in the Far Future, she was not used to the city streets, the single-level non-moving sidewalks, and the hard, dull buildings. She longed for the light cities, their energy, the floating sidewalks that climbed into the sky.

*I wish I could fly*, she thought. *Not just to escape this bruised and restless time, but to be among the stars again.*

"One more time," she whispered as the man crossed the busy intersection of Liberty and Broadway. "Just one more trip into the stars."

Shanoah had promised herself, made a vow to the universe itself, that if she ever made it back to space, if she returned to Cosega, to Trynn, she would never again venture through the Spectrum Belt.

The man slowed as he passed a chain coffee house just before Thames Street, which seemed more like an alley to her, a lane that, in Solas, would lead to a slight, which in Cosegan cities were places the engineers had missed, slivers of small areas where the light didn't reach. Normally, even in the overnight hours, Cosegan cities exuded a glow; more like moonbeams than rays from the sun, a sleepy kind of photonics hue that seemed entirely different than how it was lit during the day. However, even with their incredibly advanced artificial intelligence, and their fully engaged, enlightened minds, the engineers could not defy the true laws of physics, which resulted in places that the light could not find.

And because there was no light there, surveillance was also absent.

But in modern day America, there seemed to be no place where the citizens weren't being watched.

The man brushed up against a slender woman, who briefly made eye contact with Shanoah, but didn't seem too concerned. *I wasn't recognized,* she thought, always careful, knowing people were searching for her.

The woman slipped the man something. The exchange was swift and subtle. Most would have missed it, but Shanoah had been anticipating it. She'd followed him before.

Seven seconds later—she counted, drowning in the meaning of time, she *always* counted—the woman was long gone, blended into the moving masses down Broadway toward Wall Street.

Shanoah mused at the irony. The pulse of the world economy could be felt in the air. Money vibrates at an unusual frequency, she'd discovered, specifically the paper money and its digital counterpart that these strange and lonely Havlos descendants had created.

The man walked into Trinity Church. She knew its history, learned after the same man, who she now called Trinity, had walked into the church three years earlier.

Roughly seventy years after the Dutch settled New York, King William III of England granted a charter to the Trinity Church. The first building was destroyed during the New York City fire of 1776, which took nearly five hundred structures. The second church had collapsed during the 1838-39 snowstorms.

*They really should learn to build with light and sound*, Shanoah thought.

The Catholic Church and the Vatican had played a long and decisive part in the story of Eysens in the modern world. There was additional irony that this man had chosen *this* former church as a meeting place. Since the fall of the Vatican, the Trinity Church was now a museum, but she knew better. There were still the faithful, practicing Catholicism in secret, and this historic holy sanctuary stood at the crossroads of the old religion and the new. She'd studied enough to understand that suppressing something only gave it renewed strength, but none of that mattered today. Today, religion wasn't the topic—not directly, anyway. Today was about the future.

Then again, the future was always about the past.

Shanoah wouldn't be going inside during this visit. Too risky. Although she changed her appearance each time she encountered him, it would be disastrous if he saw her.

She liked her moniker for him. It sounded like Trynn's name, and perhaps if all went well, Trinity would be instrumental in returning her to Trynn one day. Trinity wasn't simply her best chance at getting home, he might be the *only* chance Cosegan descendants living in the 2020s had to survive beyond the coming plagues and wars.

Shanoah lived with the knowledge of many things; past, present, future, and the weight of what she knew. Passing people on the bustling streets of Manhattan, Shanoah read their faces, knowing how much time they had left to live. There was nothing clairvoyant about her ability, it was simply an understanding of the cellular makeup of the human biology.

*Eyes give a glimpse of the soul, a person's face reveals their health. It's all just knowing how to look, how to see.*

There was *more* to it, though. Shanoah thought of the church's remarkable stained-glass window, and the twenty-three bells housed in the grand tower, acting like metaphors illustrating the power of light, color frequencies, and sound waves. It gave a view into what was possible—*so many* clues were there for the modern humans to see.

*They are blind to so much . . . Like self-involved children, they worry about their toys and eating sweets. Oh, what they are missing.*

Shanoah stared at the building. Its giant antique bronze doors hid two critical secrets.

*What did the woman on the street give to Trinity, and who is he secretly meeting?*

# TWENTY-ONE

***Present Day – Grand Canyon, Arizona***

Rip and Gale continued sprinting through the woods. Desperate and winded, they took turns falling and helping each other up. Rip slammed into a tree at one point, and staggered back, dazed.

"I dodge bullets, and then get killed by a tree," he said as they picked up speed again.

They kept moving farther and farther from the site, still hoping to find a way out. Eventually they stashed the guns in their backpacks, then ducked into a long gift shop, getting lost in the crowds who somehow remained oblivious to the gun battle they'd just survived a mile away.

*The Canyon is so* big.

But it wouldn't take long for the Park Rangers to start discovering bodies in the closed section. Lock downs would be ordered. They couldn't stay long mingling with the tourists, pretending to look at Grand Canyon t-shirts, books, mugs, rocks and crystals, art, and a seemingly endless assortment of knick-knacks. Catching their breath and scoping the area, they forged a quick plan to get into the wilderness. If they headed northeast, they figured they might be able to hide out in the heavily forested areas until they found a house or got to a town.

"Stay off the roads, avoid the people. They'll search everywhere," Rip said, not wanting to get caught up in the panicked evacuations that would be coming any minute.

Gale and Rip exited the other side of the store and jogged back into another section of trees, putting more distance between themselves and the Canyon.

"I have an idea," Gale said. "Follow me."

She darted from the pines toward an open area and ran toward tracks and a departing train.

"You want to escape on *that*?" Rip yelled, pointing to the silver locomotive engine, a gold and red stripe on its side above big black capital letters that read GRAND CANYON. As it slowly rumbled around a curve, he saw it was pulling a long row of silver cars. Moving at a crawl, building up momentum as it moved away from the Canyon, they would have to chase it. "An antique train? Why not find a couple of golf carts?"

"Run!"

Although Rip thought hopping a train seemed crazy, with no better plan, he poured on the speed.

"You think we're Butch and Sundance?" he asked through panting breaths.

"They got away, didn't they?"

"No!" he snapped, now running beside the train. "They died at the end. In Mexico!"

"Luckily this train doesn't go to Mexico."

"Where *does* it go?" he asked as he pulled himself aboard, reaching back to help Gale.

They entered an old silver Pullman passenger rail car. Green upholstered seats were turned in both directions, wood and brass rails lining them, with most of the windows open to the warm desert breeze.

"It looks like it travels back in time."

"It does, sort of," Gale quipped. "If you've ever been to Williams, Arizona."

"As a matter of fact, I have. It's like 1950s America."

"Yeah, not far from Flagstaff."

"Half an hour," Rip said. His father lived in Flagstaff. The two men had been mostly estranged. Not only with deep political differences, they also disagreed on religion, Clastier, and a host of other minor and major things that had occurred during a lifetime of love and loss.

"Do you want to see him?" Gale asked as they walked down the aisle, trying to look normal among the tourists, as if they might have just come from the dining car.

He shook his head. "I don't need to bring trouble to his door again," Rip whispered, remembering when one of his father's best friends died helping him elude authorities during the early days of the Eysen chase.

"He could help us, at least until we figure out how to contact Booker," Gale said as they found a seat in the back by the lavatory.

"No," he said in a hushed tone, even though the noisy train and the din of the other passengers talking made it unlikely they'd be overheard. "We need to get to the safe house."

"How are we going to do that? We need a car."

"We need a plane."

"Maybe, but Booker's closest safe house is outside Phoenix." They had memorized the list. "We need to get there!"

"An easy drive from Williams," Rip said, scanning the crowd. There were at least another hundred people just in the pullman, and he wondered how many more were on the long train. Were any of them Vans, or from some other group who was after them?

"Easy drive *if* we can get a car," Gale said. "And if they don't catch us first."

# TWENTY-TWO

***Cosegan Time – Solas, Cosega***

Shank reviewed the contingent plans for evacuating each major city as the Havloses continued their advances deep into Cosega. "Solas will not fall," he told one of his top commanders, the Star-Leader.

"Eventually, the enemy *will* come at it," the Star-Leader said. "If they can take Fulswell and Mosbac, they will be emboldened.

"*Could* they capture Fulswell?" Shank asked, astonished at the idea.

The Star-Leader shifted uncomfortably, knowing Shank had demoted or even imprisoned other Guardian leaders who had delivered unwelcome news. "We must choose our battles," he said carefully. "It is possible we cannot save both Fulswell and Mosbac."

"Find a way," Shank snapped. "You had better save both or you won't have a job, because we'll have nothing left to defend!

"Yes, sir."

Shank regarded him with an annoyed expression, thinking, not for the first time, that he didn't need these kinds of people. Shank had already formed shaky alliances with the Etherens and those in the Far Past. He was also working with Kalor Locke in the Far Future, but the Havloses continued to advance.

*Perhaps it's time to speak with Jarvo. Maybe we need to find an uneasy peace,* he wondered silently. *I can betray him later, but first I need this bleeding to stop.*

---

***Cosegan Time - Trynn's Eysen Lab Barge, open ocean, parts unknown.***

Trynn had recently created a new section inside the Virginia Eysen. The secret contents had been uploaded exclusively for Rip, although in the event of his death, they could be accessed by Gale or Cira. Trynn had previously recorded and transferred rules and lessons for the managing and disassembly of Eysens.

Trynn reviewed the instructions again and made minor changes. "First, you will need to construct a factory. This is obviously a complex matter and requires skills, techniques, and materials that are unfamiliar and unavailable in your current time and technological state." Trynn paused and referred Rip, or another viewer, on how to find all the schematics, plans, and technical layouts for building the facility. A separate section explained how to obtain the specialized materials.

In the gravest of tones, the great Eysen maker continued, explaining how dangerous the Eysen core is, describing its unmatched destructive force. "The exposed core, if it becomes unstable or is triggered, will level an area with a radius of at least two, and potentially more than twelve kilometers." He did not tell them that his wife had died in such an accident, although he did acknowledge Cosegans had lost numerous experienced and brilliant scientists and engineers through the development of the Eysens. "Out of those horrible tragedies, these protocols were established."

Images showed blast results that appeared similar to the destruction of an atomic bomb, but much faster, brighter, and larger. Instead of a traditional mushroom cloud, Eysen core explosions radiated outward in a pattern resembling a dartboard.

"When working on an Eysen core, one must always wear a shield-suit. This is a recent invention, and not only protects the wearer from Eysen-leaks, a radiation-like effect, but also provides limited protection from a blast. Survival depends on a large variety of factors, including trajectory, angles, explosive force—the complete list is contained in the detailed instructions for manufacturing the suit. We have had survivors."

Trynn had worried that the Havlos descendants might get ahold of plans for the shield-suits and do what they did with every form of new tech they encountered—use it for military applications—and so had included an encoded DNA lock which would prevent the suit from activating for Havloses. It would also provide a warning of non-protective use, but he hoped it would not become necessary.

Trynn walked through the Eysen Factory using historic moving images contained inside the Virginia Eysen. "Do not *ever* cross into this active section," he said adamantly. "Hopefully soon, we will do a live training with your holographic avatar present at an actual factory. Even in that remote setting, your hologram could make the energy inside the active section unstable, and I don't want to show you another blast. I'd certainly prefer not to destroy our most sophisticated factory."

A series of diagrams presented, showing all the key areas. Highlighted in blinking red overlays were the places not to enter, including the active section.

"If someone is watching this at another time beyond your life," Trynn continued in his narration, "the recording of that live session will be included here."

Trynn continued to explain the Eysen manufacturing process and show diagrams and details, careful to make sure of one thing: that no one in the Far Future would ever be able to make another Eysen.

---

Before the Grand Canyon trip, Rip had watched the training over and over again. He'd shared it with Gale and Cira, warning them of the stunning power contained in an Eysen core.

"Trynn says it has the ability to open a vortex. Something that could swallow a person, or even disrupt time itself."

# TWENTY-THREE

***Present Day – The Ranch, somewhere in Montana***

Savina, the young and brilliant physicist who had previously worked for Booker, stared into an Eysen, one of the custom-ordered spheres that a Cosegan had made for Kalor. She'd learned that the task was more difficult than it might seem. Cosegan law decreed that an Eysen must be disassembled and its parts recycled upon the Eysen Maker's death. This greatly limited the number of Eysens in *circulation*. This made sense, since Eysens were the most powerful object in existence.

"This also means that each one is tracked and accounted for," Savina mused. "Therefore, the few that survived can be found using those records. *If* I can access those records."

She went deeper into the Eysen.

Each day there were many questions. Some she could answer quickly, others remained annoyingly out of reach. On this day, she couldn't get past wondering about the identity of Kalor's mysterious Eysen maker. *Who is it? How is he getting the materials to manufacture so many Eysens? What will happen when the Eysen maker dies? How does Kalor communicate with that person?*

Savina had, so far, unsuccessfully attempted to intercept Kalor's communications, yet there was no trace.

*Somehow he has an invisible channel back across eleven million years.*

Then it hit her.

*Maybe it's not someone in Trynn's time. Eysens predate Trynn by a million years or so. What if it was someone further back? Or what if it's someone* after *Trynn's death?*

*How long do the Cosegans last?*

That, of course, was the million-dollar question. She looked at the Eysen more carefully, actually *physically* inspected it, then ran through the Sequence, probing it with her own diagnostics developed over years of working with the magic orbs.

Savina smiled.

*No one's making these for you, Kalor, you lying little snake,* she thought, not daring to speak the words out loud. *You have someone stealing them for you.*

The revelation gave her another piece of the puzzle, and another level of power. Still, as with most of her discoveries, it also ushered forth a whole litany of new questions, the biggest of those being *who* was stealing them, and from *where?*

Savina had to put that mystery aside for the moment. A larger question nagged at her inquisitive mind. What would happen if she bypassed Trynn and went directly to the Far Past? She'd picked up traces of Shank's plan to do just that, and it was entirely possible, even *probable,* that Veeshal, the Eysen inventor, was also attempting something similar, or at least considering it.

*The thing is, Shank working from Trynn's time, and Veeshal working from the Far Past, might not be able to accomplish this feat without someone in the Far Future . . . someone like me.*

Knowing it could be a way to stop the Terminus Doom, she played with scenarios in a simulation program she'd created with a direct Eysen interface. The results initially poured in, and during those early experiments, she discovered Trynn had also looked at the same question.

"That's a shocker," she actually said out loud, something she never did, since she knew Locke was always listening. *Impressive,* she thought. *Willing to take one for the team, captain going down with the ship and all that? Or did you plant those results?*

Savina trusted no one, and always cross-checked everything. There was no time to double-check Trynn right then, but something in her gut told her it was real, and she soon learned that if Trynn *didn't* live, she would never have seen her first Eysen at the Foundation, never worked side-by-side with Rip as Booker's lead Eysen researcher, and would never have wound up with Kalor Locke to be placed in charge of his vast stable of Eysens.

*Okay then . . . Trynn must be protected at all costs, or I'm not in the game.*

Savina ran an analysis of all the potential weaknesses the great Eysen maker had, then set about creating ways to defend them.

Shanoah was a separate matter. If she really did still exist in the present day, she was a threat to all Savina needed to achieve.

Clearly, from Savina's point of view, Shanoah had to not ever have been born.

# TWENTY-FOUR

***Present Day – New York City***

Trinity walked up the aisles. The imposing nave of the old church always gave him pause, not because he believed god was watching, but because he was certain he was not. Trinity's belief that we were down here all alone, fumbling toward some hazy future, and more likely spiraling towards an extinction event, worried him less than what was happening now.

Ry, the man who'd come to see him, knew all about that. He specialized in *the threats,* as Trinity called them.

Trinity recalled their last meeting on a bluff overlooking the North Sea. It was cold and windy, but three artifacts had been recovered that required his attention, and inexplicably, Ry was there. Ry had not been expected. He was never to show up unannounced, as the consequences could be lethal to both of them. However, Trinity didn't think Ry quite understood that, or it was possible he didn't care. Neither reason was acceptable.

Ry acted as if he believed Trinity was too powerful to be touched, and with all Trinity's clout, that might have been true if the threats were ordinary. Yet these threats, the ones who held the world in their control during the first decades of the 21st century and would decide the fate of billions in the coming decades, were anything but typical. No, these threats were extraordinary in every sense of the word.

That day on the bluff, they'd argued.

"How the hell did you know I'd be here?" Trinity said through gritted teeth as they paced alone atop the windy cliff, still within site of the crews clearing and covering the dig site.

"I heard about the artifacts."

Trinity shook his head in disbelief. "Impossible."

"Apparently not."

Trinity scanned the area. "If you really *had* heard about it, others could have, too. People could be on their way already."

"They aren't here yet," Ry said.

"Even if they aren't, the political ramifications of a leak is a mess." He gazed back at the site, still searching. "England would scream bloody murder if they knew what we were taking from their sovereign soil. Norway might also have a claim, Denmark would want to look, and Germany . . . there could be issues with them, you know how they get. Then the French! The French will find a way to get involved."

"They always seem to."

"None of that can happen! This is too important." He didn't say why, that it wasn't the specific artifacts that had been found, but because these three ancient objects were tied to something else, to the most important object ever found, ever created: an Eysen.

"Why are *you* here?"

"Because I know what this means and you don't."

Trinity regarded Ry, a man he considered an inferior in almost every aspect with complete disdain. "You have no idea what I know."

"Maybe not," Ry said. "But you don't have a clue how close they are."

"Who?" he asked. There were so many threats, although he was certain it was one of the big ones, the Aylantik Foundation or the Remies. But there were many minor ones waiting to become major. Then there was the one he feared the most: Kalor Locke. Of all the threats, he was the biggest wild card because, unlike the others, Kalor Locke acted alone.

"The Etherens."

Hearing those words, seeing the expression on Ry's face when he uttered the name *Etherens*, had haunted him ever since. Trinity didn't know how, and didn't know who, but after that day on the bluff, he could no longer deny it. Someone had been waking up Etheren descendants, and if Etherens were rising from their eleven-million-year slumber, then it was entirely possible that others with origins from the eve of the Missing Time were awakening too.

*The great Eysen Maker may have predicted it, might even have had a hand in this, as hard as that is to believe, but this means things are about to get far more precarious,* Trinity thought for a moment. *Out of control.*

# TWENTY-FIVE

***Present Day – Northern Arizona***

Rip took a deep breath. The train had been moving for more than an hour, leaving the Canyon far behind them. "No trouble. We might be safe for the moment."

"I think so," Gale agreed. "We're sure out in the middle of nowhere." She'd been looking out the window for most of the trip. The western scenery was rugged and beautiful; scrub brush, pines, rock outcroppings, rolling desert, jagged distant peaks, with the occasional herd of grazing cattle and otherwise no signs of human activity. The cool breeze flooding into the warm pullman car carried the scent of piñon, sage, and cedar.

Half an hour earlier, they'd been unnerved when the conductor came by and asked them for tickets. They claimed they'd lost their tickets at the Canyon and gave phony names. The man called in and checked their story, but was unable to verify their purchase. He'd said he felt terrible, but told them they'd have to buy new ones. Gale and Rip each had a credit card under false identities, but were worried about them being traceable now. They used some of their precious cash to pay $140 for a pair of tickets.

"It's an expensive ride," Gale said, "but the scenery is nice, and we're not dead."

"Bring back old memories?" Rip asked, patting his pack with the Ovan sphere in it. "Running, trying to protect an Eysen . . . "

"Everyone who helped us wound up dead," Gale whispered. "Not good memories."

"Maybe we shouldn't go to my dad's."

"Let's see where we are in Williams."

Rip nodded. "What do you think this Ovan guy is going to have to say? I mean, he created this just for us."

When a young woman stopped and stood next to their seat, waiting for the lavatory to open, they quickly switched their conversation to chit-chat about Grand Canyon sightseeing.

Seconds later, at the sound of gunshots, Rip reached into his pack for the submachine gun.

"Wait," Gale said, touching his arm. "Look out the window."

Rip turned his gaze and saw two men on horseback galloping alongside the train. "Cowboys?"

The men appeared to have ridden straight off the set of a Hollywood western. "Real cowboys!" Gale agreed.

"Could be Vans in disguise."

Gale laughed. "I don't think so. Even if they are, I think he can handle them." She pointed to a man inside the train.

Another cowboy, this one dressed as an old US Marshal from the 1800s, walked toward them from the front of the car.

"Don't worry folks," the western Marshal said. "We're going to apprehend these two terrible outlaws."

"It's for the tourists," Rip said.

Gale winked. "I figured that out."

Rip appeared as if he still wasn't sure, and kept his hand on the submachine gun inside the pack as one of the outlaws burst through the doors.

"All right, this is a hold up," the cowboy said, bandana-masked and waving his six-shooter in the air, holding a loot bag. "Do as you're told and no one gets hurt."

Rip relaxed once he saw row after row of the tourists handing over one dollar bills, some sort of tip. "Seems like it's part of a western show," he said after hearing the people in front of them talk about a cowboy comedy skit in a faux old-west town they'd seen with the same players that morning before heading to the Canyon.

"So you're not going to shoot them?" Gale teased, chuckling.

"No, but I'm not tipping them, either."

Gale laughed.

After the entertainers exited, the rest of the ride went off without a hitch. Gale and Rip used the remaining forty-five minutes to plan how they'd get to Flagstaff.

Gale couldn't help but wonder about the Kincaid cavern that they didn't get a chance to visit. "Do you think the NPS 2050 archaeological review will include the Kincaid cave?" she asked, but she knew they never would.

"I believe *if* the things Kincaid described in that newspaper article were there way back then, the government swooped in and confiscated everything. If it was real, and still exists somewhere, you can bet the folks at HITE would have plundered any Cosegan artifacts, or evidence of Imaze activity, long ago."

"But even if they did, they would have them in storage somewhere, in a secret government warehouse. Maybe with more Eysens, who knows what else."

"Yeah. You want to find out where?"

"Of course. Don't you?"

Rip sighed. "Sure, but we sort of have our hands full right now."

"What if Kalor Locke already has the cavern contents?"

"It's very possible."

"It could be what he's using to stay ahead. It could be the whole secret to his success. Who knows what was in that cavern."

"If anything."

Gale raised a brow at him. "The man who discovered the first Eysen should not be so skeptical."

"Still, I like proof."

"They couldn't hide the cavern. It would still be there, maybe with carvings or things they could not remove."

"I'm sure it's long been sealed off. According to the article, it had been well concealed and difficult to locate to begin with. It would be easy to hide in the restricted area of the Canyon."

Gale was quiet for a moment. "Maybe those men weren't there for the Ovan Eysen. Maybe they were there to stop us from looking for the cavern."

"Or maybe both."

# TWENTY-SIX

***Present Day – New York City***

Ry sat in the middle of the pews on the left side of the church. He didn't bother looking up when Trinity took the space next to him. The gothic arched openings and ornate ceiling made for an imposing setting, but Trinity had seen it all before. Even the vibrant stained-glass that he loved, which dominated the wall above the pulpit, could not garner a moment of his attention today. He was too distracted, too worried, and if he was honest with himself, too scared.

"Why are we here?" Trinity asked in a church-voice whisper.

"Kalor Locke."

Trinity's fists clenched, as did his stomach. Although not surprised by it, Locke was the one person in the world whose very name could raise his blood pressure and at the same time give him an eerie sense of calm. Unlike others in the Eysen wars, Trinity believed Kalor was not a power-hungry madman. There was a chance—a rather good one, in fact—that Kalor Locke was a true savior, perhaps the best last chance humanity had to not destroy themselves.

Yet Trinity would kill Locke if given the chance. The stakes were just too high, and Locke's character flaws were too likely to cause him to lose the struggle within himself, resulting in a tear in his unifying moral fabric that would allow his ego to take control. *Power corrupts, and absolute power corrupts absolutely,* Lord Acton's words echoed nearly one hundred-fifty years after he wrote them. Trinity found Locke confounding, even mystifying, but without question, he understood Locke better than anyone else.

"Has he done it?" Trinity asked.

Ry nodded. "The Super-Eysen is nearly complete. But that's not why I'm here."

"Globotite?"

Ry hid his frustration. Trinity was smart and better versed in the complexities of the world than just about anyone, yet sometimes, his attempts at constantly needing to be a step or two ahead became annoying. "His stockpile grows, but he has yet to reach critical mass." That would be the point when he'd accumulated enough Globotite to prevent Trynn from inserting the ninth Eysen, decimating Trynn's ability to control and communicate with the ones already here.

"What then?"

"He knows about China."

Trinity dropped his head into his hands. "Damn."

China meant a lot of things. An all-out technological battle had been raging between China and the United States for more than a decade. It could ultimately lead to the end of civilization even if the Eysen wars and Kalor Locke didn't destroy it first, and the burgeoning present day Cosegan uprising had its own part of destiny to claim. However, Trinity knew Ry was not talking about any of that. Ry was talking about the holy grail, an artifact hidden somewhere in China that could tip the balance of power not between the United States and China, but something that could change the outcome of the Eysen Wars.

"We have to get there first."

Ry looked at him as if he'd just said something stupid, because Trinity had stated the obvious. For years, their teams had been scouring China in high-risk covert missions and equally dangerous digital blanket cyber excursions. "It could be time to make a deal."

Trinity stared up at the giant stained-glass windows above the great pulpit. "A deal with the devil."

"Yes," Ry said, following his line of sight, half expecting something biblical to happen; a flood, a great fire, a resurrection, even an inquisition, *something* . . .

Nothing occurred.

Except something *did*, not quite rising to the immediate level of Armageddon, but something monumental.

Trinity made a long-avoided decision that would shake the ages.

"Make the deal."

# TWENTY-SEVEN

***Cosegan Time – The Protectorate***

The island, small by comparison to any of the great Cosegan light cities, would never be able to house more than eight hundred thousand people, and it would be much more prudent to keep the population to half of that.

This restriction saddened the Arc. What would become of all the others? If the Cosegans could not win the war, which looked increasingly unlikely, then the vast majority of Cosegans would either die at the hands of the Havloses, or become enslaved by them.

Unable to sleep, the Arc was contemplating that very quandary as she walked along a starlit beach late one night. A shimmering appeared above the gently breaking waves. Even before the translucent image of Grayswa came into view, she could feel his presence.

"You did it," she whispered, as if speaking too loudly might shatter the illusion or even scare him away.

"What have I done?"

"You found a way through?"

"I am not back." Even from beyond death, he looked every bit the ancient prophet, the wizard, the seer, full gray beard, a roadmap of wrinkles on his leathery face, eyes that showed a glimpse into the wisdom of the universe and mysteries too numerous to ponder.

"I know," she said sadly. "You are not back, but you are here."

"Like a politician, your sentence is a contradiction, and yet sounds almost logical."

"I am no *politician*," she said, as if it were a dirty word.

"No, you are not."

"What is it like where you are?"

"The same as where you are, only glorious."

She nodded, unable to take her eyes off him, his radiance, the serenity of his presence. "It's not so glorious here."

"And yet it is," he said, smiling. "You are still in the full breath of life, the sweet, sweet scent of Flores." The bush produced a lemon-sized wild berry that smelled of baked vanilla cookies and tasted like chocolate and custard. "I didn't know they grew here. I would so love to taste one again."

She glanced over to the rocky cliffs, and although she couldn't quite make them out in the dim light of the waning moon, she knew there were hundreds of the bushes there. "I eat them every day and think of you."

"I know. Thank you."

"Can you help me, Grayswa?"

"You are so much better at that than I."

She smiled. "Such a Grayswa answer."

"It should be, since I gave it."

"Why are you here?" she asked, staring at him again. "Of course it is a miracle, and seeing you fills me with joy, but I'm sure it was not easy to get here, and in these times . . . there must be something very important."

"More important than the chocolate and custard taste of a Flores berry?"

She laughed.

"It is good to laugh," he reminded her, "to find goodness in the despair of the days we find ourselves in."

"Yes."

He inclined his head. "However, it is true. I do have another reason for walking the shore with you on this lovely evening."

She thought of reminding her brother that he wasn't exactly walking, but stopped herself. "It is a lovely evening."

"I'd like to suggest that you reconsider your thoughts about Trynn."

"*Trynn?*" she exclaimed, so loudly that she startled herself. "He helped Jarvo kill 3.7 *million* of our people. If it wasn't for Shank and Trynn, Jarvo would not be any threat to us at all."

"Don't be so sure of that," Grayswa said.

"They handed him the keys, and now Jarvo is weeks away from *ruining* us. Shank is a fool blinded by hatred, envy, and ambition. I cannot make those excuses for Trynn. What he did is inexcusable."

"But ask yourself *why* Trynn did what he did."

"I can't imagine a reason good enough. There is no way to justify it. How could he?" She suddenly sounded on the verge of tears. "He must have a blind hatred that fills him, that I missed all these years."

"There is no such hatred within him."

"Then *why?*"

"You might ask him that."

She shook her head. "Dear brother, you, with your deeply enlightened ways, and from the perspective of where you are, couldn't possibly understand. I don't want to talk to him, I want him dead. I'm sorry to admit this to you, but I would be happy if I could watch Trynn die."

# TWENTY-EIGHT

***Present Day – The Ranch, somewhere in Montana***

Parson scratched the back of his neck as he stood in front of a massive gray stone fireplace. Even after years out of the service, his military haircut and powerful build gave him the look of ex-special ops. Good looking like his older brother, Parson also had an easy side, coming across as polite and friendly. A pile of four-foot-long logs as thick as telephone poles burned in a crackling glow. The large man looked small below a giant Bison head, hanging above the ten-foot mantle.

"I'm sorry we haven't had any luck finding her," Parson said as Kalor entered the room.

Kalor waved his hand. "I have new information, but first I want to show you something." He hugged his brother. "Thanks for coming."

"I wish I could stay. You know I love it here at the ranch."

"Someday you will stay," he said as they walked outside. The crisp air was filled with the scent of burning wood from the fire inside, cool but not cold. "That's part of why you must learn this, in case something happens to me."

Parson stopped him. "*Nothing* is going to happen to you."

"Probably not, but we're in a perilous battle. I've made enemies across eons."

"Alliances, too."

"Yes, and I shall prevail, but this isn't about me, or about a single lifetime. It's about the future of humanity, so there must be someone else who knows, someone I trust more than anyone." He put his arm around Parson. "Just put my mind at ease. Learn these few things for me."

"Okay," Parson relented as they climbed into a shiny black jeep. Kalor sped along the rutted gravel road that led to a massive building he called *the chamber*. It appeared to be a giant horse arena, but actually housed the Eysen labs and research center.

He checked in with Savina and reviewed her latest complex equations networking their collection of now forty-four Eysens.

"Is she really onboard?" Parson asked once they'd left Savina's domain on the first level.

"Lorne checks all her work. I told you, she seems loyal to the Cosegans, which means whoever has the most Eysens wins her heart and mind—and I have the most by far."

"Hope you're right."

"Me too."

"How come she hasn't been able to find Rip and Gale through the Eysens?"

Kalor scoffed. "It's that damned Russian hacker, Alik. He's blocking us."

"I'll get him." Although he said the words with conviction, Parson knew Kalor was growing impatient. Shanoah, Rip, Gale, Cira, Alik, Booker, and others—he had yet to locate any of them.

"Hire more operatives," Kalor said. "We're out of time, you know what I mean?"

"Yeah."

"I don't care about the cost."

"I know."

"All right, this is the first of three things you must memorize," he said as the biometric scanner approved Kalor's hand-print and opened the door to the Bridge. "I've set it up so you can access this area as well."

Inside, with the lights shining off gleaming silver pipes, glowing orbs, and discs, it gave the impression of being inside a supercomputer, one built in some futuristic world with light and rare minerals, like a thing the Cosegans would construct. Parson had seen it in its infancy, but now there was a giant globe in the middle.

"The Super-Eysen," Parson said, awed.

"Yes. We're *so* close. I need to show you what to do if I'm not here."

"Why do you keep saying that?"

"No reason, don't worry. Do you remember that time when we were kids . . . "

"When you taught me to drive when I was only twelve?" Parson said, laughing.

"You knew what I was talking about?"

"Yeah, because when we were getting on the Interstate, and I asked why we had to do this. You told me it was in case anything happens to Mom or Dad and you weren't around to help."

"Right. Always—"

"I know, always be prepared."

"It's served you well."

"But not that day," Parson argued with a grin. "If you recall, we got pulled over."

"Did we?"

"You told me to try to outrun that cop!"

"I don't recall that part of the story." He winked.

"Like hell you don't. I would have wound up in jail if I'd listened to you that day instead of pulling over."

"No way! You were twelve, and the cop was Carl's older brother. You just got a warning."

"See? You do remember."

"Remember what?"

Parson punched him affectionately in the arm. They shared a laugh, and then Kalor showed his brother the procedures to start and work the Super-Eysen, telling him that it would actually teach him how to use it. Kalor further explained that the large device would act as a massive quantum computer which would siphon all data contents of the Eysens in his possession.

"We'll be able to know anything about anything that has ever been, and it will be accessible almost instantly!" Kalor said with magic in his eyes. "It will be fully functional in a matter of days. We're just waiting for one final Eysen."

# TWENTY-NINE

***Present Day – Williams, Arizona***

Inside a cheap motel in Williams, Rip unwrapped the Ovan sphere. It took only seconds before Ovan projected into the cramped room. "I feel like a genie confined to a magic lamp for a thousand years," Ovan said. "Although, in this case, millions."

"Are you here to grant wishes?" Gale asked.

Ovan smiled, but shook his head. "Glad to see you made it out the Canyon."

"Did you know we were going to face an ambush?" Rip asked.

"I thought it likely."

"Then why leave the sphere there?" Gale asked. "Wasn't there a safer place we could have found it?"

"Nowhere is safe during the Eysen wars. Kalor Locke would have zeroed in on you no matter the location."

"So it *was* his Vans?" Rip asked.

"Not necessarily. You must be aware that there are others in the fray."

"But you don't *know?*" Gale asked, shocked.

"Nothing is definite until Trynn pushes the Switch." He went on to briefly explain how difficult it would be to get to that truth point, how Kalor's Super-Eysen would make reaching Finality impossible, and provided many details about how the Switch worked and what would happen if, miraculously, Finality could be achieved.

"That's a tough one to get my head around," Rip admitted.

"That's one of the reasons I'm here."

"What are the others?" Gale asked, feeling as if Ovan was actually in the room with them. "Why are you here?"

"I chose you to be the first failsafe Eysen after the Nostradamus issues," he began. "It was me, not Trynn, who decided who should be the recipient."

Rip paced for a moment. "I've always wondered why . . . why me?"

"The process is complicated to explain. Actually, we would need some Revon and a few months before I could make you understand, and even then you would forget. As brilliant as you are, as any human is, there are many concepts too extraordinary to grasp."

"What's Revon?" Gale asked.

"Neuro-enhancing herb."

"Surely there's *something* I can understand about how I was chosen," Rip said. He parted the draperies slightly and looked out onto the parking lot and the busy street beyond. A classic car show was in town, and old hot rods spanning the last hundred years were rolling up and down the strip.

"Later. Right now you need to know that Trynn was never quite able to put his trust and faith in someone from your time, the time when the Havloses were in control."

"And you?"

"I always knew you were not an average person of your era. You are a direct descendant, which is why you will have to manage the Eysens that remain in your time."

"What's that mean?" Rip asked, turning back from the window. "We don't even have them all. You know about Kalor, so you must know he has dozens."

"Yes, I know, but you will have to obtain those, or there is no chance for the Switch."

"We've been trying."

"Not hard enough," Ovan said, producing a list, glowing next to him. "These are the Eysen Makers who have manufactured Eysens now, or soon to be, in Kalor's control."

"He's getting *more*?" Gale asked, exasperated.

"I thought Trynn or Markol made all the Eysens," Rip said.

"Oh no, there are many Eysen makers. Trynn is just the best, the greatest to have ever lived. He was born for this, for what must be done—the ending of the Doom, the Switch. No one else could have done it."

"Aren't people trying to kill him?"

"Most assuredly, but it is not so easy to kill an Eysen Maker. They can see things we do not. They know what is coming."

"But what if his death facilitates the only future to achieve the optimal conditions for the Switch?" Rip asked.

Ovan smiled. "I knew I was right about you."

"What do we do with the Eysens if we can somehow wrestle them from Kalor Locke?"

"They must be used to help save your time."

"Wait, if Trynn stops the Terminus Doom when he presses the Switch, won't our time be saved, too?"

"The Havloses are entrenched in power," Ovan said, walking to the window. "Trynn always thought it was about stopping the Doom and saving Cosega. However, I always suspected we Cosegans were already doomed in our time."

Gale moved the curtain for him. He nodded a thank you.

"So the Cosegans won't survive?" she asked.

"Survival is perhaps too simple a word. Cosega will not endure, but Cosegans . . . we are a tenacious breed. We are still here, are we not? Eleven million years . . . we slipped through the Missing Time. Trynn gave us that chance, but the Cosegans who made it through did that. Cosegans are the best of humanity."

"Then what?"

"The Cosegans had their time in the sun, an epoch, and oh, was it something," Ovan said, as if talking about the most amazing thing ever. He paused, gazing out the window onto the junky end of Williams, Arizona. "You can't imagine what we created, how we manipulated light, the way we used sound."

"Can it ever be again?" Gale asked.

Ovan nodded unconvincingly. "The minds are here still. What holds you back isn't so much the Havloses, it's the fear, the greed."

"How do we get around that?"

"Trynn did a good job getting more time for Cosegans in the Far Future by bridging the Missing Time and making sure Cosegans could keep the dream alive, but we've had our time. For me, this was about making sure in the Far Future, that Cosegans overtook the Havloses so they could correct the world they built."

"Then we have that chance?" Rip asked.

"The Cosegans could survive long into the future and lead humanity rather than Havloses. It depends on the Eysens, the Etherens, and you."

"What do I have to do?"

"It's too much, really, and that's why I packaged myself up and sent myself across the ages, so that I could help you and help Trynn."

"Does Trynn know you're here?" Gale asked.

"Not yet."

# THIRTY

*Present Day – The Ranch, somewhere in Montana*

After reviewing the operational plans for the Super-Eysen, Kalor and Parson Locke drove the jeep to another smaller cabin about a mile away. It, too, was actually constructed of concrete underneath its log facade.

"This is Wendy," Kalor said, introducing the Etheren descendant in charge of the program. "What are we reaching today?" he asked her, studying a large screen showing rolling streams of numbers. The end line of each row, expressed in different percentages, carried out to nine decimal places.

"Slow and steady," she said. "Yesterday was eleven—that's rounded, of course. Today we are already near nine."

"The amounts are minuscule," Kalor admitted to Parson, "but Globotite is millions of times more precious than gold, than anything."

"Tedious work," Parson said, pointing to images of large tanker trucks positioned around the globe.

"Very. We are literally vacuuming up the air in places where we have indications of a Globotite seam, then we've developed special equipment to extract the mineral." He pointed to another large monitor. "We even have seventeen repurposed oil tankers at sea doing the same thing."

"Expensive."

"Yes, but it's where we're getting our best results. I wish I had a hundred more out there. Historically, the air above the oceans has largely gone untapped."

"Does Globotite replenish?"

"We don't know for sure, but if it does, it takes tens of millions of years. Remember," Kalor explained, "once a seam is mined, it vanishes from *all* times, so our operations are denying the Cosegans the resources they need."

"Don't they need some to get you another Eysen?"

"Oh, the Cosegans and Etherens of that time period are experts at mining, processing, and storing Globotite. They still have enough for some Eysens."

Parson shook his head. "I don't understand . . . how are you *finding* it?"

"It's not easy. We discovered some extremely ancient Globotite maps. Of course, most of those veins were long drawn down, but we used the historic locations to build models on likely places for other deposits. That yielded us many good sites, and then we fed that data in. Turns out there are some patterns to it—very subtle, I couldn't explain it, but the AI sorts it all out. We also have Etherens, or at least their distant descendants, working for us. It's not just Wendy."

"And they're good at finding it?"

"Better than me. I mean, their abilities have been dormant, and some are more diluted than others, and they aren't *thrilled* about the job, but we've used information from the Eysens about Etherens to train them, and several have hit source sites. Some were previously mined in Cosegan times, but others were still there."

"Wow," Parson said, impressed. "But when will you have enough?"

Kalor looked at his brother as if this was a silly question. "When I have it all."

"Said the mad scientist beset on world domination," Parson said, laughing.

Kalor smiled, too. "It's not that. Don't you see? Soon the world is going to wake up to the power and importance of Globotite. The potential dangers that will usher in are almost unimaginable. Yet, if a sane, sensible person controls virtually the *entire* supply . . . the world will be safe."

"What's Lorne think of all this?" Parson asked as they climbed back into the jeep.

"I don't really care what Lorne thinks."

"Yes, you do," Parson teased. "She disagrees with you, doesn't she?"

"Lorne does not disagree, Lorne debates."

"Kalor no like debate," Parson said, laughing again.

"You may be surprised to know that Lorne believes my plans are all possible, including some form of immortality. The exact definition of how long that is might still be an open question, but the underlying premise of living for centuries is, at the very least, undeniable, even to Lorne."

"So what's the rub, Shakespeare?"

"Lorne doesn't always appreciate my methods, or my priorities."

Parson nodded. "Listen to Lorne more."

"Whose side are you on?"

"Yours," Parson said, stopping to make sure he met his brother's eyes. "Always yours."

"I know."

"That's why I'm saying listen to Lorne more. You always taught me to take advice from those who are smarter than you."

"No, what I taught you was to *seek* the advice of those smarter than you, but whether to *follow it* is the hard decision to make."

"Same thing."

Kalor shook his head. "Not even close."

Soon they visited another building, a smaller cabin about the size of a two-car garage.

"This is where the real secrets are," Kalor said, closing and locking the door behind them. "This is a backup on all my research on cell-framers, Cosegan longevity and health, and Etheren abilities." He turned to his brother. "Cosegans could live for more than a thousand years, maybe much longer, and Etherens, especially their shamans . . . well, we have no idea, but far beyond what normal Cosegans achieved."

"And you can replicate that?"

"Not yet, but it's totally possible." His face lit up like a child facing a mountain of presents on his birthday. "I'm *so close* to cracking the code. It's mostly about consciously directing the energy of our cells. It's *real*."

"How long do you really want to live?"

"Are you kidding? Forever!"

Parson frowned. "Immortality? Is that even possible?"

"I'm sure as hell going to try to find out." His expression was serious, like a scientist absorbing breakthrough lab results. "I'm so busy, there's so much to do, there's no time to die."

"But don't you think at a certain point, you'll get tired of this life?"

Kalor scoffed. "Ask me in a thousand years."

# THIRTY-ONE

***Present Day – Williams, Arizona***

Rip and Gale decided to put Ovan away. "Too risky," Rip had told him. "I'm sure you understand."

"More than you could ever know," he'd responded. "I'll be here when you get safe."

They'd already asked him if he could help them navigate their way back to Booker's protection.

"I only know what future has happened before my death." He'd shocked them with the admission that he was not like Trynn, not communicating across the void, but rather that they were dealing with the entirety of his consciousness uploaded to a micro-Eysen. "Everything has changed trillions of times since then. I'd only be guessing. They'd be very *good* guesses, however, discounting the actuality of my second-hand knowledge of your time, and you'd be left with not much better than you'll do without me."

"We might take that," Gale said, but Ovan had insisted.

Rip kept peeking out the motel room's window. "A lot of old cars out there. Maybe someone would give us a ride in one."

"We'd stand out," Gale said.

Rip thought of another ride, a lifetime ago, in the Blue Ridge

Mountains of Virginia, when they cruised to safety in a primer gray jeep on country roads. Then he recalled how that had ended. "Damn it," he barked.

"What?" Gale feared he'd seen trouble out the window.

"Rusty is dead. *All* of them are dead. Most of them were just grad students like we lost in Virginia."

"But the ones at the Canyon knew there was some risk."

"They didn't know they could lose their lives!" They were just students, trusted by Rip and paid by Booker, scattered around the globe. For years, these search teams had been pursuing leads, anything remotely Cosegan, Imaze, or simply unexplained, advanced, or OOPart. "We have to stop the search teams."

"Without them, we never would have found Ovan," Gale pointed out. "You know, the deaths—" Her voice cracked, and it took a second before she could press on. "The losses are unbearable to me, too, but the stakes . . . Cira, her future, *everyone's* future. Maybe I've grown hard over the years, but we *have* to keep going. We have to stop Kalor Locke, help Trynn get to the truth point, find Finality, and throw that Infinity Switch." She met his eyes. "*That's* when all the killing will end."

"Okay," Rip said, inhaling deeply. "Then I guess it's time."

She nodded. "Call him."

They'd picked up a burner phone at a convenience store on the walk from the train station. They'd decided not to contact Booker because they believed his communications had been compromised, and they could not risk jeopardizing Cira. But there was one other person they could trust: Rip's father.

---

"I figured you were in some more trouble, or close by," Rip's father said. "As soon as the helicopters started flying overhead about ninety minutes ago."

"You need to get to safety," Rip said, frustrated his actions had put his father in danger again.

"Already have. I'm clear of my house and the radio station. Don't want to say where."

"Good."

"And you know I always use burner phones. I'm about to dump this one now that you contaminated it. Here's my next number. Ready?"

"Go ahead," Rip said, knowing his father would use family code. A quick string of statements, such as, "The number of kids Eddie's sister has." That was easy. Rip recalled his dad's good friend growing up was a guy named Eddie. They were like family, so Rip recalled that Tina had three kids. "How many dogs Wanda owns." Rip knew Wanda hated dogs, so that was a zero. The rapid-fire clues went on like that until Rip had the new number.

With that out of the way, his father asked, "What do you need?"

"A car," Rip said. "Nothing connected to you."

"But not one you'll be returning?"

"Possibly not." Rip thought of the many vehicles he'd lost over the years. "But we can have funds sent to more than cover the replacement cost."

"I can get you something. Where are you?"

"Williams."

"Why?"

"We were at the Canyon."

"Then get *out* of Williams," his father snapped. "It's the first place they'll look."

"We *need* a car," Rip repeated, sounding more desperate than he wanted.

"Is Cira with you?"

"No."

"At least there's that. I know a guy in Kingman right now, for the car show. Have you seen a bunch of fancy rides?'

"Yeah."

"Well, he's there. Ice blue K code '66 Ford Mustang convertible."

"Anyone with a car like that is not going to part with it."

"True enough, unless the cash is right. We had dinner last night. He's got fifty or sixty into it. Said it'll bring around eighty grand, but like you said, he wasn't wanting to sell."

"So?"

"So get your buddy Booker to wire him a hundred, and I think that car could be yours."

Gale looked at Rip. "Wouldn't it be easier to rent something?"

"Do we trust any of our fake identities?" Rip asked.

"It'll get you out now, and it's *very* fast," Rip's father added. "You may well need some speed."

"We can't contact Booker right now."

"I figured, or you wouldn't be calling me. Your word is good enough."

Gale pointed up. Rip heard it too, a helicopter flying overhead not far from their motel.

"Fine," Rip said. "Do the deal."

# THIRTY-TWO

***Present Day – An island in the Philippines***

Cira called Booker. "Shouldn't they have been back by now?" She knew that since this was the first time Rip and Gale had left without her, they would let her know if they were going to be even a few minutes late.

"Your parents have encountered some trouble," Booker replied gently. "There was an attack at the Grand Canyon."

"Are they *okay?*"

"They survived the initial battle."

"That's *not* an answer!"

"Cira, I'm sorry, but I don't know where they are just now." He didn't tell her how many Blaxers had died, or that Federal agencies would now be crawling all over the Southwest searching for them, meaning even if they lived, they might wind up in custody, which in itself was a kind of death sentence from which Booker might not be able to ever extract them.

"Who did the attack?" Cira asked. "Vans, right? Of course it was Vans. Kalor Locke is evil!"

"Yes, it was Vans. We're not—"

"Where could they be?" she interrupted. "You're using satellites, right? How many Blaxers are in the area?"

"We are checking all satellite data, but you know your mom and dad are good at running, hiding. They—"

"They must be hurt. *Were* they hurt? Why haven't they called in?"

Booker sighed. "We have no indication they were injured in the attack. Not calling in, well, there's some history there going back to the first time they ran, with the first Eysen, before you were born. I think they might be worried that my communications are compromised since the Vans were waiting for them."

"*Are* they compromised?"

"Nothing we can find."

"Then how did the Vans know where they'd be?"

"We don't know yet," Booker admitted, frustrated. "And to answer your other question, we have more than a thousand Blaxers on the ground in Arizona, and your parents know where a dozen safe houses are in that region. We're *going* to find them. I promise."

# THIRTY-THREE

***Present Day – New York City***

Shanoah knew that she would have to intervene in Trinity's life sooner rather than later. *The Terminus Clock continues to tick,* she thought as she walked the busy streets of Manhattan, but it wasn't that time pressure which worried her most. *Trynn will soon reach Finality, and then he'll push the Switch. I've got to get home, and Trinity is the key.*

A few minutes later, a man joined her on Liberty Street. He matched her stride, but walked in silence until she spoke. The man, Levi, had been her first recruit. One of the easiest to spot, he was definitely an Etheren, and definitely had some knowledge of who he was, at least in an esoteric sense. Before, Levi had been leading workshops and seminars on how to identify with ones 'higher self'. She had taken one of his retreats just to be sure he was a descendant. Now, he was the head of her operations, and oversaw the nine directors. She trusted him as much as she could trust anyone in the Far Future.

"Nice to see you, Levi."

"And you," he said. "Your thoughts are full."

"You noticed."

"Always," he said as they crossed South End Avenue. "Trinity is not the only thing that brought you to New York."

"No. I came to meet you, as well."

"And another."

"Yes."

"So how is Ricardo?"

"Dark today."

"It's a dangerous game you're playing with him."

"He is Etheren," she said firmly.

"I know, but the damage . . . "

"It can be repaired."

He sighed. "You can't save them all."

"Why?" she demanded. "Why can't I?"

"There is a list of reasons," he said as they cut through the trees in Pumphouse Park. It would take longer, but Shanoah always preferred the trees over the traffic and congestion of the cities. For similar reasons, she'd rather walk than take a taxi. Shanoah longed for air. "There are too many. We're running out of time. Kalor Locke has corrupted too many. Drugs, alcohol, and mental illness is so prevalent among Etheren descendants that—"

"I know your limiting reasons," she said. "What if I had not come for you?"

"I'd be wealthy and comfortable—*not* being hunted by Kalor Locke."

She laughed. "Your books weren't selling *that* well."

"I'm hurt. Anyway, they were starting to take off. My retreats were fully booked."

"My point is, you were missing your true and authentic self. You could never have been happy or satisfied with life, no matter how rich you got, regardless of the amount of materialistic things you accumulated."

He shrugged. "It would have been fun to try."

"You know that's not true. It would have been frustrating and empty."

"True, but Ricardo is different."

"Yes, he is."

"I didn't mean that in a good way."

"I know how you meant it."

They emerged from the trees. Shanoah carefully scanned in all directions. Used to moving about freely, she also knew of the constant threats and risks. Rip and Gale might have officially been the most wanted people in the world, but Shanoah and Cira were sought by far more powerful forces than the US Government. However, Shanoah held many advantages over her pursuers, knowing much of the future, with her greatly magnified levels of perception, cell rejuvenation, and highly enhanced mental and physical abilities. And now she had Booker Lipton and a network of Etherens behind her.

There was one other strength that protected Shanoah from her enemies: Trynn. The great Eysen maker stood watching and manipulating events to keep his love safe, a chore he'd undertake even if Shanoah was not dear to him, for she was the last best hope at stopping Kalor Locke, ending the Terminus Doom, and reaching Finality so he could push the Switch.

"There's our ride," Levi said. "The pretty blue one."

They crossed a street and moved quickly to the docks. The boat waiting in the small marina was idling, captained by an Etheren descendent, a woman she'd rescued a year earlier. It would take them to a waiting yacht. Even after all the decades in the Far Future, Shanoah had still not grown accustomed to traveling in heavy vehicles; cars, boats, planes, they were all so mechanical, slow, solid in the bulky sense of the word. She missed the light, glowing vehicles of Cosega . . .

"Isn't it beautiful?" she said to Levi over the roar of the engine.

"Yes, yes," he said, not sure *why* the Statue of Liberty so captivated Shanoah. He motioned to the captain to slow down and circle the island.

Shanoah marveled at the grand lady as if she were made of

light instead of copper sheeting. The statue depicted a robed Roman liberty goddess called Libertas.

"Why do you like her so much?" Levi asked.

"It is the torch she holds above her head, and perhaps the broken shackle and chains which lay at her feet."

"Why the torch?"

"We are people of light," Shanoah said, her eyes glued to the statue as they circled Liberty Island. "She is brave, seeking freedom and justice—liberty, of course."

"Yes, and beautiful . . . proud."

"I think she is also a great symbol for hope. For so long, immigrants arriving saw her as the end of their long journey to discover freedom. She is hope, and she holds the light to show the way, enlightening the world."

"She is like you," Levi said.

Shanoah smiled, but shook her head. "She is an Etheren, like you."

"We are all part Etheren," Levi said. "The inner-self, human's true power waiting to be tapped."

"Yes, it's true."

Shanoah continued watching the Statue as they cruised under the Verrazzano Narrows Bridge, as if it might reveal something to her. The sounds of countless vehicles from thirteen lanes of traffic above caused her to look up. She was amused by the bridges these modern people made. This one was beautiful, in its way. When it opened in the 1960s, its 4,260 foot span made it the longest suspension bridge on earth.

"One day, they will use light," Shanoah said softly.

"What?" Levi asked.

She shook her head. "Nothing."

Levi pointed out to sea. Not far from where the Lower New York Bay met the Atlantic Ocean, a white, two-hundred-foot yacht could be seen. "*The Teason,*" he said.

Shanoah nodded. Although she'd never been aboard the luxurious yacht before, she had been to the actual Etheren settle-ment for which it had been named. "We must be careful of these kinds of displays of wealth."

"Tell that to Zorger," he said. "Saving the world is not easy without the proper funding."

# THIRTY-FOUR

***Present Day – Northern Arizona***

Early the next morning, after deciding to stay on back roads and navigating the switchbacks into Oak Creek Canyon, Rip and Gale relaxed a bit. However, as soon as they crossed the bridge into Sedona, traffic began to slow, and Rip gripped the wheel tighter.

"You hear the helicopter?" Gale asked.

Normally, the distant *whop-whop-whop* of spinning rotors high above would not have stood out, especially against the heavy purring of the Mustang's V8 engine, but sounds of approaching choppers was one that haunted them. "Yeah."

"Could be a helicopter tour company," Gale said optimistically. "They do that here in Sedona."

"Wouldn't that be nice? Maybe if we were two other people on a different day." Rip glanced in the rearview mirror. "Four cars back, there's an SUV. Maybe you should turn around and check, but I'm pretty sure that's the barrel of a gun sticking out the passenger window."

She spun. "Definitely a gun. Doubtful there are any other people being chased by soldiers of fortune in Sedona today."

"Probably not. So they're for us."

"This heavy traffic will buy us some time. Tight lanes, so they can't exactly race up here."

"Not enough time with the helicopter overhead."

"How did they find us? We left Williams clean. This is *why* we came on the back roads."

"We might as well put down the top," Rip said. They had debated whether to lower the convertible's top, but chosen not to in case of helicopters. "There's no telling what tech Locke's using against us. He could somehow be following us with a satellite. For all we know, the Ovan sphere *was* planted."

She squinted at him, astonished, but his eyes were flashing between the rearview and the windshield, searching for a way to escape. He worried that at their slow speed the killer could just walk up to the car and execute them at a stoplight. "Do you really think the Ovan sphere is a Kalor creation?"

"I don't know. Anything's possible. He may have wanted us to stay away from the caverns in the Canyon, or he doesn't even know about them and he just wanted us to fall into a trap." He pounded the wheel, frustrated to be hemmed in by traffic. "I mean, the Vans were there already. We've been so enamored with Ovan that we haven't gone over enough of that. Think about it. They were just waiting to ambush us and the Blaxers." He glanced in the sideview mirror. The vehicle was still four cars back. Traffic was still crawling.

"But the sphere was embedded *in* stone," Gale said. "It had to have been there for millions of years."

"Yeah, but maybe he had someone plant it eleven million years ago, taking the Eysen war to a new level. We don't know *who* Ovan is. He may never have existed—he could actually be Trynn's mortal enemy." Rip stuck his head out the window, trying to see up into the sky, hoping to spot the helicopter. No luck, but he could still hear it.

"Maybe we should dump the sphere," Gale suggested.

"What if it's the key to getting Kalor Locke? What if *that's* why he's going to so much trouble to stop us from keeping it?"

"Then let's find a place to hide it until we can figure out which it is."

Before they could make a decision, a man ran from the SUV, a submachine gun hanging at his side.

"You're riding shotgun," Rip said. "Handle it."

Gale pulled one of the Blaxer's guns off the floor. "Yeah."

Rip swerved into the oncoming lane, then hit the accelerator, putting to work every single one of the two hundred seventy-one horses under the hood. Another car veered into a stone wall to avoid a head-on with the Mustang. Horns blaring, tires screeching, sounds of crunching metal brought a cacophony of confused wildness as chaos swept the streets and sidewalks of the tourist mecca.

Rip pushed the pedal to the floor, throwing them both back hard against the white vinyl seats. As the Mustang barreled ahead, it sideswiped an old pickup truck.

"That's a thousand dollar scratch!" Rip yelled, thinking of his father's warning *not* to tear up the car.

An instant later, Gale squeezed off the first few shots, taking down the gunmen who had the unfortunate luck of getting clipped by the pickup truck before he could scramble out of the way. The truck bounced onto the sidewalk to avoid the SUV, which by Rip's best view, contained at least four other armed men in addition to the driver.

"Rip!" Gale shouted as they came out of a blind curve into more congestion.

"I see it, I see it!"

The septic truck just in front of them might as well have been a fortress. Somehow, Rip got through, swerving around it and onto a narrow concrete storm drain tinted red, like everything else in Sedona. Jerking over another curb, testing the decades-old suspension, Rip wished they'd stolen the vintage Ford Bronco he'd seen in Williams.

This time, grazing a signpost, Rip muttered loudly, "That's another thousand."

"Where are you going? Look out!" Gale yelled as the Mustang ended up on a busy sidewalk. The road, now separated by giant planters, was no longer an option even if it hadn't been packed full of cars. Traffic held at a standstill from the mess they had left behind minutes earlier.

"There's no choice!"

"Watch it, watch it!"

He cranked the wheel hard, crashing into the corner of a New Age gift shop selling crystals, touting the widest selection of rare minerals in the universe. If Rip had not been fighting to keep control of the vehicle amid a raining storm of broken plate glass, flying amethysts, rose quartz, and an extraordinary geode, he might have wondered if a store such as this might have some Globotite. Maybe they kept it in a secret backroom. Perhaps an ancient Native American toiling in the basement was conjuring up what was truly the rarest mineral in the universe.

"Look out!" Gale screamed as they slammed into the colored glass doors of an ice cream parlor and fudge shop.

Rip threw the mustang into reverse, craning his neck to look over his shoulder, hoping to avoid killing any pedestrians, and saw something worse. Another attacker, ten feet behind them, was leveling his gun, readying to let loose a stream of bullets upon them.

Rip stomped the pedal. The Mustang responded in a smoking rubber squeal as it flew backwards, burying the gun man, rolling over him and leaving his crushed and broken body among the glass and debris.

Rip's feet continued to dance over the pedals as he pushed the muscle car to its limits, fishtailing, then tearing across a fountained courtyard and into a narrow alley separating a realtor and a vortex tour company. The only thing following them at the moment was the distant sound of the helicopter.

# THIRTY-FIVE

***Present Day – Atlantic Ocean, off the East Cost of the United States***

The large Yacht seemed a magical presence on the water. Although Shanoah did not approve, she could not deny it was a beautiful craft, even if no light was used as a material to construct it.

Rob Zorger, a tall, thin man, greeted Shanoah and Levi as the cabin cruiser departed. "I see you frowning," the tanned man said. His faded gray cotton pants, rumpled white linen shirt, and weathered face gave him the look of a wealthy man who spent a lot of time on a boat.

"Too fancy," Shanoah said. "What did this cost?"

"What does it matter?"

"The money is supposed to fund the uprising."

"And it does," Zorger said, walking on the aft deck, pointing to the built-in loungers. "Sit."

"I like it," Levi said, taking a seat. A slender woman brought him a drink.

"No alcohol," Shanoah said.

"Of course not," Zorger replied, feeling insulted. "Herbs and fruits. I hope you'll love it."

The woman handed Shanoah one as well, starry-eyed, as if serving a celebrity. "Thank you," Shanoah said, making eye contact. "This is delicious."

"See?" Zorger said.

"But *this* is too much," she said, motioning with her arm, indicating the yacht.

"We need this to mingle with the elites."

"The Havloses," she corrected.

"Yes. And you know the money is not an issue."

"Of course I know. *I* provided the initial seeds."

"Yes, yes, but we have done quite well since then. Preserving a hidden culture, awakening a sleeping people, avoiding our probing enemies . . . these things do not come cheap."

She nodded.

"Consider the yacht as camouflage."

She frowned, but relented. "You're probably right."

"Shanoah, I would do my job in the back of a broken-down pickup truck, or from the seat of a rusty bicycle, whatever worked best. I admit, I don't mind working from this fabulous little ship, I enjoy being comfortable and seeing beautiful places, but make no mistake, I *am* working."

"I know," she said. Zorger was one of her favorites; an early recruit, and a straight-line Etheren descendant. Smart, intuitive, and full of energy, he had parlayed their resources and been crucial in building the organization that she hoped would one day replace the corrupt Havlos stranglehold on leadership of the modern world governments—and, more importantly, reclaim the power from the Havlos-run corporations.

"We are at capacity at the center," he said. "I've been unable to acquire the adjoining land, and I've been thinking, maybe we should *not* concentrate our numbers."

Shanoah nodded, sipping more of the concoction. "It is risky. Where should the second center be?"

"I was thinking we should open fifteen more."

She blinked back at him. "Why so many?"

"We have the people to staff them now. Let's step up recruitment, fight this world of ill intentions."

"It seems that could bring us notice. Like this yacht."

He laughed. "The yacht gives us credibility with the people we seek to undermine. But more descendants open and understanding to their ancestry, to what is possible, wanderers ready to remake the world, that is not risky. That is our *purpose*."

"You are right, but it could bring trouble before we are ready."

"If trouble is that close, then we must *get* ready."

Shanoah remained silent for more than a minute, staring out across the ocean as if looking into the memory of a future she'd seen long ago in the past.

Zorger and Levi shared a glance. They both knew her better than most, but Levi knew her best of all. He even knew about Rick Dorey, the first Far Future person she'd encountered after crashing in Florida in 1974. He'd helped her, been kind, actually fallen in love with her, like so many did, but she'd slipped out of his life, leaving that love unrequited. Still, she'd secretly kept tabs on him, anonymously helping him when he needed it.

Levi quietly checked up on him these days. Now in his seventies, it was an easier task. He'd be shocked to see Shanoah had hardly aged while he'd grown to be an old man.

"I think we are not going to be able to avoid the battles that are coming," she finally said. "I just wish I knew if we have a chance to prevail."

"That's why we need more centers, more people. It's time to fully commit to overthrowing the Havloses."

"I fear we are simply once again igniting the Havlos/Cosegan war from my time," she said.

"Maybe we need to," Zorger said.

She shook her head. "You have no idea how horrific it was. War is never the correct course."

"It's coming whether we like it or not," Levi began. "How can it not? When enough Etheren and Cosegan descendants wake up and realize who they are, where they came from, the true history of humanity on earth and the real potential each holds within, they're going to revolt."

"To the revolution," Zorger said, raising his glass.

"Always remember," Shanoah said, "'love' is written backwards within the word revolution."

"So it is," Zorger said.

"That's only to keep it hidden. That's the secret of all great rebellions . . . love."

# THIRTY-SIX

***Present Day – Sedona, Arizona***

More ice blue paint scraped off the classic automobile as it squeezed through the alley. The unforgiving red rock walls began grinding into the metal.

"That's gonna cost three thousand!"

Taking the corner too fast produced a crunching dent in Gale's door that Rip did not want to guess the repair cost of. The Mustang burst out of the alley, landing on a wider driveway.

"It's blocked!" Gale yelled. "And stop worrying about the repair costs."

Rip had already seen the UPS truck and steered onto the narrow sidewalk, unable to avoid crashing through a kiosk. Dreamcatchers, kites, frisbees, and colorful banners flew across the hood, windshield, and roof like over-sized confetti.

"I feel like we just hit a damned piñata!" Rip barked. A rainbow-colored streamer was caught on the antenna.

"There they are!" Gale yelled. "Half a block down."

"How many people still in the vehicle?"

"Looks like only two," Gale said, straining to see inside the SUV. "Where are the others?"

"Hold on!" Rip said, taking the car off the curb into the road, through a tangle of vehicles screeching to a halt in both directions. "Still not enough lane." Slamming the prized Ford through the traffic, Rip used every bit of the engine's power to forcefully move lesser cars from his path. "Made it!" As they got onto another side street, Rip exhaled for what felt like the first time since they'd reached Sedona. The rainbow streamer was still hanging on the antenna.

"Where are we going?" Gale asked.

"I have no idea. I'm just trying to keep us moving. We stop, we die."

"I don't need that reminder!"

Rip navigated to the end of the short street and clipped a row of electric rental-bikes, sending the expensive bicycles falling like dominoes as the Mustang sped around the corner.

"No! We're in a parking lot!" Rip checked the rearview, hoping the SUV wasn't there. Relieved it hadn't arrived yet, he still knew there was no going back.

"Booker knows we were ambushed at the Canyon. Where is he with reinforcements?" Gale said.

"Yeah, if Locke can find us, Booker ought to have no trouble."

Seeing the tight lanes between the parked cars was clear, Rip punched the accelerator, taking the speedometer up to fifty mph and sending their muscle car through a small split rail fence, landing in the scrub brush desert and spraying red, rocky soil.

The grade inclined gently at first, then grew steeper as the Mustang bounced over rocks, taking out small plants and crunching whatever else came under the wheels.

"Do you realize that 1966 Mustangs are *not* four-wheel-drive?" Gale said.

"Really? Seems to be doing fine."

They continued to plow through the rough terrain. Gale scanned the area in front of them. Nothing but stark wilderness. "How far do you think we can get?"

"A lot farther out here than we would back on those crowded streets."

"We may have lost the SUV, but not the helicopter!" Gale yelled, leaning out the window, finally spotting the chopper in the open sky. "They see us!"

"I know, I know!" Rip replied, wishing there were Blaxers left to save them. "Maybe we should call Booker."

"Too risky!"

"It doesn't matter if the communications are compromised. The Vans already know where we are."

"Yeah, but they don't know where Cira is. If we call in, we could be leading them straight to Cira." That was something they would not risk. "I just don't know why Booker hasn't found us yet!"

# THIRTY-SEVEN

***Present Day***

Ricardo was not the most troubled Etheren descendant Shanoah had encountered. The majority of them were coping with drug or alcohol dependency, and many had mental health issues. The common thread did not surprise her. Even after so much time, the Etheren within them remained strong and at great odds with the modern world that Havlos had forged.

Countless descendants who had been rescued described feeling overwhelmed or cut off from *reality*. There were large numbers of artists, fantasy and sci-fi authors, illustrators, video game makers and players, among *the unknown Etherens*, as Shanoah sometimes called them. It was a slow process bringing them out to the center, cleaning them up, exposing them to Etheren ideas, skills, and eventually awakening their powers and abilities. Only then was the origin story told, the truth about humanity's past. At that point, it didn't seem hard for any of them to believe.

However, the hard part was getting them to the center in the first place. There were often legal challenges and relatives to deal with. Money wasn't an issue. Shanoah had begun accumulating a fortune back in the 1970s, first to afford her own life and travel needs as she tried to thwart Kalor Locke and find her ship, and then to fund the Center and a growing network of Etheren operatives. Finally, there was the big money needed to finance a future uprising. At first, she'd traded off her knowledge of the future and made plenty of easy money. Eventually, loyalists like Zorger and others invested in a diversified portfolio of equities, real estate, and entire companies. The profits were rolling in now.

Ricardo was a troubled man with a strong Etheren lineage. His love of music brought him from the mountains of Mexico to New York City. He'd been discovered by an Etheren operative searching for other descendants. Shanoah only got involved because she recalled his name not from lists prepared by the Center's directors, but one she'd heard while studying the Far Future with Trynn.

She had told him all about the Center at their first meeting. "It's filled with creative people like you."

"No one is like me," he said in a sad, quiet voice. His accent somehow made his words sound as if he were hiding a great secret about himself.

"Of course not, but there are so many who feel out of place in this world, who only hear the calling of their gifts. I will fly you there and show it to you. If you don't want to stay, I will fly you right back here."

"I could not afford such a place."

"It's all free. We have wonderful donors. You pay for nothing, and we actually pay you to create the work you love."

"That sounds too good to be true, and they say that if it does, then it is."

But Ricardo believed it. Shanoah had a way, an aura, as if she was incapable of lying. People trusted her and believed everything she said. However, Ricardo had also fallen in love with Shanoah, a common response. He wished more than anything to make her happy by going to the Center, but his demons were strong, and addictions held him tight.

Shanoah struggled with Ricardo. She wished to tell him everything, even before he got to the Center, believing the truth of where he ultimately came from would be enough to cure his addictions, or at least convince Ricardo to go so that the specialists at the Center could help him connect with his true self and rebuild his life. But he wouldn't go. She had discussed actually having him kidnapped and taken there forcefully, but Levi had been adamantly opposed to such a radical plan, saying it would violate the trust within the whole program.

"Please trust me," she told him that morning in New York.

"I do. It is me I don't trust."

Shanoah felt Ricardo was very powerful, and speculated he was descendant from an important Etheren. She recalled what she'd seen with Trynn that day. Ricardo might not survive, but if he did, the future would go easier for many other descendants. Ricardo could become a great and gentle leader, one they desperately needed to navigate the tumultuous decades ahead.

# THIRTY-EIGHT

***Present Day – Sedona, Arizona***

The Sedona desert landscape grew steeper and the boulders and outcroppings became bigger.

"We're going to run out of navigable desert pretty quick," Rip said. "I'll take us into those trees."

Gale glanced ahead. The only trees she saw were scrubby little pines, nothing that she would actually call a tree, but she figured that once they were on foot, there might be enough foliage to keep them hidden from the chopper.

"The only way we get out of here is to bring that chopper down," Rip said.

"How are we going to do that?"

"Bring the guns. We've got to get up to the high ground."

"You're going to shoot a helicopter out of the sky?"

"Unless you have any better ideas." Rip drove the car until it wedged in between the dry, hard trunks of ancient, gnarled pines. The classic car now looked like a battered junker from a salvage yard. "Oh well . . . at least it's still in one piece."

"Do you think those men will chase us on foot?'"

"Absolutely."

"Then what's to stop them from catching us?"

"Only our head start."

Sticking in the trees as best they could, running as fast as possible in the hot morning air, they gained elevation rapidly. The shadow of the circling chopper washed over them.

"What about Ovan?" Gale asked as they reached a small boulder field.

"I got it," Rip said.

"Shouldn't we stash it?"

"I don't know what to do," Rip admitted breathlessly. "But I keep feeling like we're on some sort of parallel with the first Eysen, when we ran in the mountains in Virginia. What if we hadn't taken it? Humanity might already be lost."

A hundred scenarios flashed in her mind. If she and Rip had never come together, Cira would not have been born. She thought of all the people who had died protecting them along the way; not just Blaxers who were professionals and knew the risks, but all the good and simple people, the kindness of strangers who had died only because they were doing what they thought was right.

Maybe they never should have taken the first Eysen that day.

"We need to decide," Rip shouted over the echoing sound of the helicopter.

"What if it's a plant? Tracking us somehow? The Vans were there too quick. They knew in advance we were going to be at the Canyon."

"It's the communications, not the Ovan Sphere. Kalor's smart, but he's not going to wait eleven million years to see if we'll find this obscure sphere. He wants Ovan."

"You think he knows about it?"

"I think he knows about everything," Rip panted. "What if he needs the Ovan sphere to complete his Super-Eysen?"

"We need to stop talking and save our breath. We need to keep moving faster than them."

"So we hold onto the sphere?"

"For now."

The steeper and higher they went, the more labored their breathing became. They stopped four minutes later, when the trees ran out.

"It's right above us!" Gale yelled, pointing to the helicopter.

"As soon as we leave this canopy, that bird is going to spot us," Rip said scanning the area for options. "Those sharpshooters will pick us off!"

"They know we're in these trees anyway," Gale said. "We have to chance it."

"There," he said, pointing to a narrow gap between two high rock pillars.

"You and I have both hiked enough canyons to know that could be a dead end. We could easily get bottled up in there. Then the Vans come and we're done."

"We could stay in these trees, wait for the Vans to come, maybe get lucky if there aren't too many of them. We might be able to take them by surprise . . . it's not too hard to be accurate with a submachine gun."

"Let's make a run for that opening next time the chopper makes its pass," Gale said. "If we have to fight them and kill them, I'd rather do it from inside the canyon where we'll have real cover, not count on bark and pine needles to stop bullets."

# THIRTY-NINE

***Cosegan Time – Jarvo's bunker Complex, Havlos Lands***

Jarvo stood attentive, a hard smile on his face as the military leaders reported the long list of Havlos successes against the Cosegans.

"Excellent," he said often, looking tough as always, like a street fighter ready to brawl. His bald head and stubbled beard, along with the angry creases on his face, told all that this was no man to cross.

Cass, his deputy, a slim, red-haired woman, stood nearby, wearing a confused expression. She was happy at the achievements, yet burdened by the knowledge that so many were suffering. She could not imagine how Cosegans, totally unaccustomed to war, even killing in any form, were coping with the atrocities both sides were inflicting.

*We are the cause of the Terminus Doom*, she thought, hiding the mounting dread behind an approving nod.

The leaders took turns relaying the latest territories occupied, towns annihilated, enemy technology and equipment captured or destroyed. Prisoners taken. Cosegans dead.

Jarvo hid his shake by clasping his large hands together

behind his back, but anyone watching him closely might have noticed the twitching around his eyes. Next time he would conduct meetings such as this outside so that he could wear sunglasses. "Excellent," he said again, concealing the quaking in his voice by speaking in short bursts rather than long sentences. He was sure no one would notice. Of course, he couldn't hide it forever, especially from Cass. She might have already picked up on his condition.

*Soon, I'll need to tell her, but then . . . then, I'll be forced to have her executed.* He glanced her way. Fortunately, Cass was looking at the woman speaking. The idea of watching her die saddened him. Perhaps he would imprison her with orders that she be shot upon his death, but what if they failed to carry out his final orders? No, that would be too risky. She'd have to be removed soon after he informed her, before she noticed.

*But what if she already has?*

*I could just sentence her tomorrow, just get it done, maybe not even tell her why.* He didn't *have* to tell her before they ended her life, but he owed her that much. She had been a good confidant and strategist, *too* good.

He'd heard rumors of a miracle drug, Revon, and wondered if it could help his condition. There was a team looking for it, but his experts told him it likely didn't exist anymore, if it ever *had*.

*I do have an Eysen,* he thought, pretending to listen. He wanted to *actually* be listening, but his health had become a major distraction. *My little crystal ball was made in the Far Past. Veeshal must know of this Revon. However, that witch would like nothing more than to see me suffer, see me dead.*

Each direction he turned in search of an answer, a way to survive, a chance to live, there only seemed to be dead ends. Doctors had already told him that the damage to his cells was beyond repair, even with advanced Cosegan medicine. Yet he'd sent a unit to capture several Cell framers, the Cosegan health scientists who had long ago devised methods to manipulate human cells, and could teach people to do it themselves.

"The last twenty percent of a territory is always the hardest to take," Jarvo said before gasping for air. He covered it by quickly drinking some water, then dismissed the war committee.

A few hours later, his plans of concealment fell apart when he was notified that Nels, the lead scientist working on his Eysen, had died. She'd left a confidential letter for him detailing all she'd learned about the mysterious and deadly Eysen disease. Her closing sentence left him in despair: *We've been poisoned. The pain is too much to bear. You would be wise to end your life before you worsen, because you are next. You could have no more than a few days remaining.*

Cass joined him soon after the news.

"I think I'm dying," he blurted out.

"How?" She knew he was sick, but the severity of *how* sick shocked her.

"The original Eysen . . ." His strained expression turned to one of amusement. "The irony is almost enough to save me. An Eysen, from the beginning of Cosegan expansion, has been slowly killing me." He laughed bitterly.

"How?" she asked again, sad, but also not. Surprised, yet not.

"The original Eysen cores were not stable. They used too much power. They leak a kind of poison. Not radiation, but something similar. Globotite fused with other things makes poison vapors so subtle that only through physical contact with the Eysen is one contaminated."

"I'm sorry," she said, her sincerity true. Cass loved Jarvo. She hated him, too, but the love side was front and center in the face of his death.

"Thank you." He did not dare tell her that the original Eysen, what was now his murderer, would also make a massive weapon, that the instability of the core could be channeled, that energy properly set and adapted to one of his strike weapons imbued it with ten times the destructive force of what they'd used to obliterate Tunssee.

He would lose the Eysen war, but this revelation in faulty

technology would, with all certainty, allow him to win the Cosegan war.

The question was, would he live to see it?

# FORTY

**_Far Past – The Works_**

Inside the Works, the view of endless stars seemed to be the only thing keeping Veeshal steady.

"There you are," Kenner said to his mother as he walked into the main lab. "You'll like this news."

"Good news? Yes, please, all you've got."

"Turns out we don't have to try to kill Jarvo. We already did it," Kenner said.

"How?"

"Eysen poisoning."

"The core?" she asked.

He nodded. "It was one of the first."

"I'd forgotten," she said. "The unstable core."

He looked surprised. "How could you *forget* such a thing?"

"We went so far beyond that. I don't dwell on the failures, I build upon them."

"His death won't be quick."

"No," she said, doing calculations in her head. "Depending how much time he has been in contact . . . "

Kenner gave her the figure.

"That would mean, given his weight and general health, quite good for a Havlos . . . oh dear."

"What?"

"Well, it will be a slow and excruciating death for him."

Kenner shrugged. "Karma."

"He *has* been a monster."

"Are you surprised? He is a Havlos."

"Not all Havloses are bad."

"Hitler was a Havlos descendant."

She relented that one. "True."

"Every evil person in human history has been a Havlos," Kenner went on. "Not one Cosegan among them."

"There have been plenty of bad Cosegans."

"But none have crossed the line into *evil*, and relative to the number of bad Havloses, there has virtually been no bad Cosegans."

"Sure, relatively speaking, but there have still been more bad Cosegans than there should have been."

"Depends on what happens with Trynn, doesn't it?'

"And us."

"Can we do anything to speed up Jarvo's demise?"

"Not soon enough to change the outcome of the war."

"Unless . . . " He looked at her, finishing his thought with his eyes, as only a son could do with his mother.

She nodded knowingly, and hesitated before responding. "That would be a dangerous game to play."

"We must try." He looked at her pleadingly, but at the same time, his tone made it clear he was not asking permission. "We can control it. We've done it before."

"Days." Her voice rose impatiently. "We've played with *days*, but you are talking about a million years. Time is very unpredictable when you stretch it out, dangerous, unstable—"

"Like the cores in our first Eysens?"

"Much worse!" Her expression flooded with fear. "Much, *much* worse."

"It doesn't have to be a million years," he said. "Not if we do it right."

She stared at him for a moment, her brilliant mind catching up to his scheme. "Maybe," she said, some excitement returning to her voice. "But the complexities are enormous. We'd have to build an Eysen just to contain and extrapolate all the variables."

"Good thing the Works is equipped for just such an endeavor."

"Oh, this is far more than an endeavor. This is a *quest*."

"To save the world," he said, emboldened.

"By changing it."

"We can do it."

She suddenly turned somber and serious, her expression extreme. Her words came focused and slow. "If we fail—"

"I know," he said, anticipating her words. "So we won't fail."

"But if we *do*," she said, pointing a narrow finger at him. "If we fail, even making a single little mistake, any miscalculation at all, then we will become the Terminus Doom."

# FORTY-ONE

***Present Day – Sedona, Arizona***

The canyon turned out not to be a dead end. It was worse. It quickly opened, leaving few places to hide. The vistas were breathtaking as Cathedral Rock and Coffeepot came into view.

"I guess this isn't where we make our last stand," Rip said, looking around.

"Keep moving," Gale said, thinking of Cira as Rip's words, *last stand,* echoed in her head. "We have to survive this day."

The chopper circled continuously, but so far Rip and Gale had been able to stay in the shadows and edges, avoiding detection.

"We're running out of cover," Rip said. "Unless we can get across to there."

"Wait until the helicopter makes its long sweep. We might have time." They'd been watching the pilot's small flight patterns, most likely ex-military, trained in grid searches. Just after it flew overhead, they counted to ten, then bolted.

The scenic panorama visible from their elevation stretched in all directions. It seemed they were a million miles from anything, especially a way out. On the other side of the ridge, the terrain transformed again. Now they were walking on smooth rock surrounded by red boulders ranging in size from small cars to enormous, house-sized monoliths.

"Lots of hiding places here," Rip said.

"Then this is where we do it." Gale looked at him as they ducked into a low overhang just before the chopper returned.

"Yeah," Rip said. "We're going to need some luck. It'd be a lot easier if the Vans walked into this area while the chopper was on the away-sweep."

She closed her eyes for a moment. "We're going to need more than luck."

"We can do this," he said, giving her the better gun.

"Do we have enough ammo?"

"We're going to have to. Don't worry about it. Shoot as much as you need to."

"And if it runs out?"

He shook his head. "I'll be shooting."

"From where?"

He pointed to another alcove, diagonally across from her. "If they come this way at all, they'll most likely go through here. We should be able to see them before they see us."

"Okay."

"Remember, try not to shoot until they get here." He indicated a line in the trail from where they would both have the clearest shot. He found a lighter colored rock and placed it so they could both see it.

She nodded.

"Good luck."

After a seemingly endless six minutes, three Vans appeared. The well-trained men approached the area cautiously, but Rip had been right—they funneled up the trail between the large stones.

Rip fired first, but instantly two of the Vans and Gale joined the battle. The symphonic sound of four submachine guns raging in close quarters echoing off the stones at dozens of different angles made anything beyond instinctive thought impossible.

The thundering fury put reality in slow motion for several seconds. When silence returned, two of the Vans were on the ground, bloody, already looking violently gruesome. Rip and Gale had seen plenty of blood and death since that first Eysen discovery, but something this close, casualties *they'd* caused, took a cruel stab at their souls, another bit of peace surrendered.

The stone next to Rip suddenly chipped and cracked in a hail of bullets. The third man had found cover. "Come out!" he yelled in accented English.

"You first!" Rip countered.

He laughed. "You're dead, man."

Rip couldn't deny this, and he heard the man calling in coordinates and realized the helicopter could easily land back in that clearing. Rip caught Gale's eyes and signaled her to run. He held up three fingers and then lowered one, counting down as he closed his fist, representing zero, then jerked his fist and pointed hard down the trail, mouthing, "*Go!*"

She took off. The man heard and peered out of his hiding place, already shooting. Rip shot at the same time, but he'd anticipated where the Van would be, and his bullets tore the man's face open. Rip was there almost at the same time the guy's body hit the ground.

"Gale, come back, quick!"

They both pulled the guns and ammo from the dead men, repulsed by the deed, but determined to survive.

"Here comes the chopper!" Gale said.

"Stay here and just keep shooting toward it. You'll be shielded by these rocks."

"Where are you going?"

"Up there."

"Climbing?"

"It's been a while, but I think I can still get up a cliff face."

"They'll be shooting at you."

"That's what you're for."

"Still, they'll—"

"Not if I'm fast enough," he said, already six feet up and looking for his next handhold.

Rip's position during the climb, with Gale providing cover, made it impossible for the chopper to get around to a vantage point where they'd be able to spot him. Minutes later, he was at the top.

*Now, all I have to do is figure out how to shoot a helicopter out of the air.*

*One chance . . . I'm only going to get one shot.*

# FORTY-TWO

**Present Day – Sedona, Arizona**

Arriving like a desert thunderstorm, the chopper banked sideways and flew in closer than Rip had anticipated, clearly attempting to provide the Van manning the guns a better view.

*It's seen me . . . Damn it, they're going to get Gale, I need to—*

A hail of bullets blasted into the red rock all around him. He rolled on the hard ground, nearly going off the edge of the high pinnacle.

The airborne Vans had eliminated Rip's only advantage. The element of surprise gone, he scrambled to the single piece of cover the top of the pinnacle provided. Bullets sprayed the dusty surface as he dropped down onto a contour shelf. The narrow ledge made him invisible as long as he didn't fall. The artificial wind produced by the rotors whipped at him, pushing his body hard toward the cliff's edge. Somehow, he held on until it passed.

Rip knew from geology courses he had taken that the entire Sedona area had once been sea bottom, and that the formation he was on was hundreds of millions of years old.

*Cosegans could have stood here.*

He silently thanked the elements and conditions that had come together to save him in that moment. The trees on the opposing cliff prevented the chopper from positioning so that it could get behind him, at least until they could get at a better angle above. He knew they'd circle and slow in a hover, giving him his only chance.

The Vans took some shots at Gale, and he heard her returning fire, telling him they had missed. The chopper came around again, machine gun fire striking the top of the pinnacle, pinning him down, leaving him unable to attempt a shot, knowing each minute it took to end the siege was a minute closer to more Vans reaching Gale below.

*Soon we'll be outnumbered. I've got to take the next shot.*

Rip crawled to the corner of the ledge. Stealing a look at the sheer drop, he lowered himself down to a smaller ledge, this one about as wide as his feet. It also left him more exposed.

*If they didn't see me before, they probably won't see me until they pass. Hopefully by then they'll be crashing.*

If they'd seen him move, however, that all went out the window.

He listened closely to another futile exchange between Gale and the helicopter while counting the seconds until they came back.

The thudding thunder returned with the chopper swooping lower this time, panicking him. He feared they'd seen him reposition. It turned out they were actually angling for a better shot at his old location. The bullets obliterated his former hiding place.

Rip used the bullets as a gauge, timing his play. As the chipping rock and dust ran farther from him, he sucked in air and risked making his move. As he rose, bullets landing inches in front of him, the chopper just past its lowest and closest point, Rip fired, not stopping until there were no bullets left.

The storm opened. Like standing in a hurricane on a shooting range, Rip collapsed as the noise, the pressure and stress, caught him. Not knowing if he'd been hit, every part of him ached and burned, but the chaos quieted slightly. As he lay on the rocks, wondering if he was dead or alive, he realized there was a new sound, a whining, droning, screeching sound. He managed to roll over, getting to his knees, and saw the chopper going down, trailing black smoke, twisting and hurtling like a deranged creature as it sunk. Rotors clipped the rock wall. There was still gunfire. He leaned toward the edge, desperate to know where Gale was, horrified she might get crushed by the falling wreckage.

# FORTY-THREE

***Present Day – Washington DC***

The nation's capital was the most surveilled city in the United States, and one of the most in the world. Shanoah wasn't overly worried, though. She regularly changed her appearance, and as far as she knew, no one had any idea what she looked like.

She spotted Levi at the café two blocks from the White House and joined him at his table. He'd chosen the place because they served freshly squeezed orange juice, her favorite. Shanoah still missed the elixirs made by Etherens and Cosegans. She'd settled for drinking herbal teas and smoothies since arriving in the Far Future, but there was no way to duplicate the beverages from Cosega since most of the ingredients were missing.

*It seems all the best plants, fruits, flowers, and herbs did not survive the Missing Time . . .*

Booker's efforts to re-establish many of those species pleased her, yet left her a little wary.

"What are we doing here?" Shanoah asked, taking a sip of the orange juice.

"I've located another Etheren," he said.

She looked at him, waiting for the rest of the story. Locating descendants was no longer a newsworthy event.

"This one already knows he's an Etheren." He smiled, certain this would pique her curiosity.

"Really?"

He nodded, taking a gulp of his organic coffee.

"That is a first," she said, more concerned than excited. "How does he know?"

"Because he's been in communication with an Etheren shaman from Cosega."

She glanced around the busy café, worried now that somebody could overhear them. In Washington DC, people were always listening, always watching. "From what time period in Cosega?"

"I'm not sure. Perhaps the shaman's name will provide a clue."

"You know the name?"

"I certainly do."

"Is it Grayswa?"

He shook his head.

Her expression fell, her disappointment evident.

"Who's Grayswa?"

"Perhaps the greatest Etheren shaman to ever live."

"He lived in your time?" Levi asked. "You knew him?"

"Yes."

"The Shaman he's communicating with is called Adjoa."

She gasped.

"You know of him?"

"Adjoa is a female shaman. She was Grayswa's last apprentice, probably his favorite."

"So a powerful shaman?"

"Definitely," Shanoah said, watching the nearby pedestrians carefully. "Why is Adjoa contacting this descendant?"

"The shaman is having him follow Kalor Locke."

"Are you sure?" she asked.

Levi nodded.

"I had no idea Grayswa and Adjoa were pursuing Kalor Locke. I wonder if Trynn knows this," she said, mostly to herself. Shanoah finished her orange juice. "Let's walk."

Levi was not surprised. Shanoah didn't like sitting in one place for too long, especially crowded places.

"Would you like to meet the descendant?" Levi asked, leaving cash on the table for the bill.

"He's here?" she asked excitedly.

"Close by."

Shanoah motioned her arm for him to lead the way.

After going more than a block in silence, Shanoah grabbed Levi and stopped walking. She quickly steered him into a doorway to get out of the flow of well-dressed pedestrians.

"Wait, if this Etheren is tracking Kalor Locke for Adjoa and we're going to meet with him, doesn't that mean Kalor Locke is in Washington?"

Levi blinked back at her. "I . . . I don't know."

She stared at him, startled for a moment. "How close is the Etheren?"

"Close by. It's a couple of blocks from here."

She looked at the throngs of people on the sidewalk behind them, scanning across the street, paying closer attention to the crowds than before, looking for Kalor's thugs. She spotted three of her own security. There was a fourth somewhere else whom she did not see.

*Perhaps I should've brought more . . .*

"They don't know you're here," Levi said. "Only I knew about this meeting.

"I don't need any accidental encounters."

"Come on." He guided her back onto the sidewalk. They'd gone only a few hundred feet before they encountered a large contingent of law enforcement—DC Metro, Capital Police, Suits wearing earpieces who could have been with any number of government agencies.

"What's going on?" she asked, seeing everything now as a Kalor Locke trap.

Before Levi could answer, they saw the protesters. "Looks like a pretty big antiwar demonstration."

It reminded her of the demonstrations Trynn had told her about. He'd actually shown her images of young people just like these back in her time, protesting the Havlos war against the Cosegans. "It's always the young who die in wars." She watched them chanting slogans, carrying signs for peace. "It's no wonder they're the ones most against senseless wars."

"And their parents," he said, pointing to a contingent of older demonstrators singing protest songs.

"Why do humans continue to believe killing each other can somehow resolve a problem?" She looked back at the students once more. "By the time they get older, most of them will be brainwashed into supporting a *necessary war,* when no such thing exists."

# FORTY-FOUR

***Cosegan Time - Trynn's Eysen Lab Barge, open ocean, parts unknown.***

The small boat found them in the middle of the ocean, in the middle of nowhere. There was little doubt it was someone friendly. The boat was too small to be anything military, anything to do much harm at all. However, all doubt was cast off once they were in strandband range.

"We've come a long way," Welhey's voice said.

Trynn, who was standing on deck with Mairis, watching the approaching skiff, smiled and looked at his daughter. Her hopeful expression tore at him. He knew there was a decent chance Mudd was on that boat, but he had no idea what condition he'd be in, and it was also entirely possible he wasn't onboard at all. It had been a long time, and their plane, the heavy mechanical kind, had gone missing. It might have even crashed.

"We are sure glad to hear your voice," Trynn replied over the strandband. It was a secure, encrypted frequency, but he still thought it better not to discuss any details in the open. They'd be alongside in a few more minutes.

"Do you think Mudd is with him?" she asked. "He said *we've* come a long way."

"I hope so," Trynn said. "We'll know soon enough."

Nassar came topside to see what the boat was all about. He looked over to the laser station and saw that Trynn had ordered the gunner to stand down. He was still not used to the weapons, and not sure he agreed with having them, but he was definitely glad they had them on the barge. "What's going on?"

"It's Welhey," Trynn said, motioning toward the boat preparing to moor to the broadside.

"Are Mudd and Julae with him?" Nassar asked, heading to the gunwale to help them. Mairis was already there.

"Not sure," Trynn said, joining them.

A minute later, Welhey emerged from the small boat's cabin, followed by Julae. Mairis stared expectantly. Nassar gave Julae a hand up, then Welhey.

"Where's Mudd?" Mairis asked, looking at Julae and then back at the boat.

"We were hoping you had word," Welhey replied.

"What?" Mairis asked. "Mudd was with you, on the plane. Where is he? What happened?"

"I'm sorry," Julae said, hugging Mairis. "The last time we saw him was on the plane. We crashed into a big river. It was all so fast. So bad . . . "

"It was horrible," Welhey said. "All this time, we thought maybe he survived, too, and just got separated, found his way back."

"But didn't you look? Couldn't you find him?" Tears ran from her eyes. "How could you just *leave* him?"

"We didn't leave him," Julae said. "Not by choice, anyway. I tried to find him. The river was . . . it was heavy rapids, a huge waterfall, it was mayhem. The plane, the water . . . we got carried off. He would have, too. He might still be alive."

"But he would find us."

"That's not easy," Welhey said.

"And maybe he was captured," Nassar added, trying to be helpful, but regretting his words immediately.

"Captured by the Havloses? They had just released him!"

"Maybe by them, but it could be the Cosegans. Mudd is a Havlos, after all."

"Oh no!" Mairis cried.

"It may not be the worst thing," Welhey said. "We came down in Cosegan territory, so if they did find him, he'd be safe now. Cosegans treat prisoners well—at least that's what we hear. But we can talk to the Arc. She still has lots of contacts, she can find out."

Mairis began to calm down.

Welhey gave her his warm smile that everyone loved. "It'll be okay," he told her. "Now let's get inside and figure out just how we can reach the Arc."

"There might be a problem with that," Trynn said. "She has a price on my head. She'll be doing no favors for me or anyone in alliance with me."

"Why? What happened?"

"You haven't heard about Crimsonsor?" Trynn asked.

"Of course we did. We were with Etherens, and they caught us up on all the war news. But Crimsonsor . . . that's too much to bear. Jarvo is pure evil."

"We can't figure out how he got through Crimsonsor's defenses," Julae said.

"It's a long and ugly story," Trynn said, exchanging glances with Mairis and Nassar. "Come inside and I'll tell you everything."

# FORTY-FIVE

***Present Day – Washington DC***

Shanoah stared at the crowd, hoping Kalor Locke's Van army was not using the anti-war demonstration as cover. "Do we *have* to go through that?"

"No, we're this way." Levi led her to H Street, then down 15th Street. Soon they were in front of a beautiful historic building constructed at the beginning of the last century.

She looked at the number, 725, and the small brass sign indicating a stock brokerage firm was housed there. The receptionist told them that Mr. Wood was expecting them. Moments later, a young man came down the hall and introduced himself as Mr. Wood's assistant. He ushered them toward a private elevator, which took them to the third floor. The posh room was beset with antique leather furniture, lavish Persian rugs, dark wood paneling, and moldings reeking of money. The assistant led them to a small, private, windowed conference room.

Shanoah looked out through the antique panes, searching for any sign of Kalor Locke's men. She paced nervously. Being inside buildings made of solid objects left her feeling trapped, caged, closed-in. She missed the light, the vibration and flow of energy in Cosegan structures.

Only a few seconds passed before Wood entered the room and introduced himself. One look at him and Shanoah knew he'd been aware, or had known for quite a while. "Shanoah, it is wonderful to meet you." She sensed hesitation, as if Wood had to stop himself from dropping to his knees, bowing before royalty. "I simply cannot believe I am in your presence."

She looked at Levi, somewhat annoyed that he had obviously told Wood that she was an actual Cosegan. That information was rarely divulged, and in those rare cases it was always left to her to do so.

Wood quickly saw the displeasure in her eyes. "Oh no, Levi did not tell me of your true identity. Adjoa did, when she suggested I find you."

Shanoah was even more surprised by this, and quite intrigued. "Why did Adjoa arrange this?"

"So I could help you."

"Why didn't she just contact me directly?"

"It is much more difficult, since you are not Etheren. There is also the matter of security."

"Mine?"

"Yes, of course. Kalor Locke has many Etheren descendants working for him."

She nodded, having already discovered this.

"He manipulates them, tells many lies . . . they do not know all of who they are."

"We're working to find and wake as many as we can."

"Yes, I know this. That is why I contacted Levi."

"How did you know where to find him?"

He looked at her, puzzled. "You know there is talk among the outcasts, misfits, the creatives, the alternative communities, that there is a center, that things happen there."

"That's a little more public than we'd like to be," she said, shooting Levi a concerned look.

Wood nodded his agreement. "It is only a matter of time before the wrong people begin looking, calling, checking."

"But it led you to us?"

"It could have, but Adjoa told me how to find Levi, and that he would find you."

She checked out the window again. "You are tracking Kalor Locke?"

"Yes. It is not always possible, but he is a man of habits, and a man of self-importance. Both traits lend to a satisfactory trace, and eventual discovery."

"Where is he now?"

"Don't you know?"

She shook her head.

"He is at the White House, meeting the president."

"That's probably not good," Levi said.

Wood shook his head. "The president is a Havlos."

Shanoah already new the president was descendant from the Cosegan's enemies. Almost every world leader was, nearly all members of Congress, governors, most everyone in serious politics, and down through the ranks of military, police, bureaucrats . . . the world was a mess. She'd also been aware of a connection between Kalor Locke and the president, but a meeting, *today?*

*Why?*

"I believe Kalor Locke knows of your presence," Wood said. "And he suspects your efforts to bring about enlightenment en masse."

"So he is enlisting the president's help?"

Wood shook his head, as if that was a silly notion. "Kalor Locke is ready to consolidate his power. He is moving toward blocking Trynn, Booker, you, and all our efforts."

"What can be done?" Levi asked.

"This is why Adjoa thought it was time we met," Wood said. "We have another option."

"Option?"

"There are shadow shifters here in this time. They are involved in—"

"Wait, what are shadow shifters?" Shanoah asked.

"Shadow shifters are people created from the ethers by Etheren shamans," Wood replied. He walked across the Persian rugs and became quite animated. "They appear as real people, you could not tell the difference, and these *beings* are actually capable of physical activities."

"What kind of activities?" Levi asked.

"If the shaman who created them is powerful enough, they can drive a car, fly a plane, fire a gun, almost anything."

"And who was the shaman?"

"Most were done by Grayswa."

"But . . . how have they survived Grayswa's death?"

"No one really dies," Wood said.

Shanoah nodded. "But to control these ether people from the other side? It seems beyond remarkable."

"Grayswa was an extremely powerful shaman. He is even more so now."

"You said *most*," Levi said. "There are more Shadow Shifters that other shamans have sent?"

"Adjoa has some, and I believe other shamans from even later times have put some here. It's like a spirit army. I have no idea how many there could be."

"And what are they doing?" Shanoah asked.

"Same as you, as me. We are in this effort together." He looked at her, seeming momentarily confused, as if suddenly she might not be aware of all the forces being brought to bear on this epic. "They are pushing to save humanity by tilting the world back to the Etherens."

"Cosegans," she said a little self-consciously.

"We are all Cosegans," he said. "Even Havloses are Cosegans. You are an Imaze, and have seen the wonders of the universe, soared in the starlit heavens and crossed the boundaries of time and space." He looked at her again as if he might drop to his knees. "We all have the propensity for so much within us, but

each of us is also flawed. If we can recall where we came from—
Etherens, the oldest of the Cosegan lines—we can return to the
glory of the light and the endlessness of the stars."

# FORTY-SIX

***Present Day – Sedona, Arizona***

The normal quiet of the beautiful and wild lands surrounding the picturesque town of Sedona, already shattered by the gun battle, collapsed completely as the crashing helicopter went down hard. Its scraping rotor snagged against the cliff and forced the mangled chopper to shift, pushing it far enough so that it rolled away from the pinnacle and dropped into a section just beyond Gale.

Rip yelled down to her, but got no response. He quickly checked himself for injuries. There was blood, but not too much. He'd definitely been hit, but not by bullets, just rocks, maybe metal and glass. The multiple lacerations on his arms, legs, and torso, plus a pretty good scrape on his face, stung, but it was nothing bandages couldn't handle.

After a quick look to make sure the sphere was still intact, he headed down the pinnacle, which he found to be much more challenging than going up. He slipped once, straining his arm as it caught a thick seam. Soon, he heard Gale calling, but couldn't make out her words. Finally, he dropped the remaining eight feet to the ground.

"Are you okay?" She inspected him. "Are you shot?"

"No, just cuts and scrapes. You?"

"Fine. You shot a helicopter out of the sky!"

He smiled briefly. "I'm a tough guy." He gave her a quick kiss. "We've got to go."

"You know there are more coming. Where are we going? We have no vehicle."

"We have to go back the way we came. The other way is blocked." The twisted, smoldering wreckage of the chopper had sealed off that section of the small canyon. "That's probably the only place we'll find a car, anyway."

"Yeah." She held up her hand. "Sirens!"

"Law enforcement doesn't tend to ignore machine gun fire and crashing helicopters, not to mention the car chase through downtown."

"We can't get arrested." They were still wanted by every enforcement agency of the US government. If picked up, they would never be freed, and even Booker, with all his connections, would not be able to save them without an all-out war between his Blaxers and government forces.

Scrambling through the brush was easier going downhill, and a lot easier without a helicopter chasing them. They were quickly back on the edge of town, moving swiftly, skirting the gated homes and paved roadways in search of a car.

They froze at the horrific sound of another helicopter overhead, then dove into nearby shrubbery. Rip twisted his head through parted leaves to get a view of the sky. "Good news/bad news," he said. "It's not Van's, but it is a police helicopter."

"Probably flying to the crash site in the canyon," Gale said.

"Yeah. Keep moving."

A couple minutes later, they were in a paid parking lot behind a row of shops. A woman was approaching her white Tesla.

"Excuse me," Gale said. "Our car broke down and we *really* need a ride."

The startled woman looked nervously at the bedraggled pair.

"I'm sure someone in one of the shops can tell you where to get a car rental, tow truck, whatever you need." She moved toward her car.

"Please, wait," Rip said.

The woman, about to get in her car, looked around as if wondering who might hear her if she screamed.

"To be honest, it's not just the car. We're actually in trouble. There are people after us." He held up his arms in surrender. "We haven't done anything wrong, but they're not *good* people."

She studied him for a second. "Oh my god . . . are you Ripley Gaines?"

It was Rip's turn to panic. For a moment, he didn't think he should admit to such a thing, but they were desperate. "Yes, I am."

"But they said on the news that you were dead years ago."

"Well, they've been trying to make that true for a long time."

"I'm a bit of an armchair archaeologist," she said. 'I was just at the Honanki Heritage Site, the seven-hundred-year-old Sedona cliff dwellings built by the Sinagua people." She pointed up into the hills.

"Yes, an intriguing dig. I consulted."

She nodded. "I know your work. I've always been so fascinated by archaeology and things like that. I still have a stack of Archaeology magazines with your face on the cover. That's how I recognized you."

"Could you give us a ride?"

"How far?"

"Silver City."

"New Mexico?" she asked, surprised.

"Yes."

"And we need an answer now," Gale added.

She could see the distress on Gale's face. "Well, get in, and let's see how far we get. I'm Joan, by the way."

"Joan, are you *sure*?" Rip asked, thinking if she said no, they'd probably have to take her Tesla anyway.

"Silver City may be beyond my range. I just charged her, but we'll see."

"It could be dangerous," Gale said as she climbed into the front seat.

"Life is dangerous," Joan replied. "But I'm up for a little more adventure."

Rip sat in the back behind Joan. He exchanged a quick glance with Gale as Joan pulled onto the main road, both thinking of all the people who had helped them, all who were now dead. The guilt always lost out to the importance of their mission.

"So why is everyone in the world really after you two?" Joan asked.

"Long story," Gale said.

"We've got six hours. Gives you a lot of time to tell it."

"Well, uh . . . ?" Rip stuttered.

"I don't need the classified version, but at least give me the broad strokes. Let me know what I've stumbled into here."

"Fair enough," Rip said.

He started in Virginia, how he and Gale met that day they pulled something remarkable from the cliff in the Blue Ridge Mountains. He thought she'd like the romantic part, and she did. But she really wanted to know about the find, and Rip decided to tell her more than he should have.

*If she's going to die,* he thought, *she might as well have some idea why.*

# FORTY-SEVEN

***Cosegan Time - Trynn's Eysen Lab Barge, open ocean, parts unknown.***

After Trynn explained his reasoning for sacrificing Crimsonsor, Welhey and Julae, two of his most ardent supporters, had a difficult time understanding how anything could be worth the lives of so many.

"You gave away Cosega, and for what?" Welhey asked bitterly. "For a future dream millions of years away?"

"The universe . . . time is not . . . millions of years are not the same," Trynn finally said, struggling to explain. "It is part of now. It is *here*."

Welhey possessed a trace ability to use Myree, the talent to read minds. Although rare outside the Etherens, it was not unheard of, and he used it to gauge Trynn. "I see your heart is pure, and that is as I expected. But Trynn, are you *sure* this was the correct course?"

"This fell to me because through my work with Eysens, the endless days I've spent inside the Room of a Million Futures, I see time differently. We are not giving Cosega away. This was the only way to *save* it." Trynn thought of the Switch, knowing that unless he could press it soon, all would be lost anyway.

"I trust you old friend, but the Arc . . . "

"She has ordered me detained, declared me an enemy of the people. I would face trial, almost certain execution—"

"We don't execute."

"I would be made an exception."

"Yes," Welhey agreed after a long moment. "Of course they would."

Julae, who'd been silent during the conversation, looked at Trynn sympathetically. She possessed a strong Myree ability, yet had no need to use it on Trynn. "I had friends in Crimsonsor."

"I know," Trynn said softly. "I did, too."

She nodded. They shared much in common. "What an awful choice you were forced to make." Her mother being a Dream Sender gave Julae a very different perspective on time as well. "We all exist at once."

"Yes."

"The Far Future is not so far away. Fear makes people short-sighted, but we must do what is best for all of us, not just those in Cosega's present day."

"We've already made a mess of the present day," Welhey said. "Haven't we?"

"If we fix everything at once," Trynn began, "everything will be fixed."

Welhey couldn't help but laugh. "Is that all we have to do, then? Just fix everything?"

"Yes," Trynn said, without the slightest hint of amusement.

"Is that truly possible?" Welhey asked skeptically.

"All we need is one instant when everything is as it should be, a cosmic unified moment."

"You can measure that?"

"Yes."

"And how long would such a perfection last?"

"It's called Finality, and if we find it, I can make it last forever."

"*Really?*" Welhey asked, stunned.

"That's not to say there will not be suffering, mistakes, war, and the rest of what we humans do to foul up an otherwise wondrous existence," Trynn cautioned. "However, we will survive, and inch back toward where we are destined to be . . . a highly evolved species spreading love and wisdom among the stars."

"A beautiful vision," Julae said.

"How close are we?" Welhey asked, holding onto the notion because the alternative meant a horrendous extinction event.

"The window is closing, and many are working against us."

"Does the Terminus-Clock affect this?" Welhey asked.

"The Terminus-Clock affects everything."

Trynn went on detailing all that must happen, but stopped short of explaining the Switch. A short time later, an assistant interrupted them with a report that someone had found Mudd's body in Cosegan territory, downstream from the crash site. The area had active Havlos-Cosegan battles, so not much could be done for recovering it. The somber news ended the meeting as Trynn went to tell Mairis.

---

Mairis stared out on the glassy sea as the sun set, painting the waves with streaks of red.

"Thinking of Mudd?" Jenso asked, joining her at the gunwale. Her shock of white hair was such a contrast with the darkening water and her own mahogany skin. Everything about the great architect screamed exotic, power, and mysterious brilliance.

"How'd you know?"

"The dreamy, faraway look, the gorgeous sunset, and it's exactly what I would be doing."

"He was so kind to me," she said, voice sad.

"Mudd adored you."

She nodded. "There are so many things I wished I'd said to him, things we should have done together."

"You two found each other in the most tragic of times. War romances are filled with more passion because of the danger, knowing any moment might be the last, the distance, the risk of everything we do."

"But I would have loved him even on a quiet and pleasant day in the forest outside Teason."

"I know," Jenso said, putting an arm around Mairis. The two of them watched the sun sink into the great ocean, a fast flash of green as the golden-orange orb vanished.

"He was so brave," Mairis finally said.

"He sure was."

"And funny."

"The whole time we were locked up, he made us laugh constantly," Jenso said. "I see why you loved him. I'll miss him, too."

"We can miss him together." A few tears fell.

Jenso hugged her. "We will."

# FORTY-EIGHT

***Present Day – Washington DC***

Wood told Shanoah everything he knew about Kalor Locke and his operations. "I've lost him again," he admitted. "It happens often. However, there are many ways to find him. His organization is very large."

"Do you know Booker Lipton?" Shanoah asked, wondering if this information was being shared with him.

"Not personally, but of course I know *who* he is, and I know people who *do* know him personally."

"He's looking for Locke, too. You need to tell him all this."

Wood shook his head. "My purpose is to stop Kalor Locke from getting Globotite."

"But if you give him to Booker, he won't *get* any Globotite."

He shook his head again. "I'm sorry, but such a decision would lead to increased violence. We will not advance if we partake in violence."

She studied him, trying to decide if he was a saint or a fool.

"Sometimes there is little difference," he said, reading her thoughts. "And true answers come much too late. Am I a fool? We may not know for a hundred years."

"If you are not going to help us stop Kalor Locke, why are we here?"

"I *am* helping. Kalor Locke needs Globotite. I am attempting to slow his acquisition levels. The universe—as Booker Lipton is no doubt aware—has a plan, and if we work from love—"

"Kalor does not work from *love*."

"This does not mean we leave our principles. Love is always the answer."

"Then why not let him get all the Globotite he wants, and trust the universe to take care of it?"

"The Globotite is not his. His intentions are out of universal alignment." He smiled serenely, like a monk. "We each have a part to play."

Shanoah did not want to argue philosophy with an Etheren, and she ached to get out of the solid building. "Okay." She thought about the Etherens propensity for non-violence, and realized she had incorrectly assumed that had ended with the Havlos war. Prior to the war, the Cosegans had been peace-loving people. Those days were sadly over. "Then what can we do to assist with your mission?"

He shook his head yet again. "My apologies. We are not meeting for me, we are meeting for you. Let me explain. In the course of pursuing Kalor's activities, we came across information. There are Imaze artifacts in Costa Rica."

"My Costa Rica?" she said involuntarily, recalling her mission there almost fifteen hundred years earlier, which to her had been closer to sixty years ago.

"I don't know anything about that, but here is the location." Wood handed her a paper filled with coordinates and other details, including a satellite photo.

"Does Kalor have this information?"

"Not yet." He gave her a look that indicated she should leave immediately.

"I thought the ship was destroyed."

"Parts remain."

### Present Day – Costa Rica

Being back in Costa Rica after so many years had passed since her visit with the other Imazes seemed so strange. To her, it had only been a matter of decades.

*In some ways, it seems like only days since we were all here with the now extinct Diquís culture.*

The Diquís had been Etheren descendants, and the mission had been to have the counter-weight spheres made, but a secondary reason had been to protect them from Havlos descendants. It saddened her that the culture did not survive. Those sweet indigenous people had no weapons or warriors, as they had no enemies before the Spanish came seeking gold and riches.

The Conquistadors were direct Havlos descendants.

The stone spheres she'd had the Diquís people make had become a minor sensation, particularly within Costa Rica, where they were regarded as a kind of national symbol. Like so many things from the ancient world, archaeologists had no real explanation for how or why they were created. More than three hundred of what were now known as the bolas de piedra, meaning stone balls, had been located. Shanoah knew there were *many* more still buried. They'd been made to her specifications and coated with a micro-layer of Globotite. It had been done to offset the energetic presence of Eysens. In that way, to her, the bolas de piedra were more like energy Eysens or stone Eysens.

She recalled those nights of the rituals, the chief, the great shaman, and the Imazes who had been there with her. Then she thought of Sweed's betrayal and grew angry.

Shanoah pushed it from her mind. Time was limited, and if she found the parts from the *Stave*, there would be difficulties getting them out.

The area seemed so familiar, yet everything was different. Fortunately, she knew where to go because of the stone spheres.

Although not all the stones were where they'd been left, enough remained to guide her to the *Stave's* location.

Shanoah pushed through the jungle. Her GPS, set with all the locations of known stones, had been supplemented with ones she knew to still be buried undisturbed. She came upon the exact spot where the *Stave* should have been and closed her eyes.

*I should have come sooner.*

The freshly disturbed ground meant someone had recently been there. Curiously, though, the area was charred, as if the remaining *Stave* parts had been destroyed rather than taken.

Shanoah knelt down and touched the dirt.

*Warm.*

She realized someone might still be there, that she could be in danger. Scanning the area for threats, Shanoah figured out that this was no coincidence, knowing that whoever destroyed the ship did so perhaps only minutes ago.

*They knew I was coming.*

*This is a trap!*

She got to her feet and ran.

"Stop!" a woman's voice commanded, a voice Shanoah recognized almost as well as she did her own. Shanoah stopped and turned to face the person who had betrayed her, and wished she had an Infer-gun, but she'd been unable to bring it on the plane.

Sweed *did* have an Infer-gun, and she pointed it at Shanoah.

# FORTY-NINE

***Present Day - Silver City, New Mexico***

Joan pulled the Tesla into a ranger station. "Thank you, Elon Musk," she said. "The Tesla made it."

"Might have to get myself one of these," Rip said. "We sure appreciate all you've done."

She waved him off. "Loved every minute. You sure *this* is where you want to be let off?"

"Yeah, we'll make it from here."

"I've got a bit more range remaining." However, Joan knew they'd say no. They'd all decided it was best if she didn't know exactly where they were going. She'd seen on the dash-map that the closest Tesla charging station was only a few miles back, so she would be fine. They each hugged her. "You stay safe. And don't worry, I'll keep your secrets."

"I know you will," Rip said.

Joan watched them disappear into the woods, then pulled back onto the road and headed to the charging station. She'd decided to get a hotel in Silver City. It would be a long drive home.

After hiking a couple of miles, Rip and Gale reached the safe house.

"There's a light on," Rip said, studying the structure. "And what's that? Looks like an observation tower."

"Must be quite a view," Gale said, checking the list. "This safe house is occupied. That's good news. Whoever's here will be able to help us get to the next facility, maybe even back to Cira."

"How do we know whoever it is is alive?" Rip said, scanning the heavily forested area. "For all we know, the Vans have beat us here, killed the person, and are in there, just waiting."

"You read too many *Chasing* books," she told him. "This is a safe house. No one knows it exists. It isn't connected to Booker or us. Let's go. I'm hungry. A person also means real food, not the canned stuff like at the unmanned safe houses."

Rip still wasn't convinced. "Just walk up to the front door, then?"

"Looks like there's a security gate. We've got a code."

"There'll be cameras."

"I certainly hope so."

After successfully entering the code and walking up the long gravel driveway, Rip and Gale reached the house. Standing on the front porch with the door wide open was a man they knew well, a man they had not seen for many years.

A man they loved.

"Aren't you two about the biggest surprise in the world," he said, smiling, a dog yapping at his feet. "Quiet down, Perro. Saw you on the camera and didn't believe it. Had to come out and see for myself. You know how they can fake video now."

"Grinley, is that you?" Gale said, running toward him. She almost knocked him over with her hug.

At the same time, the big scruffy dog at his side decided Rip needed some attention. Rip petted the dog to stop him from licking him. "What are you doing here, Grinley?"

"Apparently I'm stealing your wife," he said, still wrapped up in Gale's arms.
</caption>

"Sorry." Gale let him go, but then quickly pulled him back again, this time giving him a quick kiss on the cheek.

"Yep," Grinley said, blushing. "I'm definitely stealing your wife."

Rip laughed. "Okay, but I get the dog."

"Hey," Gale said, giving Rip a playful kick, which made the dog bark.

They moved inside and reminisced about when they'd first met Grinley after winding up at his house—really more like an outlaw's hideout than a house. In fact, Grinley was an outlaw himself. He'd spent time running drugs, guns, and had been involved in numerous adventures in and out of prison before disappearing into the high desert outside Taos, New Mexico, where Gale and Rip found him while on the run themselves. They'd barely stayed one step ahead of the FBI and Vatican agents when he'd fed them, hid them, armed them with both cash and a gun, then held the attackers at bay while they escaped out one of his tunnels. The attackers had killed his dog.

"You're the one that lived," Gale said, reliving it all again. Every person who'd helped them on their initial marathon run with the first Eysen from Virginia to new Mexico had been killed, all except for Grinley. "There were so many good people."

"Hush," Grinley said. "Anyone who knew what you two were trying to do, what you *are* doing, would do it again. They would risk their lives to help you. I know I would."

"We don't want you to," Rip said. "We wouldn't have come if we'd known it was you. We can't put you at risk again."

"But you'd put a stranger at risk? Nonsense. I'm over the moon that you're here. Perro and I are all alone out here. A few times a year, someone shows up for the safe house, one of Booker's schemes needing some help or something. I don't ask too many questions, but it's awfully quiet here."

"Do you ever get back to Taos?"

He shook his head sadly. "It's too risky. People are still looking. I did sneak back there one autumn a few years back for a couple of days, wore a disguise, but it wasn't the same."

Rip pointed to a floor-to-ceiling bookcase covering one wall. "You do a lot of reading?"

"Love reading. I travel the world and never leave this room. I march with the armies of history, real and those from fantasy realms, and never am injured. I meet the greatest of characters, and never give up my privacy. I do all this because I read."

"We're the same," Gale said.

"When someone comes through here, if they don't read one or a few of the books, or at least take an interest in that library, I don't trust them."

Rip smiled. He loved books, too.

"Let me show you up in the tower," Grinley said. "Then we'll figure out how to get you where you need to go."

"We need you to get a message to Booker," Rip told him.

"It's a safe line. You can talk to him yourself."

"No, if someone's cracked his communications systems, an AI can pick up our voices. We've got a coded message only he would understand. Family code. If you give it to him, he'll know what to do. Then we can get out of here before someone finds us."

"Booker has an entire armory stored here. He's afraid the end of the world is coming." Grinley laughed. "If someone was to come here and try trouble, there's no end to what they would find."

"It's only the three of us."

"Oh yeah, but to protect the armory, he's got a fully auto-mated army response. I'll give you the tour, but you sure picked the right safe house. This is Booker's top site in North America. If he's stuck in the country and it hits the fan, this is where he'll come." Grinley gave them a serious look. "No one is getting in here."

# FIFTY

***Present Day – Costa Rica***

Shanoah stared at Sweed, restraining herself from attacking her former best friend. "It would be worth dying if I could kill you!"

Sweed laughed. "Same old Shanoah."

"You destroyed the remnants of my ship. That was my way home."

"You're not going home."

"Oh, you're going to kill me like you killed Glenn?"

"I didn't kill Glenn." She paused, looking as if she might cry, her voice strangle-quiet and weak. "Not personally."

"Are you kidding? You had him killed to cover your crimes! How *could* you? Glenn was like a father to all of us."

"I'm sorry about Glenn!" she barked. "But we're talking about *billions* of lives, the future of our people. Glenn would have gladly died for that cause if he'd understood it."

"Really? Did you bother trying to explain that to him?"

She shook her head. "He never would have understood. He's brainwashed—so *many* of you are brainwashed by the comfort of your easy lives."

"And Maicks? Was *he* brainwashed, too? So you sent him and the entire *Bullington* crew to a time prison?"

"I did what I had to do. You always think you're right, but you are blinded by love."

"Love? I loved you like my sister. And then even when I thought you were helping me, you sabotaged the *Reno* knowing it would strand me here. And you just did it again!" She motioned to the obliterated parts.

"I run the Imazes now, and after all this time, we can finally use them in the effort to save us. The love that blinded you wasn't you and me, it was you and Trynn. He is wrong. Trynn is killing us."

Something in Sweed's combination of words triggered a horrific realization. "How long have you been . . . Did you kill Stave?"

Sweed hesitated long enough that Shanoah knew it was true. Her best friend had killed her husband. "Stave died, uh . . . he died in the Spectrum Belt."

"I know *where* he died, but he didn't *have* to die," she snapped. "It never made sense, and I blamed myself, but it was *you*, wasn't it?"

"What if it was?" Sweed said. "Hasn't your life been better since he died? You found Trynn."

"How dare you . . . wait . . . you *wanted* me with Trynn. You wanted to use me."

When Sweed didn't respond, Shanoah lunged for her.

Shanoah managed to kick the Infer-gun out of Sweed's hand. The two women had always been evenly matched in their fighting skills. However, Shanoah had grown accustomed to the air in the modern world. Time breathing, the difficulty in adjusting to a different "weight of air" from vastly separate eras, meant Shanoah now had a big advantage in a physical match-up, especially with the gun out of the way.

The fight, vicious and hard-fought, lasted ten minutes, back and forth, until Shanoah reached the Infer-gun and fired as Sweed dove for it.

Sweed, gasping for air, stared down at the laser burn and blood. "It's a mortal wound."

Shanoah nodded, panting. "I'm sorry, Sweed, but you deserved this end. You deserved far worse, actually."

"Maybe," she said in a strained voice.

"I'll take your ship," Shanoah said, realizing only in that moment that Sweed had to have come on an Imaze ship. She was free to leave for home and Trynn immediately. "Where is it?"

Sweed's eyes closed.

"Oh no you don't—you're not dying until you tell me where the ship is! Have the code locks changed?" Shanoah knew the ship was likely self-buried, and it could take her months to locate it without Sweed. The codes, if changed, would also be difficult to crack.

"Sorry," Sweed said, opening her eyes. "It's wired. It's a new policy because of Maicks and you . . . If my heart stops, the ship will blow up."

"*What?*"

"You may not believe me, but I wish you could go."

"I don't believe anything you say! Where is it?"

"Shanoah . . . the coordinates are on my strandband, but it will blow. And it will kill you if you're anywhere near it."

"I'll go get it now, while you're still alive."

"No time. I'll be dead in a few minutes. But listen to me. Maicks' ship is still there."

"Where?"

"China."

"After all these years?"

"Yes. I was going there next to destroy it."

"You know where it is? You *found* it?"

Sweed nodded slowly.

"Where is it?"

"Coordinates on my strandband." Sweed tried to take it off, but was too weak.

"Why tell me? You were about to kill me."

"I never wanted to hurt you."

Shanoah laughed. "But that's all you've done! You killed my husband, sabotaged every mission for years, you killed Glenn, you've tried to stop all Trynn's progress, you condemned all my friends to die on the Bullington, and you trapped me here in the Far Future. *Everything* you've done has hurt me. I loved you, and that hurt most of all. I just still don't understand how you could be so ruth—"

A large explosion interrupted Shanoah. Not knowing its source, she threw herself on the ground.

Then she remembered the failsafe.

Shanoah crawled to Sweed and checked her pulse. Nothing. Sweed had died.

Shanoah took Sweed's strandband from her wrist, glanced at the pain on her face, then turned and left.

---

On the plane home, she reviewed the contents of the strandband and found the China file.

*Maicks, old friend, did you really leave me something in China? Something that can get me home?*

*I'll find out soon . . .*

# FIFTY-ONE

**Present Day – Philippines**

Parson Locke took a final look back into the plane to make sure all the equipment had been deployed. He was the last man remaining onboard. Having done hundreds of these high-altitude jumps, the challenges this one provided were evident. The dangers rattled in his high-strung mind: size of the island, the defenses in place, it being a primary hold, meaning Booker Lipton was present, which meant full Blaxers blow back to be expected.

Yet the one thing he knew to be present on all missions ate at him the most—the unknown.

"All manner of hell is waiting for us down there," he'd told his men, some of the best of the best of the Varangian Guard.

This invasion, the culmination of years of intelligence work, had overcome Booker's own top intelligence, his highest level defenses, his Cosegan-based tech security, and the Blaxers, a private army second to none. Kalor Locke had managed to breach Booker's encryption, and everything now fell into exposed risk.

Parson had long been holding back the Vans, never using the full force of what he and Kalor had built—a lethal, specialized army of elite operatives that could topple most small countries and successfully take any US military base on the planet. He'd made sure never to show Booker all his cards, making sure his enemy would always underestimate him, waiting until they had a confirmed primary hold.

"Booker is there," he whispered, the one man who could stop his brother from fulfilling his incredible destiny. "I'm coming to kill you!"

Parson sprang out from the opening, the cold, thin air pummeling him, as if conditioning him for the fight ahead. He soared toward the island below, toward the end of Booker Lipton.

A laser battle already raged by the time Parson landed. Speeding stealth combat ships had delivered more troops and weapons while the jumpers were hitting the ground. Now attack choppers filled the skies. They took out embedded anti-aircraft guns, which had been ready to defend them from sea or air attacks, with the aid of laser-sighted Magneto Hydrodynamic Explosive Munition, or "MAHEM" weapons, which used a magnetic flux generator to fire projectiles without the need for chemical propellants. The balmy nighttime air transformed into a scene from Star Wars.

The Blaxers standard response to a barrage such as they faced this night included the release of Hybrid Insect Micro-Electro-Mechanical System, or "HI MEMS." The buzzing swarms flew out like murder hornets. Invisible in the darkness, without their typical micro-LED lights illuminated, the tiny killers attacked with deadly electro-dart stingers infused with poison.

This time the Vans were ready for the HI MEMS, spraying a red-laser aerosol from portable tanks that completely neutralized any of the "insects" that came into contact with the massive red glowing clouds.

Soon the Blaxers were overwhelmed by thousands of Vans.

---

Inside Rip's Eysen lab, a computerized system automatically locked the Cosegan spheres within a hardened failsafe vault capable of withstanding a nuclear strike. The interior of the mechanized vault shifted, and the Eysens dropped down a long tracked shaft similar to a bowling ball return, winding up fifty feet below the island's surface.

---

Parson, now hunting the many structures on the island for Booker, spoke to his crew. "Do not let any craft, either by air or water, leave this island." It had been the priority standing order before the attack, the critical part of the mission: kill Booker, kill Cira.

They knew Rip and Gale were not there, but those two would be dead in New Mexico very soon.

Parson moved swiftly, even with his full-body armor. The specially designed kevlar material meant he was almost entirely bulletproof, and its black mirrored digital coating meant he was almost entirely laser-proof. Although technically Parson's gear and clothing made him nearly invisible, he didn't feel that way. Though he couldn't pinpoint the exact cause of his unease, the knowledge that he was about to kill a teenage girl didn't help.

Inside what he believed to be the residence of at least Rip's family, his night vision picked up a heat signal. He didn't need to confirm identity before the kill. This was a full zero mission, meaning no survivors, but Parson had to know if he was killing the girl.

Rip's teenage daughter would turn out to be a bigger threat than her parents in the future. She *had* to be eliminated. However, Parson had never knowingly murdered an innocent teenage girl before. His training, his experience, his instincts all told him *Take the shot, kill her and keep moving, find Booker, kill him, get out*—but she was just a girl.

Something in him needed to know, to feel the regret. Even though Parson had prepared for more than a year that he would likely be the one to kill her, and he thought he was ready, but that slight hesitation . . .

*Hesitation kills*, he told himself.

———

Cira thought of running, but she had seen enough nature documentaries to know that animals were always attacked when they darted. So she waited.

*Maybe he hasn't seen me.*

She'd also seen enough thriller movies to know he had night vision, and that he knew her exact location. She tried not to breathe.

———

Parson walked around the bed and saw a girl cowering in the corner. She turned and made eye contact. He quickly determined she was unarmed, then, keeping the laser gun pointed at her, double checked the photo in a digital processor mounted to his wrist.

Parson didn't need the confirmation from the photo. He'd long ago memorized her pretty face, but he did it anyway.

*She looks even younger in person*, he thought. She reminded him of a girl he once knew in his youth.

Cira shook her head very slowly, begging him not to do it with her teary, but brave eyes.

He hesitated again. "I'm sorry," he said. "You may not understand now, but you present great trouble to us in the future, present great trouble to the future itself."

"No," she pleaded.

"Sorry," he repeated.

His finger moved.

She screamed at the sound of a single gunshot as Parson's laser obliterated her nightstand.

Parson Locke crumpled to the ground.

"Cira!" Booker yelled. "We have to go!"

A flashlight beam cut into the darkness. She caught a quick glimpse of the man who'd been about to execute her. His face was gone. Booker's bullet had found the only vulnerable spot on Parson Locke's body.

Neither Cira nor Booker knew who he had killed. All they knew was a hundred more Vans were running all over the tiny island, and the gunshot meant they would all be running to the residence, all with orders to kill the two of them.

# FIFTY-TWO

***Present Day – Southern New Mexico***

The plan was to stay the night with Grinley at the safe house, surrounded by nothingness, in the Gila Wilderness, which in 1924 became the first wilderness area in the National Forest System, and had remained isolated and remote.

Rip and Gale would take a car to the airport first thing in the morning. Grinley had chartered a plane under a cover name so well layered that even he didn't know where the identity ended.

While Grinley made them dinner, his famous Taos green chili enchiladas, Rip and Gale could not resist delving back into the Ovan sphere.

"I feel like a genie emerging from a lamp in one of your tales of *One Thousand and One Nights*," Ovan said. "Please, make sure you continue Trynn's training on how to handle the Eysens. If you survive, then you *must* know how to handle the Eysens that survive."

"Why is this all converging now?" Gale asked.

"Because your world so closely mirrors that of my time," Ovan replied. "The Havlos culture and their seven sections are similar to the United States, China, Europe, Russia, the Middle East, and the rest of it."

"But the Cosegan side," Gale said, "where does that fit in? Where does that mirror?"

"We fractured in our time, Cosegans and Havloses. We coexisted until we could no longer. In your time, you went all one way, all Havlos. There were those of you who felt the pull, knew there was something more, knew there was something different, better, that society had chosen the wrong track. Everyone has some Etheren in them—the spiritual, natural side—and everyone has a little Imaze in them—the adventurous, curious side. Everyone is a Cosegan, but the scared Havlos side has been allowed to dominate your people. It is the easy path, the lazy route."

"I don't understand," Gale tried again. "How does the Cosegan side mirror us?"

"Because that is where you should be. Your society should be like ours. If your leaders, and the majority of the population, had chosen differently, rejected greed and fear, corruption, hatred, anger, and laziness, you would already be living in the utopian."

"Wow."

"But then how did you lose it all?" Rip asked.

"We allowed the Havloses to suffer. We accepted separation. We forgot we were all Cosegans."

---

The attack came in the middle of the night. Rip, Gale, and Grinley were sound asleep. However, Booker's automated defenses never slept. Using Cosegan and Havlos technology, a system of seven Killtrons immediately engaged with more than one hundred heavily armored Varangians.

Grinley had shown them the bunker, a safe room inside the safe house—a vault for people. It was almost impenetrable, the only real threat being a massive ordinance directly hitting the place, and even then, there would be a chance of survival. Still, the three of them found watching the battle on the closed-circuit monitors nerve-racking.

The Killtrons mopped up the initial waves of Vans, but it seemed that Kalor's army had some tricks of their own and were able to fry several of the killer AI bots with an energy weapon the Killtrons had not previously encountered. For more than three hours, the war raged in the remote sections of New Mexico, spilling into the Gila Wilderness.

Near sunrise, the tide turned. Only one Killtron remained, and it looked as if the Vans might win.

That's when the choppers arrived.

"More Vans," Gale said.

"Then we're in trouble," Rip said.

"These Vans sure fight dirty," Grinley said. During their hours locked in the safe room, where they also had the dog, Perro, Rip and Gale had given him a decent overview of their history with Kalor and the Vans.

"Ruthless," Gale said.

"But they won't get in here," Grinley assured them. He had long ago pushed the panic button, so they all knew whatever Blaxer squad monitored the safe houses would be mobilized. Booker himself surely must have been notified by now.

"Incredible!" Rip said.

"What?" Gale asked, studying the monitors to see what had caused Rip's optimistic exclamation. "Is that . . . ?"

"The man who's saved us even more times than Grinley."

"What, I'm not your favorite?" Grinley said, petting Perro.

"You will always be my favorite," Gale said, giving him a kiss on the cheek.

"That's better, as long as you don't kiss this guy." He pointed at the monitors, which were now lit up with a new battle. "Wow, your hero sure is beating those surviving Vans pretty good."

Ten minutes later, it was over. The man they'd watched command the forces who'd destroyed the remaining Varangians looked into one of the cameras. "Rip, it's safe to come out, but I don't know how long it will be, so . . . "

Rip looked at Grinley. "Let's open up."

"This guy really trustworthy?" Grinley asked.

"Yeah, he's FBI."

"Are you kidding me?" Grinley looked as if he'd been shot. "There ain't an FBI man alive that's trustworthy."

Rip laughed. "I knew you'd say that. But really, this one is different."

Grinley turned to Gale, as if seeking confirmation.

"He is," Gale said. "Saved our lives fairly often."

"Okay, if you say so. But don't blame me if this heads south." Grinley pressed the button to open the massive vault doors.

A minute later, they were standing in front of Dixon Barbeau. "You make a habit of being there when we need it most," Rip said, shaking Barbeau's hand. "How'd you find us this time?"

"Two ways," Barbeau said, sounding like a military commander. "We are tracking Vans, and we got a message from Booker's operations that this place was under siege."

Perro went up and licked Barbeau's hand. Barbeau kneeled down and scratched the dog behind the ears. "Border collie mix, good looking animal."

"Okay, so then Booker knows where we are," Gale said, hugging Barbeau as he got up. "We need to check on our daughter."

"Let's do it from the air," Barbeau said firmly.

Grinley glanced at Barbeau, then back to Gale.

"Don't worry," Gale said, laughing. "I promise he won't arrest you."

Barbeau looked Grinley over. "Really, buddy, I have so much on my plate right now, I don't even want to know your name."

Once they were in the air, Barbeau made arrangements to get them on a flight out of the nearby White Sands military base that would take them to the Philippines. Then they called

Booker and were horrified to get no answer. Barbeau accessed satellite images.

"If that's the island where Booker and your daughter were," Barbeau said, showing them the images, "I'm afraid it's not pretty. Every structure on the island has been completely destroyed."

# FIFTY-THREE

***Cosegan Time – Solas, Cosega***

The Shields protecting Solas had held, but Jarvo decided occupying the Cosegan capitol was too great a prize to pass up. "We won't destroy this one," he'd told Cass. "We're going to take it the old-fashioned way, like they do in the Far Future."

Cass supported the idea because it meant far fewer deaths, but it would be a brutal battle nonetheless.

The Havlos leader sent battalions of Enforcers and dozens of units of Coils to take the legendary light city by conventional means. Shank had legions of Guardians ready to defend the capitol. Those soldiers were supported by newly formed citizen militias.

Unbeknownst to Shank, the former Arc had returned to Solas, determined not to see *her* city fall. Shank believed the citizen militia had grown organically from patriotic Cosegans wishing to save their way of life. However, these bands had been pulled together and trained by ex-guardians still loyal to the former Arc.

With little regard for her own safety, immediately upon the Arc's arrival in the city, she began leading counter attacks and strategizing defensive measures, including guerrilla tactics, and repurposing Cosegan tech into weapons.

"I will never allow Solas to be occupied by the Havlos scum," she vowed.

---

### *Present Day – The Ranch, somewhere in Montana*

Kalor received word that the assault on the safe house had failed, that yet again Rip and Gale had slipped through. There were more reports coming in on other operations, but he still hadn't heard from Parson, and his mood was not happy when Savina asked to see him.

Savina pondered the Super-Eysen constantly. It excited her to be involved in such an ambitious undertaking. She believed it would change the world, and now that it was close to completion —literally days from powering up—her excitement became laced with a certain amount of fear—not that it would be dangerous, but that it might not live up to its full potential because of the power source.

"The problem is we don't know where these Eysens are coming from," Savina said. "They aren't all first quality."

"Trynn isn't the only one who can make an Eysen," Kalor shot back.

"Of course not, but the makers are of different skill levels, manufacturing Eysens in a range of qualities."

"You can tell these apart?"

"Yes, but that isn't my point. These Eysens . . . some of them are seconds."

"I have personally worked with each of them. They function perfectly."

She shook her head. "This kind of instrument requires a precision that takes many of our lifetimes to master. Cosegans live in durations many times that."

"Yes, I am well versed in the Cosegan longevity."

Savina smiled and nodded, knowing his obsession with living forever, but not picking up that thread. "During an Eysen Maker's training, there are many Eysens created which lack the requisite levels of perfection."

"And you think that's what they're giving me?"

"I believe many of them are . . . defective."

"*Defective!* What does that mean? How can an Eysen be defective?"

"It produces interference."

"With?"

"Other Eysens."

"Finish your thought, Savina," he demanded. "Don't make me guess."

"It dilutes the strength, and while I'm still unsure how exactly this plays out, I believe it will default your Super-Eysen to something far less than you envision."

"The amplification?"

"It won't be there."

"Because?"

"The flawed Eysens produce a drain, a net negative result," she explained.

"Are you certain of this?"

"Yes."

"Have you sent the data to Lorne for review?"

"I just did. I'm confident she will confirm."

He nodded, disgusted, yet resigned. "How many are this way?"

"I'm still testing, but preliminary checks show thirty-seven with issues."

"*Thirty-seven!* That's ninety percent!"

"Yes."

Kalor fumed. "This is no accident."

"Unlikely. However, it is possible that your source only had easy access to the failed models. The others are highly regulated."

"No," he said, stomping the wood floor like a child throwing a tantrum. "This was intentional. This is Trynn, *he* sent me these."

"Does Trynn even know you were amassing Eysens?"

"What kind of question is that?" He turned toward her as if he might lunge and make a venomous strike. "Trynn knows everything."

She nodded slowly. "Only broadly."

"I am an area of extreme study," Kalor hissed. "He is attempting to sabotage me."

"He might see it differently, a vice-versa kind of view of this."

This made Kalor laugh. "Yes, he might."

"Perhaps you could get other Eysens."

"Don't you think I'm already in that arena? Each piece of Cosegan magic I can obtain is in process. What the hell do you think I do all day?"

She wanted to reply that he watched her all day, but didn't believe the comment would elicit a second laugh from him. "Then perhaps there is still time."

He shook his head. "We must get the others."

She knew he meant Booker's spheres. They were all of the highest quality, all created by the ultimate master, Trynn. "We've tried and failed."

"Then this time we shall succeed."

"You have a new plan?"

"I have a new ally," he said. "Someone who hates Booker almost as much as I do."

"Who?" she asked, knowing it could be any number of hundreds of the world's most powerful people. No one had more enemies than the wealthiest man in the world.

"The president of the United States of America."

# FIFTY-FOUR

***Present Day - Philippines***

Cira ran into Booker's arms. He gave her a tight hug. "Are you okay?"

"No, but I'm not injured."

"Remember the evac door?"

"Yes. I tried to get there, but he was coming."

Booker pulled a computer tablet out of a large front pocket on his black jacket. The screen showed images from dozens of cameras. "We can't go this way."

"But that's the closest evac."

"We won't make it," Booker said. "I can't shoot that many of them."

The image showed more than twenty Vans coming down the hall. They went another way. Booker had a submachine gun strapped to his back in addition to a Glock in his hand. He had thousands of hours of shooting range practice, and would have killed them if it were possible, yet knew he'd lose that battle and lose Cira in the process. He didn't tell her that shooting the man in her bedroom was the first time he'd personally killed someone. He'd ordered thousands killed by his Blaxers, and those deaths weighed on him, but this felt different.

Less than a minute later, they were in another hall. They reached the closet just as a dozen Vans streamed in the other end.

"There!" one of the Vans shouted. The men ran toward the closet.

Booker and Cira were already inside the second door, a heavy steel and concrete barrier. They slid down a long turning tube, like one might find at a water park, only smaller and without the water. However, they did land in a sand pile next to water. Booker ushered Cira into the small, high-speed submarine docked inside the cavern. This feature had been used on many islands he owned, and he worried that the Vans knew about it, and would be waiting.

"Aren't you coming? she asked.

"In just a minute." He unlocked a small vault door and unloaded the Eysens, which had dropped there from above and landed in two cushioned cases, onto the sub, then got in.

"Are we safe?" Cira asked.

Booker engaged the autonomous captain, then looked at Cira with a deeply sad expression. "Not as long as we're still alive."

––––

### Cosegan Time – Unknown location

Dreemelle stood before Trynn, shimmering like a myth.

"I sometimes wonder if you're even real," Trynn said. "Or perhaps just a Revon-induced hallucination."

"A great man of science such as yourself should know better," she said, smiling, glowing, seeming to be just what he claimed. She opened her arms, always greeting him with an embrace that was at once healing and shattering, because as soon as it ended, the separation of it highlighted a void within him that otherwise went unnoticed. It didn't matter, though, because while in it, he became part of the light and felt infinite. Trynn would do anything for even a few seconds of that completeness.

"I need to know where it comes from."

She knew he meant Revon, but she played with him to make a point. "The light?"

His confused expression made her laugh.

"The *Revon*."

"Where do you think it comes from?" she asked.

"You aren't going to tell me, are you?"

"There is one thing in all existence, and you know what this is."

"You speak of light."

"Yes."

"What of darkness?"

"It is only the perceived absence of light."

"Then Revon is light?"

"Of course," she said, suddenly seeming translucent, as if he could see the trees through her instead of just behind her. But it must have just been the iridescent glow that surrounded her at all times, an aura of sorts, fluctuating with her energy and mirroring the environment. "There are two things that rule your life, Trynn."

"Revon and Globotite."

"Yes, and it could not have been otherwise. These are the same for Cosegans. Revon and Globotite are the story of your people."

"What is the story of the Havloses, then?" he asked, worried Jarvo would soon destroy all of Cosega, desperate that his own part had not been miscalculated, that they might still survive to one day rebuild the society of light.

Her smile widened, as if she'd been hoping for just that question. Dreemelle always appeared calm and exuded a mystical wisdom. Trynn had described her to Shanoah as a woman of light, and that's how he thought of her, as if the radiant woman had arrived in a sunbeam that would never diminish in its magic.

"Havloses are no different. They are merely the perceived absence of light. Havloses, Etherens, Imazes, Cosegans, they're all caught between different ways of seeing the light, but they are all one people. Your differences have driven you each to a kind of madness, to the point where you have forgotten that you are all one, all Cosegans."

# FIFTY-FIVE

***Present Day – Southern Caribbean***

On a lush private island called Tujeres, located in the southern Caribbean, off the coast of Venezuela, Cira waited for a helicopter, not unlike the one that had flown her and Booker to the tropical hideaway hours earlier.

She was still recovering from the night before, when Booker had shot the man in her bedroom. The sub, equipped with a Cosegan propulsion system, had taken them to the middle of the Philippine Sea, where a waiting speed boat transported them to a rendezvous point with a helicopter, which dropped them somewhere else. Cira wasn't sure if it had been another island, or part of the mainland, but there'd been an airstrip. A private jet flew them a long way, and during that flight she finally slept. Then a landing—or had there been two landings?—and finally a helicopter ride to yet another island, the one on which she now stood, halfway around the world.

*How many islands does Booker own?* she wondered.

Somewhere along the line, she'd learned from Booker that her parents were alive. Dixon Barbeau had safely extracted them out of another Varangian massacre. Rip and Gale had also taken multiple hops to get back to her, including a plane, a car, and at least a couple helicopters. She watched the chopper land, still shell-shocked, relieved it belonged to Booker and not Kalor Locke's Vans.

Gale was the first to reach her. They both cried, but mostly happy tears. Then her father lifted her up like he had when she was a child and kissed her cheeks.

"I guess it wasn't such a good idea to split up," Cira said.

"Maybe not, but it all worked out," Rip said, squeezing her tight before putting her back down. "But we'll have to think twice about *ever* doing that again."

"Yeah," Cira said, taking their hands and leading them up to the beautiful white stucco house built into a seaside cliff.

Tujeres had no structures built for secure Eysen storage and research like so many of his islands did. Although it was protected, Booker was definitely on edge when they joined him on a vast balcony at the main house where he'd watch them land.

"Are you okay?" Rip asked.

Booker nodded solemnly.

"Cira told us about how you saved her. Thank you." Rip knew what most would never believe about Booker. In his heart, he was a committed pacifist. How that belief so completely contradicted the huge army Booker had built and the incredible number of lives they'd taken played a part in how complex a person he was, how difficult his life was to understand. And yet Rip somehow did. He knew the cost that taking another life would have on Booker, and worried about his old friend.

Booker patted Rip's shoulder. "Cira's smile is all the thanks I require."

Gale came across the balcony and hugged Booker. Rip thought he saw a tear in Booker's eye, but an instant later he wasn't sure he had ever seen it.

"The Blaxers have been decimated over the last few days," Booker told them. "Kalor Locke made a massive push, but we survived. At least for now. I have people scrambling, and efforts are underway to pull together enough forces to protect us. In the short term, we will be fine." He paused and stared out to sea, his voice uncharacteristically strained. "But hard times are ahead."

"We're going to need some good hiding places," Gale said.

"Don't worry about that. I've been preparing for this for longer than I've known you," Booker said. The weight of his statement lingered in the air.

"We've got to get the Eysens back online," Rip said, and then he and Gale proceeded to tell Booker and Cira all about what they'd found at the Canyon.

"The Ovan Sphere," Booker said, awe returning to his voice. "To be able to have endlessly long discussions with a Cosegan sage . . . "

"We have to get in touch with Trynn," Rip said. "This isn't over yet, and we have important things to do, vital actions to take."

Booker led them to a makeshift room that had been some sort of private movie theater for the island's previous owners. As they'd done so many times before, the four of them set up a small Eysen research facility from scratch.

"The Blaxers are getting things secure," Booker said, checking his tablet, hoping there was time before the next siege.

"Are there enough of them here in case *he* attacks again?" Cira asked.

"Don't worry. I chose this island because it has our newly developed satellite defenses," Booker said excitedly. "And it has the most advanced Eysen EAMI protective systems in place."

She smiled.

"But wait, there's more," he said, sounding like a late-night infomercial. "There's also a great accumulation of Cosegan weapons and technology here."

Cira laughed, still nervous, but assured for the moment.

Once the Eysens initiated and completed the sequence, Rip sent a message to Trynn.

Trynn, having just arrived at the ultimate Eysen lab and manufacturing center in Solas, was not surprised by the timing. He looked into the original Room of a Million Futures for almost thirty minutes before allowing Rip's holographic avatar to come through. "It looks as if we've both had a rough couple of days, and your daughter, too."

"It's good to still be alive," Rip said. "I have a message for you from Ovan."

Trynn smiled. The words comforted him. They also astounded him. Even with all the experience the great Eysen maker had in dealing with events and people in the Far Future and the Far Past, he still marveled at it all.

*Just days ago, Ovan died in my arms. Now he speaks to me from eleven million years into the future.*

Trynn stood in front of Rip's hologram and whispered as if imparting a great secret. "Ovan's entire consciousness, life's history, vast knowledge of Cosega, the universe, the sciences, Eysens, events in the Far Future, of *everything,* is now sitting in your hands. You have no idea the *power* you hold."

# FIFTY-SIX

***Present Day – Central China***

Shanoah walked through the marshy field, recalling the caves they had built in China so many thousands of years before, wondering what had become of Maicks.

*What kind of life had he lived? How did he eventually die? Who did he love? Did anyone ever figure it out? What had he influenced?*

Maicks had been the first Imaze to live among the Far Future. She had judged him harshly then, and now she had committed the same crime. Sure, Trynn had convinced them both she was still on a mission, but that was just an excuse, especially after Kalor Locke had wound up with the sphere anyway.

*I would not have been able to implement the final protocol, to suicide.*

Even her own thoughts were a lie. She could have done it in those early days, back when her training was still fresh and life in Cosega remained a raw memory. Now, though, after so many years, this life seemed as real as her life in Cosega.

And Maicks had a child. And that child had children. And there were others until today . . . The excitement and anticipation of meeting his descendent, the first of a direct line, was almost too much.

From twenty feet away, incredibly, the man looked shockingly like Maicks. "*Wow*," she mouthed, surprised by the resemblance. Shanoah had worked on what she would say to the man called Cabe Adams, practiced it during the long flight, but now words escaped her.

It didn't matter anyway. Cabe had much to say. "So you're really from there?"

She nodded.

"Cosega? Eleven million years ago?"

"Yes," she said in a voice barely above a whisper.

"You knew him?"

"Maicks, yes. We were friends."

"Then why didn't you ever come back for him?" he asked accusingly.

The question startled her. She stuttered a few seconds before responding, "It is against the rules." As soon as the words were out, she realized how silly they sounded.

"Rules?" he asked rhetorically. "Yet *you're* here."

"My mission is ongoing."

He nodded exaggeratedly, as if agreeing with her. "Oh, I'm *sure*."

"That mission is why I needed to see you," she said, missing his sarcasm. "I need your help."

"*My* help?" He glared at her. "Like *you* helped Maicks?"

Shanoah paused, still trying to understand the man's anger. "It's been thousands of years. Other than the stories of Maicks' passing down through the generations of your family like a myth, you have no connection, nothing that would warrant your obvious anger, so please tell me what's going on."

"You left him to die. You never came back."

"I'm sorry about that, but Maicks knew the risks."

"Tell me something. If the Cosegans were *so* brilliant, *so* advanced—I mean, *time travel?* You don't *look* eleven million years old."

"Technically, I'm not—" she began to explain, but he waived a hand to quiet her.

"With all your technological achievements and space travels —the Imazes, right?"

She nodded, this time careful not to speak.

"How did my ancestor crash so far off the planned trajectory of the mission? What happened? Why did he get trapped here?"

"It was . . . sabotage. Someone we all trusted betrayed us."

"That was in the story. But tell me, how did you *miss* it?"

She shook her head, tears welling in her eyes. "I don't know. It . . . it was a difficult time. The world was ending, the war, the Doom, so much was happening . . . " As she rambled, her voice dwindled.

He saw the authenticity she was trying to offer. "You want to know why I'm so angry?"

"Yes," she said, wiping away a tear. "Please."

"Because I'm a Cosegan. I should have grown up *there*. Lived *there*. Hundreds of generations of my family should have been *there*. Instead, we got this disaster, this Havlos world."

"If Maicks had gone back home, he most likely would have died on another mission to the Far Past, and even if he'd somehow survived that, his line would have died off in the Missing Time."

"Missing Time?"

"There is a vast period separating our existences," Shanoah said. "Everything was lost there."

He stared at her for a long time, wondering if he should press for more on the Missing Time, but mostly letting his anger go, realizing there was too much he didn't know, didn't understand.

"What was it really like?" he finally asked, sounding like a kid asking about magic.

"Cosega was the most remarkable achievement by any known life form in all the universe," she said. "The only point of reference you might be able to associate it with was a land of gods."

*Present Day / Far Future / Cosegan Time*

Rip, via hologram, followed Trynn through the most incredible place he'd ever seen. Only through the cosmic Eysen trips could he even imagine such a facility existed, and to see that many raw Eysens at one time was completely overwhelming. Knowing the power in each individual Cosegan sphere, and the exponential increase when linked to others Eysens, the sheer volume of the hundreds there before him was simply beyond comprehension.

"Recall all your training?" Trynn asked.

"Not all, but . . . "

"No? Why not? Do you understand what we are up against? The stakes? What has been sacrificed by so many? Is this not a serious endeavor to you?"

"Yes, of course. I mean, I *do* remember most of it."

"Most?" He stopped and stared into Rip's hologram. The passion in his eyes made Rip feel as if the great Eysen maker actually stood less than a foot from him in real life, in real time. Trynn raised his voice. "Do you have any idea how much this has cost? My life, *centuries* of it, folded into this cause." He paused, looking past Rip for a moment, as if seeing the hauntings of his past. "The peace lost, the friends and loves gone . . . Without a tether to my own time, I have witnessed the brutality of the future of humanity, the surrender of what it is to embrace light. I am hunted by those I've never known, from a time before memory, and oh, this terror does not simply belong to the past, it has burned holes in the present from which I see into the darkness of man throughout all history, particularly those centuries darkened and surrounding your lifetime."

Trynn stopped speaking as the Eysens swirled with light, leaving an imprint the Cosegan seemed to glean meaning from. Rip thought of replying to his words, but Trynn continued the rant with a stronger voice and harsher words.

"I have traded the souls of millions, stomped on a reputation so wearily earned, watched the suffering, assured the existence of our species, yet constantly have I been berated and betrayed by one-time friends—do you see? Can you *begin* to grasp that I have done all this not for glory, not for recognition of any kind, but because I *must*? It is all I can do."

Rip nodded. "You are a great man, Trynn."

"No," he said, shaking his head. "You have missed the point. I am *nothing*. Nothing at all."

Shafts of light poured in the facility from all directions, like spotlights cutting through a darkened auditorium filled with the dreams and illusions of thousands of beautifully unique souls.

# FIFTY-SEVEN

***Present Day – The Ranch, somewhere in Montana***

Kalor Locke's hands gripped the gasping man's neck. Three other Vans pulled him off just in time.

"It's *not* true!" Kalor screamed, fighting himself free from the rough hands trying to subdue him. "My brother is *alive!*"

"I'm sorry," one of the other men said. "We have his chest cam footage."

"Show me!"

"Perhaps this is not the best time," the man said, not wanting to upset Kalor further.

Kalor stepped toward the man. "There is no *best time* to see my brother die."

"Of course, I just—"

"Let. Me. See. It."

It took a couple of minutes to bring it up on a small tablet. Kalor watched in horrified silence.

"Booker Lipton killed my brother," he said, as if uttering an incantation. "Booker Lipton killed my brother. Booker Lipton killed my brother. Booker Lipton killed my brother."

### *Present Day – Central China*

The knobby hills of rural China, framed by cliffs and jagged mountains both remote and stark, offered Shanoah a glimpse into exactly what it must have looked like to Maicks when he crash landed, lost in time, sabotaged by a trusted friend, thousands of years earlier.

"Is it really still here?" Shanoah asked.

"My grandfather came," Cabe said. "Like all of us, he'd heard the stories his whole life. Maicks had made sure that each generation would tell the next. That the story would never be forgotten, never altered. Someone a few hundred years ago finally wrote it down, but my grandfather wanted proof. I guess before him . . . imagine for hundreds of years, such a thing seemed unimaginable, before the inventing of the airplane, before going to the moon. So maybe it had just become a story, a myth among family lines, but my grandfather wanted to believe it, desperate that we had come from greatness, from something of living gods. 'Gods walking the earth,' he sometimes said to me. My grandfather made a decent fortune in the automotive industry, and he had money. He flew to China. He found this place."

"And he found the ship?"

"Yes."

"You've seen it?"

"I have. My grandfather brought my mother. My parents brought me."

Shanoah's excitement built. *There is a chance.*

"A distant cousin owns the land, keeps the secret." Cabe looked sad. "I am the last of the line."

"You have no children?'

"No."

"Brothers, sisters, nieces, nephews?"

"No, just the cousin. And he is very old."

Shanoah was not surprised. Time worked that way. She was here now, meaning the secret did not need to be kept any longer. It had been maintained all these many centuries for her arrival, to facilitate her return. She could not escape the irony that if Sweed had not betrayed her and sent Maicks and the *Bullington* crew to their wasted lives in the Far Future, then Shanoah might never be able to escape it.

"Maicks made this sacrifice for me," she told Cabe.

"Why?" he asked as they climbed a hill covered with tall grass and spiky flowers.

"So that I could leave."

"Why was it more important for you to leave than for him and his crew?"

"Perhaps so that you, or your grandfather, or someone else in your family line, could live. If not for the crash, you never would have been born."

"I would have been born in Cosega, millions of years ago."

She stopped, mostly so that Cabe could catch his breath. "I suppose you are right. Your life would have been very different."

"Perhaps I would have travelled the stars like my ancestor did, like you did."

"Very possible. Most Imazes come from a long line of Imazes."

He nodded, lost in thought, as if the idea pleased him and made him sad at the same time. "Can I go with you?"

She had been expecting the question for several minutes. "It is not so wonderful there right now."

"Nor here."

She smiled. The regulations flooded her mind, all the reasons this idea was outrageous and impossible. "Yes."

He stopped. "Really?"

"If I can get the ship working, you can come."

"Okay," he said, shocked at her easy agreement. They were silent for a while.

"How much farther?" she asked gently.

"When we reach the top, it is a short walk to the cliffs. It is near there." He pointed.

Ten minutes later, they entered some trees. Boulders littered the area, most the size of city dumpsters, a few even larger. Their brown and white color matched the cliffs, but soon they were surrounded by several dark gray truck-sized stone slabs that seemed out of place. Leaves and grass covered the lower parts.

"Just over here."

But when they got to the other side, Shanoah knew the ship was no longer there. A large section of earth had been disturbed, and tracks from at least two backhoes were present.

"Oh no!" Cabe said. "What happened?

Shanoah saw the tracks only went as far as a small clearing, and knew the heavy machines had been flown in. This was no accidental discovery. Someone knew the ship was here, and they'd known she was coming. The ground had not even seen rain since it was opened.

*This could have been hours ago, no more than a day or two.*

Kalor Locke was not her first thought.

"Trinity," she whispered, and hoped it had been him. Kalor Locke or anyone else meant more than she wasn't going to be able to fly home on the *Bullington*, it meant *real* trouble.

# FIFTY-EIGHT

***Cosegan Time – Solas***

Standing in front of one of the most secret buildings in all of Cosega, Shank marveled at how it appeared so ordinary, so boring.

"And yet from this location, all of the disasters of Trynn began," he muttered, his voice rising. "He killed his wife, perpetuated the Doom, wrecked the Far Future, contaminated the Far Past—" he was shouting now, "—and eventually these epic blunders led to the murder of 3.7 *million* innocent Cosegans, a deed he undertook with malice and forethought and in collusion with our great and mortal enemies, the Havloses."

Several in his entourage looked confused, as if an answer might be required, but nervous they might say the wrong thing. All remained silent but for a few nods.

"He's in there?" Shank asked the closest Red Guardian, amazed the great Eysen maker would be so foolish as to return to Solas and then to breach security at his original Eysen facility.

"The FlyWatchers picked him up," the man said, referring to the self-propelled flying cameras with 360-degree view.

"Everyone thinks Trynn is so smart. Turns out he's not."

"He may just be desperate," the Guardian replied.

"I don't care about your thoughts," Shank sneered. "Was I talking to you?"

"My apologies, sir."

Shank, carrying a newly modified laser weapon, approached the doorway, a double blind, triple layered light sheet sealed with four sets of encrypted sonic curtains. Few would have the privileges and clearance to bypass one of the most secure facilities on earth. Using his all-access override entry code, Shank was one of the few with the credentials to enter.

"Trynn should already be dead. All this incompetence," he muttered. "I'll do it myself."

The corridor leading off the entrance would not prepare a visitor for what lay ahead. By Cosegan standards, the long hall was almost bland; columns of light low on the color spectrum, translucent walkways of sound channels equipped with vibration baffles discreetly concealed under laser pulses. Ordinary, quiet, and Shank stormed through it as if he'd been there a hundred times, when in fact he'd only been there once, years before, when the full Circle had toured the facility back when Eysens were still approved for negotiating the Terminus Doom.

He didn't recall much about his earlier visit, since he'd been seething at Trynn's glory—his undeserved, incompetent, manipulated glory. *How had Trynn fooled everyone?* Shank wondered as he marched toward the float, which would take him to the lower floors.

But he knew how. It was the fancy, glimmering magic of the Eysens.

*So easy to spellbind simple people with such an incredible device. Although it really isn't as much use as Trynn and his cohorts would have us believe. Oh, there's plenty that can be done with an Eysen, but Trynn has always gone about it the wrong way. These scientists don't understand the practical applications of their creations, rather they get caught up in the research of it, the transformative power, when it's really the control they miss.*

*I will not miss it. Once this techno-freak is finally dead and out of my way, I will use the Eysens to control my people.*

The float felt like being enveloped in warm, soothing light. It gave no sensation of moving up or down, even hundreds of stories. Instead, it just seemed comfortable, relaxing, private. No matter how many people were on it, there was total privacy for the brief ride.

The three Red Guardians accompanying him each arrived on the lower lab floor at the exact moment Shank did, although they had gone down separately. Each Guardian was armed with two Infer-guns and a Spartan laser rifle. Shank had chosen them personally. They would not hesitate to follow any order. *Execution.* When and who?

Another thirty Red Guardians were outside, securing the building. *There will be no escape for Trynn this time.* There were only two entrances, and the Cosegan dictator had issued an explicit order that anyone attempting to exit the building without Shank would get cut in half by a laser.

He smiled just before the float opened, thinking of how Trynn would be dead very soon.

The lab level was something different altogether. Shank gasped at the spectacle. He would not have forgotten this place. Either they had not come to this floor on the Circle tour, or it had been dramatically modified in the intervening years.

The colors were the first thing to hit him. A dazzling array that never seemed to end flowed across the ceiling, or where the top of the massive room really started or stopped. Whatever it was, it appeared like thousands of rainbows interweaving with one another, rippling like a river. He knew just enough to understand it somehow created a power generating form. In the Far Future, they would toil for decades trying to master nuclear fusion, when the answer to endless and free energy could be found in photons, much simpler and safer.

The next thing he noticed were hundreds of what appeared to be floating vats of bubbling liquid, each larger than a fifty-five-gallon drum, but without walls to hold the contents, yet nothing spilled. The colored liquids churned in an apparent air vacuum. Shank couldn't tell if it was done with light or sound, but it didn't matter. Beyond the extravagance of potions existed the reason he'd come to this dream works.

With his back to Shank, bent over working on one of dozens of levitating Eysens, Trynn stood defenseless, blind to what was about to befall him.

Shank decided in that instant it would not be nearly as enjoy-able to kill his longtime foe without the pleasure of watching Trynn die. He would go around and face Trynn so that the Eysen maker would know his life had been ended by the Cosegan leader's hand, choking on the knowledge in his final breath that Shank had defeated him.

# FIFTY-NINE

***Cosegan Time – Solas***

Shank paced in the hall of the factory, deciding how best to approach Trynn, when he suddenly spotted another person in the room. An instant before firing his Infer-gun, he realized the person was just a hologram. A split second later, he recognized *who* it was.

"Oh, Ripley Gaines, you startled me," Shank said. "But that's okay." He flashed a forced smile. "How fitting we should meet after all this time." He shook his head cautiously, still quite surprised that Rip was there, at least in holographic form. "Here is the legendary archaeologist," Shank said, as if the Guardians cared, then he looked at Trynn, who had strangely not yet turned around. He had not yet fled either.

"Always obsessed with your work," Shank barked. "Your wife died because of that selfish trait. Your daughter will likely be next. You care about no one, just your huge ego, that precious reputation, and glory—you can never seem to get *enough* glory, can you, Eysen maker!"

No response. Only the soft sounds of neon colors, streaking rain from micro clouds of misty golds and silvers, took the silence from the closed vacuum.

Rip, knowing his hologram could not be killed, still felt a tinge of fear standing face-to-face with such a dangerous Cosegan who he knew wanted him and so many others dead.

"And you, of course, are Shank," Rip said, wondering if Trynn would abandon his operation and attempt to flee, or try until the last second to complete it.

"Apparently my fame has lasted all these millions of years," Shank said, sporting a politician's smile.

"No," Rip said. "I'm fairly certain that I'm the *only* person in the Far Future who knows who you are."

Shank scowled. "Is that so? Well, don't worry. Things keep changing, so soon you may be the forgotten one, never to have existed, and I will be a legend. Then you'll remember this moment when you foolishly thought you were superior." He spat on the floor. "You are nothing. I am a Cosegan. I am your God."

Rip laughed.

"What's funny? Am I a clown? You're so brave, hiding behind the curtain of time because you think I cannot kill you. Maybe not at this moment, here in the lab, but I can and will make sure your life ends or does not ever begin. Have no doubt that I will do this."

Rip laughed again.

"I amuse you, do I?"

"Yes, very much. But in spite of your entertainment value, I have a question."

"What is it?"

"How did a Cosegan turn out to be such a maniacal dunce?"

Shank walked closer to Rip, which meant he was also closer to Trynn, who was still ignoring the scene, content to let Rip buy time so he could complete the procedure.

"What did you do, Mr. Well-known archeologist? You attended a college for four years, maybe went on to graduate school, earned a masters in something or another? Let me tell you, little Far Future man—all of that, including whatever your work experience has added to the quaint, trivial amount of education you *think* you have, is the equivalent to the amount of knowledge that comes out of our *stupidest* Cosegan's nose when they sneeze. It is *nothing*. You are barely brighter than a stone. The collected brain power of your entire civilization—and I use the term *civilization* loosely—is not equal to what I knew when I was six years old, and that was a very, *very* long time ago."

He walked closer.

"Therefore I am happy I make you laugh, that I provide some levity to your otherwise mundane and simpleton existence. I truly am. You see, all appearances to the contrary, I am a benevolent god. Just remember that whatever you have in your world today only exists because *I* granted it to you."

Rip looked confused. "I'm sorry, I couldn't hear you with all the machinery. What did you just say?"

Shank shook his head, a furious expression, and waived Rip off. He turned to Trynn.

"Hey, Trynn, I'm here to deliver your own personal Terminus Doom."

Trynn, unable to move or stop his delicate work, said nothing.

"Nothing to say? Strange for you." Shank studied Trynn to make sure he was also not a hologram, content that this was, in fact, the authentic Eysen maker standing before him. Shank continued. "Ironic that I will now be considered a hero for executing the murdering traitor that everyone knows you to be. I always knew you were dirt, it just took the average Cosegan a lot longer to see it. I'm curious, though. *Why* did you do it? So many foolish people still revered you, and then you turned around and killed 3.7 million Cosegans. Wow. I mean, even for you."

Trynn did not respond.

"Disappointing, but your words are less than meaningless to me anyway. Have fun in the Missing Time."

Shank aimed his gun at Trynn's head.

# SIXTY

***Cosegan Time / Far Future / Present Day***

Rip, caught in the pathway between times, watched the greatest Eysen maker manipulating the most fantastic and amazing device ever created in a seemingly magical factory that actually used stardust as an ingredient. In that glowing vortex of light bending, twisting photons, searing liquids of every color, swirling crystals, and a spectrum of rare air minerals, a mad man, wielding a futuristic laser weapon, stood poised to end it all in an instant.

"Wait!" Rip yelled.

"You can do nothing to stop me," Shank said with a laugh. "You're not even here."

"But I am here," Rip said. "And I know things that you don't. I know what happens eleven million years from now."

"I'll change all that," Shank sneered.

"Possibly. But you do not know the *most* important thing."

Shank glared at him. "And *you* do?"

"Yes."

"You don't know."

"You wouldn't be standing here if you didn't need the information you believe I possess."

"I don't need *anything* from you, archaeologist."

"What about the Missing Time?" Rip asked.

Shank's eyes flickered in the light. "What do you know of it?"

Behind the Cosegan dictator, translucent hues of a thousand colors surged through gleaming glass tubes processing captured starlight.

"I have solved it. I know the Missing Time like I know my own time, and you, who believe only you know the path forward, will be walking blindly in the fires of the Doom unless you know what takes place in those middle eons."

Shank moved his gun so it was pointed at Rip's head. "Tell me what it is."

"Or what? You're going to shoot my avatar? I assure you, eleven million years from now, I will be laughing as you pull that trigger."

"I have people in your time. I don't have to pull this trigger, they will do it for me. Assassins will find you and Gale and your precious droop-eyed daughter and first torture you, then slice you in half with weapons you only think you understand."

The volcanic cauldron thousands of feet below them sent incredible levels of thermal heat through advanced boilers made of comet-mined crystals, which allowed for further heating of the Eysen cores and hardened unibody Eysen shells, hastening the manufacturing process to a level just this side of reckless.

"If they could have found me," Rip said, "they would've found me by now."

"My people didn't know where you were before. But they know right where you are this very moment."

"And how's that?"

"Because I just told them," he said, pointing to his friend. "Say goodbye to the Far Future. The only thing that can save you is the information you possess that I *might* be willing to trade for your life."

"Trynn's purpose is far more valuable than my life."

"How noble," Shank said sarcastically. "What about the life of your daughter, Cira?"

Rip was quite unnerved by how much Shank knew about him and his family, but he needed to keep talking to give Trynn more time to finish the dismantling and reconfiguring. He knew from Ovan exactly what Trynn was doing, and the vital importance of it.

"Shank, with all that you have at your disposal, the vast technologies, the extreme depths of knowledge available in Cosega, how can you not understand that your past is us, and our past is Cosega? We are all connected."

Shank laughed. "Why are you stalling? What is the very fallible Trynn attempting? Why is he here, in Solas, during such dangerous times?"

Then, suddenly afraid Trynn had found some way to destroy him, erase him, Shank moved back toward the Eysen maker and aimed his gun.

Rip recalled what Trynn had told him about the energetics of the place. It was in the plans he'd studied. There was only an instant left to stop Shank.

Had Trynn completed enough? Was his consciousness uploaded? Would his protective suit be enough? Could he even survive the cataclysmic upheaval that was about to occur?

Rip knew none of the answers, but knew the time to act had come, and not one breath more could be permitted to pass through the Cosegan dictator's lips.

Rip moved, causing his holographic avatar to step across the no-boundary, what Trynn had called *the point of no return*.

An avalanche of photons exploded in a shimmering, spiraling vortex. The last thing Rip saw before being thrown back onto the floor in his own time on Booker's Caribbean island, was Trynn seemingly disintegrating into a blinding flash of light.

The connection between Cosegan time and Rip's time in the Far Future severed. What the archaeologist missed would have been too crazy to believe. All apparent matter in the vicinity of Trynn, working on an exposed Eysen core, erupted. Fissures opened in the air itself, allowing lightning bolts to escape into the space until everything fought for the remaining recognizable reality. Darkness, naked voids, supernova brightness, floating seams of glowing starlight, an unexplained screaming of thousands, and suffocating silence congregated into a death spiral. A funneling vortex formed then collapsed below the Eysen center. It swallowed Shank in a terrifying capture, inflicting upon him a kind of infinite death from which escape would be impossible, even with all the immense energy of his tragic soul.

# SIXTY-ONE

***Present Day – San Diego, California***

Waves La Jolla restaurant overlooked the Pacific. Shanoah had been there several times before, preparing for this meeting. Each time she could not help but recall how the area had looked in her time when it was part of Cosega. Geologically much had changed, but it was still the ocean, just shaped so differently, and the level so much lower.

She took her seat at the table and tried to enjoy the view. Trinity would arrive in a few minutes. His plans could have changed, as they had last month when she'd set up a similar encounter in Palo Alto. He hadn't shown up. Trinity was one of the most important people in the world, and hardly anyone had heard of him.

Of course, he hadn't been aware he and Shanoah were going to meet. He never would have agreed to grant an audience to a nobody, and she could never let him know who she really was.

Shanoah looked across the terrace and saw Levi. He nodded. Familiar faces sat at all the close tables. Nearly every other person in the restaurant, including the servers, were Etheren descendants.

It would be an expensive evening, but money didn't matter.

Money was easy, other things were hard, such as slowly piecing together the details of Trinity's life, his habits, his likes and dislikes, the people he trusted and those he did not. Years, *decades*, had gone into this moment.

*Is he going to come?* She sipped a mineral water with two lime wedges. She could never get enough lime.

The server approached and asked if she was ready to order. Shanoah had taken the extra difficult step of making sure the server was one of her people, and the maître d' as well. These tasks required more than money; moves like this could only be accomplished with contacts, connections, staff, an organization, and Shanoah had that now. Far from the woman who crashed landed in Florida more than a half century earlier, she was the key player in an organization. By keeping the mission alive, Shanoah kept herself alive.

"Yes," Shanoah said to the server, a woman she'd known for four years, one of the rescues; a woman who was as much an Etheren as some she'd known in Cosega. Shanoah gave her order, all vegan, although she likely wouldn't eat a bite of it. The woman thanked her and disappeared.

"*Where is he?*" she mouthed to Levi.

Levi moved his fingers as if playing the piano in the air for a fleeting half-second. Their signal for *patience*, or *everything is okay*, or *the stars are in alignment*. She smiled, but knew it could take months, even a year or more, to get another chance at Trinity.

The planted diners, only there to make sure no one else got close enough to Trinity and her to hear their conversation, were eating by the time her food came. Still, his table sat empty.

Levi gave her the signal again, but she now believed it to be a bust. *He's too late. He isn't coming.*

If he didn't show, she might have to resort to a more aggressive approach. She'd been considering a proposal from one of the organization's security people: an abduction—just to speak with Trinity, not to harm him—but his security was too good. Not that it *couldn't* be done, but probably not without bringing attention and possibly losing some people on both sides. Not a good outcome, especially the attention part. That was the last thing Shanoah wanted.

Then she saw him enter the terrace. The maître d' escorted him to his table. She watched his security scope out the terrace. It was small, with up-scale diners there for the incredible food, the breathtaking view, and the sunset, which was less than ten minutes from peaking.

The woman he was with was not his wife, but not an affair, either. She was a former top intelligence leader who now worked freelance. They'd known each other for years. Shanoah wished she was not present, but it couldn't be helped. There would be an incident less than sixty seconds after they were seated that would send the woman to the restroom within a few minutes. Nothing so crass as spilling red wine or anything noisy like that. She'd be subtly brushed, hardly noticeable, and a solution would enter her skin that worked in combination with a tasteless, colorless additive to her drink. No harm done, just giving her an immediate sensation of needing to pee. She would excuse herself. There would be a quiet delay in her returning, but nothing unusual. Shanoah would be gone when she returned.

Trinity sat, made quick, polite eye contact with Shanoah, as one sometimes does with the people closest to them in a restaurant. Shanoah registered a brief smile in line with proper etiquette for the situation.

The server, Shanoah's Etheren woman, breezed by, and fortunately, a minute or two after, Trinity's guest took a sip of her water. The backup had been injecting the substance in her food, but that would take much longer, and Shanoah was relieved his guest had been thirsty.

Levi gave a signal that all was going according to plan. She surveyed the room, looking for anything that might go wrong. Her face-reading ability showed her two men who would likely die within a year or two. It was not that unusual. There were so many modern humans with health problems. She wished she could teach them all how to control their cells, but it seemed overwhelming when the largest percentage of the population could live longer by just eating differently, but chose not to.

*Would they even take to the discipline required to manipulate and heal their own cells?* she wondered.

Trinity's guest excused herself, rose, and walked across the terrace. The restrooms were off the back of the inside dining room. Shanoah knew she would be gone for eight minutes, with the option to detain her for up to three more if needed.

Shanoah stood up and took the three steps to Trinity's table. She sat down in his guest's empty chair.

"Hello, Holt Gatewood. May I join you? My name is Shanoah. We have something extremely important to discuss."

# SIXTY-TWO

***Cosegan Time – Solas***

In the exploding light of what had been the Eysen Research and Manufacturing Center, Trynn clawed at a shifting wall, trying to avoid the simmering caldron swirling toward the vortex that had swallowed Shank.

"The tunnels!" Trynn heard someone yell, a voice he could not recall, and never heard again. Trynn hadn't used them in decades, but remembered their location now. The Eysen labs were connected to the Solas education building, and from there eventually reached a transportation hub.

But first, still in the heavy protective suit, he had to get through the bending, contorting, melting light.

The explosion Rip had caused channeled its force and energy downward because, knowing what was coming, that's where Trynn had pointed the exposed core. If not, several kilometers of Solas would have collapsed instantly instead of a slow fall of the neighboring few blocks.

"Not much time," he said as he fought the refracting light waves still bouncing in the narrowing corridors. Limping from some injury sustained in the blast slowed him down.

Soon, though, he'd escaped the immediate danger by slipping through a sonic tunnel connecting the outer reaches of the education building to the Leadership and Circle campus. Trynn ran across the slowly collapsing great hall, then, rounding a corner, he suddenly came face-to-face with the end of his life.

"*You!*" the Arc said, flanked by a full contingent of loyal security forces, ex-Guardians who would execute Trynn on the spot on the Arc's word, or for the slightest provocation. "What in the stars are you doing here? Solas is the last place you belong."

The suit that had protected him from the blast meant the Guardians would need to restrain him and remove it before killing him, but he had no doubt they would be happy to go to the trouble.

More than a dozen Screamer-guns and Infer-guns aimed at him, and the continued crumbling of the buildings around them made Trynn wonder if dying at Shank's hands would have been easier. He shifted, trying to conceal the large pack filled with crucial Eysen materials and Globotite. "I could ask you the same."

The Arc glared incredulously, stunned by his audacity. "I am trying to preserve my city, to save as many of my people as we can!" She stepped closer to him. "Are you here to destroy Solas, too?"

"No."

"Surprising." Yet she could see he was telling the truth. "Shank is hunting you, too. If he found you first, he'd have shot you on sight. I'm just going to take you into custody. When we return to the Protectorate, we'll put you on trial."

A section of light wall shifted and blinked at the far end of the corridor, as if signaling its imminent failure.

"Shank is dead."

Shock, then relief flooded her face. "How? When?"

"He found me. He didn't survive."

"You killed him?"

"Not exactly." Trynn glanced at the armed ex-Guardians,

silently wishing Rip was there. "It's complicated. There was an accident."

"You're sure he's dead?"

"Obliterated in an awful death—painful, frightening, almost endless suffering."

"Karma has a way," she said, staring deep into his eyes. "You did what he did. Karma will find you, too."

"I have no doubt," he said, never breaking her stare. A section of the ceiling cracked near them.

"Why did you destroy Crimsonsor?"

"I had to let them remove the energy of Crimsonsor. It was the only way to compress the Missing Time, otherwise the Cosegans would go on living, but humanity would become extinct."

"What sense does that make?"

"I did it to save us all," he said in a voice filled with regret.

"Who made you god?"

He shook his head. "I never asked for this responsibility."

"Yes, you did."

He shook his head again.

"Shank was working to prevent you from reaching Finality. Now you are free to push your super Switch. But I wonder . . . will you do it and relinquish all your power?"

"You know about the Switch?" he asked, completely stunned.

She laughed. "Poor Eysen maker. You know so much, and yet miss so much. Your view of the world is limited by what you see in the orbs and perhaps what a few close confidants whisper in your ear. I have networks of tens of thousands of informants and great minds built over centuries. It was no surprise that Shank underestimated me, a man blinded by hatred, ego, and ambition. However, you should have been less close-minded."

"I have never underestimated you," he said. "Don't confuse disagreeing with you for thinking you are weak."

"Disagreeing with me is fine, but you didn't trust me, and that is the same thing as underestimating me."

Another section of wall blinked out. A nearby column of light collapsed into photon dust.

"There is too much," Trynn said. "The complexities are beyond—"

"You scientists believe only what you can test, measure, or witness." The Arc narrowed her eyes. "Trynn, I expected so much more. It's a shame. However, I know what it takes to compromise and put the good of the collective ahead of oneself, so before your trial, I'm going to give you the chance to push the Switch and end this. But you'll do it from the protectorate."

"How can I throw the switch when Ovan and Grayswa are dead, when Shanoah is trapped?"

"Is it beyond you?" Another ceiling came down. "We should go," she said, motioning for her guards to take Trynn into custody. "We'll continue this conversation once we are safely outside the city."

Trynn looked for a way to flee, but there were too many of the guards. He complied, and was grateful they left him unrestrained, at least for the moment. Still, two walked on either side of him, with three more ahead and three behind. They were not going to allow him to escape, and he had no doubt that many, if not all of them, would love the chance to kill him if he so much as stepped even a few centimeters out of place.

When the man on his left suddenly collapsed, Trynn hesitated to drop, not sure what had happened. An instant later, he saw one of the women ahead of him fall, but this time he'd seen the laser hit. He scanned the area as he dove to the floor.

"Enforcers! The Havloses have breached the capitol!"

# SIXTY-THREE

***Present Day – San Diego, California***

Holt looked flabbergasted, but not threatened. Although he glanced around for his security people, there was something very unthreatening about Shanoah. Holt Gatewood knew his enemies well, knew how they operated, and this was not how.

"You've obviously gone to quite a bit of trouble to have this conversation, so please don't waste any more of my time. It would be wonderful if you were gone before my dinner guest returned."

"You have something I would like to acquire."

"By me, you mean—"

"HITE."

"I see. Well, then our conversation is over. I do not have the authority to discuss whatever it is you wish to discuss."

"You are the director of HITE?"

"I cannot confirm that."

"Please don't insult me."

He studied her for a moment, wondering if perhaps she was an enemy. "In either case, it should be of no surprise that even discussing these matters with a woman who lacks proper clearance and is using an assumed identity, is not a bridge I wish to cross."

"It's a lovely sunset, don't you think?"

He grumbled. "My guest will be back any moment, so your time—"

"Your guest will not return until we are done."

"Really?"

"Really."

He took a sip of his water, stared at her for a moment. "What is it you want?"

She noticed the first few stars beginning to poke through the sky. "Have you ever flown into space?"

He narrowed his eyes, glancing around as if trying to decide the best way to rid himself of this nuisance who he believed with each passing second might be a few cards short of a complete deck. "No, have you?"

"I have. And I'd like to do so again, but I have a problem. Do you know what that problem is?"

He shook his head impatiently.

"You have my ship."

If he hadn't been convinced she was serious, he might have tried to laugh off her comment as absurd. But his curiosity was too great, and yet he could not respond in the most obvious way he wished by asking her, "Which one?" HITE had many spaceships. It was at the core of the agency's existence.

He stared at her a little longer this time, wondering who she really was, *what* she really was.

"As I said . . . "

"I understand you cannot simply acknowledge the theft of my ship," she said, then smiled. "You, of course, have other ships, so you'd need to know which one. I can provide you with the date and location of the find."

"Okay, listen, assuming any of this was true—and I am not stipulating to that in any way, I am simply playing along with you for the sake of argument—hypothetically, *if* HITE existed, and *if*

I was the director, and *if* we had a specific ship, which you can provide the details of to verify that it belongs to you, why on earth would we agree to simply turn it over to you?"

"For one thing, it belongs to me. But your government doesn't seem to care about ownership. I mean, just ask the native people who were populating these lands before the Europeans arrived."

"Wait, you want to debate the treaties and treatment of historical indigenous peoples in the middle of a negotiation for a spaceship?"

"No, I want *my* ship, and I am willing to trade for it."

"Trade? I must say, I'm intrigued."

"Is that really the first thing that has intrigued you about this conversation?"

He smiled. "What are you proposing to trade?"

"Information."

He laughed. "If we had such an advanced thing as your spaceship, which was capable of bringing you from where?" He paused and cocked his head, as if waiting for her to respond.

"My home."

He smiled. "Okay, but an advanced spaceship, correct?"

"Extremely advanced compared to your limited capabilities. Beyond your top scientists' comprehension, in fact."

His smile cinched. "Yes, with such a wildly advanced asset such as that, why would we trade it for information?"

"The information will change the world, possibly even save it."

"Of course."

"Listen, Holt. You are the one person on this planet who knows enough of your people's secrets to know that I am speaking the truth. You are my best hope."

"Hope for what?"

"To get home." Shanoah stood up, placed a small envelope on the table in front of him, and walked out of the restaurant.

"Well?" Levi asked as he drove Shanoah to the airport. "That went . . . ?"

"We have a new secret weapon in the battle against Kalor Locke."

"Gatewood gave you something?"

"No, not yet," she said, smiling. "Holt Gatewood is the secret weapon."

"How so?"

"He may be the one person who can out-technology Kalor Locke."

"But will he do it?"

"I think he will agree to it after our next meeting."

"You have a next meeting?"

"Yes. He doesn't know it yet, but we are definitely going to meet many more times." Her expression turned sad, fearful. "That is, if he lives long enough."

# SIXTY-FOUR

***Cosegan Time - Solas***

In the ensuing chaos of the Havloses overrunning the area, Trynn managed to slip away.

Although several buildings nearby had disintegrated, it was clear that the Havloses intended on taking Solas intact. Trynn escaped the collapsing Circle campus and thought of how very different things would be with Shank gone.

*If the Arc gets out of the city alive, she could now have an opportunity to unify the Cosegans in the face of the looming Havlos victory.*

He climbed over the bodies of fallen Guardians, knowing some likely belonged to Shank's faction, others to the Arc's. It didn't matter any longer where the loyalties of the dead lied. There wasn't much Cosegan time remaining, and Trynn was sad to admit he'd helped it pass.

Havloses would win.

The Arc had no choice but to retreat into exile, forming a hidden civilization. To survive through the Missing Time was the only feasible goal now. As trivial, and even selfish, as that goal sounded, there was nothing more important in all Cosegan history, and humanity's existence. His chest tightened as he considered the absolute need for that relatively small group of

Cosegans to carry their knowledge and culture past the Missing Time.

His thoughts were interrupted by tumbling columns of light, the once great and mighty Hall of sciences partially destroyed. He wondered if Havloses would rebuild it. He had seen in the future the short-term structures partially built from light and stone combining the two techniques, but eventually it would end. The Havloses would lose the Cosegan's ability to fashion and form light in a matter of a few hundred years, and then the long decline would officially be underway.

As he worked his way through several slights, the places in Cosega cities where light and surveillance could not reach, he recalled his times meeting Globotite smugglers. Then he thought of Shanoah, how many times they had strolled these streets, planning grand ideas not just for Cosega's future, but for their own.

He wondered where in the bleak Far Future she was at that moment.

*The Far Future*, he mused. *A time when light is hardly used, and when it is, the people mostly waste it. How can they not understand the potential they squander?*

He thought of the touch of her hand, the softness of her lips, and wondered, *Will I ever see you again?*

Could he get the Switch just right . . .

On the outskirts of town, he found the place that had once belonged to Ovan, and technically still did. His goeze was waiting unused, charged and ready. Trynn got inside the light vehicle, thinking of his old mentor, envying Rip for being able to have conversations with him. Trynn knew it wasn't exactly the same. Ovan had died in his arms, yet still the consciousness of that great man remained accessible.

*If only I could seek Ovan's guidance once more . . . What would he say of this, of my plan?* Maybe he'd get that chance, but first he had to make it back to the barge. Trynn had two great tasks remaining. *Two things I must live long enough to complete: Insert one more Eysen, and time the perfect moment to pull the Switch.*

---

Trynn endured a harrowing journey with some close calls, but aside from dodging mop up patrols of Enforcers, he was able to blend in with streams of refugees as thousands of goezes fled Solas. The majority of Havlos forces were busy taking neighboring cities or securing the central sections and government centers of Solas.

---

The Arc's Guardians were able to defeat the storming Havlos Enforcers, and even decimated a full unit of Coils. Her security team convinced her to, reluctantly, leave the city.

"We've done all we can," one lieutenant told her.

"You cannot rule if you are not alive," another said. "Even more urgent with Shank dead."

She knew they were right, and there were too many Havloses in Solas now. Most likely it would fall before morning.

On the outskirts of town, her contingent discovered Markol's family suspended over the river. The Arc ordered her people to free them.

"Find out where Markol is," she added to her intelligence chief.

A short time later, while members of her team were giving Markol's family provisions, the intelligence chief came back with a sad report.

"Markol died when the Solas Eysen Center exploded."

"He was *there*?" the Arc asked, astonished that Trynn had not mentioned it.

The man shook his head. "High Peak," he said, as if the name of Trynn's former secret Eysen lab would explain it.

She looked at him, confused.

"Some kind of simultaneous chain reaction through the Eysens . . . I don't understand enough of the Eysen science to explain it. However, High Peak was completely destroyed."

The Etheren in her understood the irony of Karma. Shank and Markol dying from the same Eysen was a related tragedy.

"One day, I will see Trynn again, and he will tell me how these two met their end," she said, not loud enough for anyone to hear.

"We must keep moving," a lieutenant told her, "if we are going to make it back to the Protectorate before sunrise."

*The Protectorate,* she thought. *The Cosegans' only hope.*

# SIXTY-FIVE

*Cosegan Time – Havlos Lands – Jarvo's bunker complex.*

Jarvo did not know any details of the battle for Solas, only that it raged. It had been half a day since his last update. Pain medication confused him.

"I can't see!" Jarvo screamed. "I'm blind, deadly blind!" He let out a kind of primal howl.

Cass ran in to see him.

"Who's there?" he demanded.

"It's me," she said. "Can you see anything?"

"It's a purple, sucking darkness. Ugly, shifty, smothering darkness. The dark wants to strangle me!" His arms flailed. He tore at his eyes, furious they would no longer work.

A nurse arrived and attempted to hold his arms back. He fought her. "His vision has been worsening, blurring, making people look like shadows," she said to Cass, as if Cass did not already know this. "But now . . . nothing."

"Worse than nothing!" Jarvo cried. "It's disgusting purple, closing in, sliding, swirling clouds of putrid purple. I wish it would go black! Why won't it go black?"

He pushed the nurse away and lunged out of bed, as if forgetting he was laying down. Crashing to the floor, he shrieked with pain. The nurse hit an alarm.

Both women saw the bone protruding from his arm. It had snapped. There was not as much blood as normally would have presented with that kind of injury, and what there was seemed oily and dark.

Several orderlies ran in. Two of the big men held Jarvo down while the other got a mask over his nose. He fought, shaking his head for almost a minute before they managed to keep the mask on long enough for the gas to take effect. For days, they had been unable to sedate him with needles. His veins were too weak and thin.

"How long will he be out?" Cass asked, watching him slip into a fitful sleep.

"Does it matter?" the nurse said.

Cass would normally discipline that kind of indifference and blatant lack of respect, but she didn't have the energy just now. Jarvo would be dead soon. There was much to do.

She took one last look at him, totally unrecognizable from the man who had shown her his secret Eysen months before; the thing he believed would reveal how to own the world, but instead had turned out to be the thing that would end his world. She was tired of watching him suffer, tired of the brutal war, but mostly she was just *tired*.

Cass wondered if she should have him put out of his misery. It would be simple to do, but she decided against it for two reasons. First, if she was to assume power after his death, her rivals might claim she had killed Jarvo to seize leadership. However, the main thing that stopped her from the mercy kill was that Jarvo had earned this agonizing, tortuous death, and she had no intention of denying him a moment of his suffering.

Late the next morning, Jarvo gasped a last choking wheeze of air, then his heart ground to a stop.

"Jarvo is no more," Cass whispered to the empty room.

Before they cleared his ragged body away, an aide brought news.

"Solas has fallen," the man said matter-of-factly.

"Did the Cosegans surrender?"

"No."

"Of course not," Cass said. "They will never surrender."

"Apparently not today," the man said, a scowl on his face as he watched them roll their deceased former leader away. "We are in almost complete control of the city."

"Almost?"

"There are pockets of resisters. We will root them out within a few days."

"Minimize casualties."

"Ma'am?"

"*Minimize casualties*," she repeated. "There has been enough death."

"Yes, ma'am. Uh, beg your pardon . . . who's in charge now?"

"I am," Cass said sternly. "Have no doubt. *I* rule the Havloses now."

He nodded slowly. "Then, uh, I guess you . . . well, with the fall of Solas, victory is at hand, and . . . Ma'am, that means you are the ruler of the world."

Cass forced a smile, having achieved what Jarvo could not. "All his dreams came true the moment he died," she muttered.

"What's that, Ma'am?"

"I'll announce his death. Call an immediate full meeting of the military commanders."

"Of course."

Cass knew there would be power struggles among the Havloses, that many would seek to fill the vacuum created by Jarvo's death, but Cass herself would step into that role.

She would have very little time to prove herself, to somehow fix the horrible chaos the world had become.

"Maybe," she whispered. "Maybe there's one thing that can save us after this, the most devastating war in history. There is something *everyone* shares a desire for: a lasting peace."

# SIXTY-SIX

***Present Day – Sacramento, California***

Alik had been searching for months, trying to discover the location of Kalor Locke's quantum AI computer that had brought continuous havoc and caused the deaths of so many Blaxers. The frustrating disruptions to Booker's Eysen operations and threatening their controls had become an even bigger problem.

From the darkened room of an industrial park outside Sacramento, his latest city in his constantly evasive movements, he found something promising for the first time in weeks.

"What's this?" he said out loud. "Something isn't quite proportionate."

Filters siphoned the data in through his own super-computer. "Wow!"

He'd never seen anything this sophisticated, and its capabilities went way beyond the current technology. However, Alik had grown used to seeing unbelievable tech advances ever since Cosegan inventions began seeping into the modern world, which oddly dated to even before the discovery of Rip's first Eysen. He now knew that was due to HITE. The ultra-secret organization had accumulated several Cosegan artifacts from an unknown number of prior Imaze trace presence appearances in ancient times.

With the start of the Eysen wars, Kalor Locke and Booker had ratcheted up their weapons and computing prowess based on Cosegan technologies, causing dramatic increases and moving everything beyond a sensible trajectory. Now levels stood hundreds of years ahead of where they otherwise would have been.

"But this . . . this is remarkable." He checked his readouts, stunned by the massive computing power. "It's almost dangerous . . . not just to us, but this thing could take over the world by itself."

He was so impressed with the quantum AI that was running Kalor Locke's empire and armies that he almost couldn't bear to destroy it. Yet he knew whoever possessed that kind of power was potentially already out of his range.

"I may not be able to stop it. How do I take this out?"

Alik ran hundreds of scenarios simultaneously, increasing those results, and again increasing the results of those increases, each time by tenfold, and then he repeated that process over and over. The objective was trying to zero in on the exact location of where the quantum AI was hiding.

"Where the hell are you?"

The AI had a creativity line that made it conceal its physical origin point, but this was Alik's specialty. He'd invented the cloak.

"I'll find you."

With the aid of Booker's arsenal of hundreds of supercomputers, he continued both lines of pursuit.

"Seek and destroy," he mumbled repeatedly. "The way to destroy, the way to find."

Eventually Alik realized he was getting closer. The mistake that Locke's QAI made was in its frequent visits to a certain North American quadrant.

"The same area I first narrowed down when Kalor came at us

with that flare." They had been unable to find the exact location, but the server patterns had given the opportunity to lay a trap. "I've got to be clever here."

Looking for a way to destroy it, sweat formed on his brow. "Time. Time. Come on, don't lose me."

Terrified the QAI would slip away again, it dawned on him. It was so big it had to have something to do with the flare. It had gotten that name because the Eysen flares acted similar to solar flares. It was the death of his predecessor, Huang, that gave him the idea, and although he had no way to expose the quantum AI to an Eysen core, there was another way.

"All I have to do is convince you it's an Eysen core, feed you that data. Since an Eysen core shares many attributes with a solar flare, if I simulate that, multiply in the added data, it could . . . be too much for you. Maybe. *Maybe*. If you survive this, then god help us."

Alik set the trap, knowing the Quantum AI was hunting him just as he was hunting it.

"We'll find the data, then you'll find it, and this will overload programming and force an override, an erasure of your operating system."

He looked at the settings, the layers of data, a variable matrix of incredibly complex shifting sequences of code that almost no one else on the planet could understand, and chuckled.

Then he sighed.

"It's complicated, maybe too crazy. I could . . . I don't know. This probably won't work."

———

Lorne saw Alik's attack coming in and warned Savina. That warning cemented the end for Locke's QAI. Alik knew exactly what steps Savina would take. She'd shut down the after-logs and synched Eysen transferences, including several other predictable steps which allowed Alik's program to isolate the location and send the full volley of flares.

Lorne realized the incident was a trap, but it was too late, she'd *swallowed the pill*. There would be no turning back. Within two minutes, Lorne had exhausted the defensive measures inherent in her programming, and all those learned during the three years of her existence. A moment later, the frantic unraveling initiated, and Lorne, the Quantum AI Kalor Locke had built to facilitate the fulfillment of his destiny to live forever and control world events for the betterment of humanity, essentially swallowed the energy of a yellow dwarf star while attempting to compute an escape from the massive surge of power.

In simple terms, Lorne killed herself trying to save herself.

Her final message arrived on Kalor's personal laptop, informing him of her death and who was responsible. He stared at the screen in disbelief. To him, Lorne had been a living person. Because she was actually a Quantum AI, he had visualized her by his side as the centuries of his future passed. She would be the one entity who would always be there, who could understand him.

In a strange way, Kalor Locke had fallen in love with Lorne.

"No!" he screamed, mourning in agony, not as primal as his wrenching moans had been when he learned of Parson's death, but it was a shockingly painful loss considering Lorne had never really existed.

## SIXTY-SEVEN

***Cosegan Time – War Zone***

Cass looked out over the ruined city, the place where she had grown up. It looked like photos she'd seen of the Far Future in Japan after World War II, of the ruins of Nagasaki and Hiroshima.

Scorched earth, twisted metal, rubble, disaster.

The smell of burning skin, of rot, of death, filling the air.

Smoke and haze. Despair.

The woman standing next to her, one of Jarvo's top generals, showed her similar images of formerly great Cosegan light cities.

"What have we done?" Cass said.

"We have won," the general said.

"Won what?"

"The war."

"And now what?"

"Havloses rule the world. Jarvo's vision has come to be reality."

"Really?" Cass said. "Do you think Jarvo wanted this much destruction, this much death and suffering?"

"The price of war is high. He understood that."

"Did he?" Cass turned away from the hellish scene and stared at the general. "Because I don't think he ever believed it would go *this* far."

"He knew the risks needed of the war to finally defeat our oppressors."

"They were not our oppressors, they were our inspiration, showing us what is possible. They were us in a different way, a better time."

"They were the enemy. Now they are defeated. They must be subjected to inspections, monitoring, reeducation."

"You are relieved of duty."

"Excuse me?" the general said.

"We have no place for people like you in the future of our rebuilding and reconciliation."

"Cass, I don't think you know how important it is for you to keep the support of the military."

"I believe I enjoy their loyalty."

"Not if you don't have mine."

Cass raised her hand. Several seconds later, two armed men were there. "Please arrest the general," she said.

They did not hesitate.

"We'll see how long you last!" the general said as they escorted her away.

Cass turned back to the destruction. She thought of Jarvo, saddened at his agonizing death, because she'd known his good sides. She didn't like to see anyone suffer, but seeing what his wrath had brought onto the world, she concluded that he had deserved his fate.

She now had the awesome responsibility to lead the world, a world she no longer recognized. Facing a Havlos revolution, with millions of refugees on both sides, decimated agriculture and manufacturing sectors, divisions within the leadership of the seven sections, a fractured Cosega she hardly understood . .
.

There were still countless Imazes in the stars, and then there were the Etherens . . .

Cass had no idea how to handle those extraordinary people. She would seek peace with them at her first opportunity.

———

Her new deputy found her on the simmering battlefield. "There are messages from the Far Past."

Cass shook her head. Veeshal had effectively killed Jarvo and brought Cass to power. Could she be trusted?

*Doubtful, but maybe . . .*

She had a team in protective suits working the Eysen, trying to glean answers—ironic, in so many ways. A Cosegan device, the thing that had killed Jarvo, and in a sense what had caused all this destruction, the Eysen wars, and now it might be the only thing that could help them get through the apocalypse.

*If there is a way through.*

Cass saw a burning bed in the distance, as if it had suddenly self-combusted days after the last attack. *The Doom*, she wondered. *Is this the Doom? Is worse coming?*

"What did they say?" Cass asked of the message from the Far Past.

"The same as before. They insist that you have to give the Eysen to the Cosegans. That it must be dismantled. That it cannot be allowed to survive into the Missing Time."

She nodded. "So nothing new."

"You have to talk to them," the deputy implored.

"They don't want to talk, they want to dictate."

"But they will talk if you insist."

"Will they?'

"They'll have to."

Cass shook her head. "I'm not so sure."

Another aide approached. This one, a young man, could not have been more than twenty-five. He looked haggard, nervous.

"Anything?" Cass asked when he was close enough, but she could tell just by looking at him what the answer was. Failure.

"No sign of him," the man said. "We have one report that he was killed when Lownfer was destroyed."

"Why would he have been in Lownfer?"

He shrugged. "Why would he be anywhere? He's hiding, running. Lownfer is as good a place to hide as any."

"Not anymore," Cass said.

"No, I suppose not," the man replied, obviously bothered by his error.

"Trynn is not hiding or running," Cass said. "Trynn does not do those things, at least not as his primary actions. He's still working, still trying to save us all."

"But the war is over."

"One war, perhaps, has finished. There are other wars that continue, and more to be fought. The biggest is with ourselves. Do we, as humans, allow the worst of our impulses to guide us, or do we let the best of our inner beings go forward to seek the greatness we are meant for, to strive for the highest possible enlightenment we can achieve?"

"And the Eysen maker can help us with that?" the man asked, confused.

"I don't know anyone else who even understands the complexities of humanity's plight."

After the man left, Cass summoned her most loyal friend, a woman she had known since childhood, and charged her with what she considered the most important mission of her new administration. After giving clear instructions and complete safety precautions, Cass turned Jarvo's Eysen over to the woman with a final directive.

"Encase it in lead and concrete, then make certain it sinks to the bottom of the deepest part of the ocean."

# SIXTY-EIGHT

***Cosegan Time – Etheren Territories***

The Arc, still having difficulties shaking the horrors from Solas, deeply inhaled the organic air of the wilderness. Coming home again, to the safety of an Etheren settlement, the first time without her brother Grayswa there, was harder than she expected. She was grateful, though, to be among the trees she so loved, knowing that every moment in these natural and beautiful lands would be healing.

Kavid and Prayta greeted her in a ring of trees that had, for centuries, been a meditation center point for Etheren shamans. Incredible stonework completed by their ancestors thousands of years earlier accented the natural setting, creating an ancient place of peace.

"Thank you for seeing me," the Arc said warmly.

Prayta embraced the Arc and whispered into her ear, "Kavid is under a lot of pressure. He doesn't always mean what he says. Please be patient with him."

The Arc nodded, upset that Prayta felt she had to apologize for Kavid's harsh manners. However, she soon learned why.

"You are not welcome here any longer," Kavid barked, giving her a spiteful look. His boyish appearance countered his forceful leadership style and the seething anger with which he addressed the Arc. Then, waving off her security entourage, he continued, "You bring trouble upon us. We have a treaty with the Cosegans."

"I am aware."

"Then you know that I am obligated to notify them of your presence here. Out of respect for Senni, I will not do that so long as you leave *immediately*." Senni, Kavid's late great-great grandmother, had been a close friend of the Arc's. "And take *them* with you." He motioned toward her security force. Since his imprisonment, he viewed all Cosegans with Infer-guns as thugs.

The Arc glanced back at her team, all of them veterans of the siege at Solas, the few survivors. She didn't bother telling him about the more than one hundred good people who had died to protect her, to help evacuate her and so many others from the city that she loved.

"You mean you had a treaty with Shank," she corrected, choosing not to tell him of Shank's death.

"Shank rules Cosega, therefore my treaty is with Cosega, since their leader—"

"*I* am Cosega!" she interrupted. "There is no treaty with Shank. He does not represent Cosega."

"Shank rules!" Kavid repeated. "He is in charge now. You may not realize that, you may not like it, but that is how it is!"

"We don't need to argue about this," Prayta said. She, too, like most Etherens, appeared far younger than her age, lean, fair, and golden.

"The Cosegans are split in a shadow Civil War. It is hidden only by the invasion and destruction brought by the Havloses," the Arc said. "You have wisely chosen peace for the Etheren people by this treaty, and whatever means were necessary for you to obtain that peace. It is not for me to judge. I come here for a different mission, but one also born out of peace."

Kavid glared at her security people. "You have two minutes

to speak, and then I will be left with no choice but to honor my commitments and turn you in to Cosegan authorities."

The Arc took a deep breath, summoning patience, denying herself the luxury of debating further what was Cosegan authority and what his loyalties should be. Instead, she made her offer.

"There is a place. A Cosegan protectorate, shielded and invisible to this war, to the eventual takeover by Havloses of our previously utopian world."

He stared at her, aghast at her apparent surrender.

"It is a small place," she continued. "We are fully self-sufficient. You, Prayta, and up to twenty thousand Etherens are welcome there."

"Welcome there? For what? To hide with your band of cowards?"

"Kavid, let her finish," Prayta said.

"We are not cowards. We, like the covenant Etheren doctrine, seek peace, enlightenment, understanding of the natural universe, and the preservation of our people. This war, the Terminus Doom, will swallow everything. Our protectorate is the one chance we have to persevere and survive this dark period. *Please*, Kavid, put aside our disagreements. The Havloses will destroy all of this. The Etherens will be ravaged. *Come with us.*"

"But we cannot all come," he said, as if this was a great insult.

"The space is limited," she said regretfully. "It is a hard reality that burdens me deeply. There is not enough room for all the Cosegan refugees, or for all the Etherens . . . only a portion of each."

"And how do I choose twenty thousand? Who gets left behind? Who will lead them?"

"That is your decision."

"Oh, how magnanimous of you to allow me a decision for my people."

"Please don't make this about you and me. We should be

friends. Our differences of the past remain in the past, buried there."

He laughed. "Nothing is buried in the past. You know what Shank is doing. He has sent Imazes to the Far Past." He checked her expression, trying to gauge if she already knew this, before continuing. "Shank is attempting to manipulate the outcome of our entire existence."

"And you have proof of this?" The Arc had been afraid Shank was doing these things, but had yet to confirm it. Her hopes lay with Grayswa's shadow shifters. He had sent some into the Far Past before his death. She didn't know how, but believed that those shadow shifters would be able to act even with him no longer alive. If true, she thought it possible those shadow shifters would be able to stand against what nefarious deeds Shank's rogue Imazes were inflicting against the current time and Far Future.

"Shank himself told me this. I have no reason to doubt him."

"He would have told you anything to entice you into signing the treaty."

"It was but one factor. Havloses and Cosegans will destroy one another. They will erode their time here. Shank foolishly thinks this war is survivable. I received assurances that Etherens would be left alone from any Far Past manipulations."

The Arc gasped, realizing what he had done to get those assurances. She looked to Prayta to see if she knew of his dangerous acts.

Prayta seemed confused. The Arc searched the trees, wishing Grayswa would appear, wondering if the truth of Kavid's egregious error would destroy the Etherens immediately, or painfully slow.

# SIXTY-NINE

***Cosegan Time – Etheren Territories***

Kavid motioned for a group of his "warriors" to approach, then turned to the Arc. "It's time for you to leave."

The Arc stood firm, demanding an answer. "What did you give Shank in exchange for his assurances?"

"Nothing, only that Etherens will effectively remain neutral in this conflict, thereby not losing people or territories. In fact, I have gained territories. Do you know this?" He went on to list the areas he was granted from Cosegans.

"You used sacred Etheren abilities to gain advantage."

He shrugged.

"You engaged in soulful combat. How could you do such a thing?" Her voice raised, appalled. "This is against our creed."

"I don't even know who came up with these rules, but I'm not bound by them. I'm only bound by saving my people, and when the Etherens rise out of the Cosegan and Havlos ashes, the world will be a better place."

"The ends justify the means? Always the mantra of a corrupt ruler."

Kavid looked back at her stonily. "Oh really? Would you like to talk about corruption? You began your political career in corruption and lies, betraying your Etheren heritage, rising to a position where you could have elevated our people. Instead, you further punished and enslaved them."

"What I did was for the good of all," the Arc argued. "Not everyone can win every time. *All* people need to be protected under a good ruler—not just those who court her, not just those from where she came."

"Even Havloses?"

"Even Havloses," she said. "They need the most help of all."

"You would seek alliance with Jarvo? After what he has done?"

"You insult me, yet your comment is forgivable because you are young. Jarvo is a criminal, a thug. He is not representative of his people. He rules by force, by coercion, manipulation, bribery, and blackmail. He is the antithesis of what I'm talking about. To lead, one must sacrifice, compromise, and elevate. You will learn this one day."

"One day?" Kavid scoffed. "When you are long gone, and I am leading this beautiful planet populated entirely by Etherens, and you are a forgotten memory, hardly a footnote in history filed under *great mistakes*, I won't even *remember* your visit here today, because you will be *that* insignificant." He glared at her, and then smiled. "Mistakes have a way of fading from memory, and that is something *you* might learn one day."

"I'm sorry that this has once again dissolved to our differences. We have much more in common, and should be great friends. I ask you again, please consider coming to the protectorate, bringing our people to safety."

"*Our* people? They are not *your* people anymore! You made that choice long ago. And *my* people, the great Etheren people, *are* protected. I have made sure of that. While you have failed to protect the Cosegans, I have brought an expansion of our territories, an elevation of my people, and positioned them to inherit the earth."

The Arc shook her head. "Poor Kavid. You have done

nothing but buy a little time. You are making deals with untrustworthy people, trading Etheren core power for months, maybe a handful of years at best."

"I don't think you understand."

She held up her hand. "Please, I no longer wish to argue. Time for all of us is short. There is another reason for my visit today. I need Globotite for our dome."

He shot her an incredulous look. "*That's* the only reason you came here. Your real and desperate plea."

"No, I came to offer you protection for twenty thousand Etherens."

"Ha, that's a lie. You knew I would refuse your empty offer. You need Etheren resources to protect *Cosegans*."

"No, we have enough for now. But you should know there are people in the Far Future, Kalor Locke and others, attempting to obtain all the Globotite."

"Kalor Locke?"

"A crazy man in the Far Future who seeks to monopolize Globotite, the most important air mineral in existence. It cannot be allowed."

"What, only *you* should be allowed to hoard and decide its use?"

"Who would you rather have in control?" she asked.

"Etherens."

"I *am* an Etheren."

"*Real* Etherens!" Kavid snapped.

"Kalor Locke enslaves Etheren descendants."

"I doubt that."

"What happened to make you so arrogant? So foolish?"

"*You* happened!"

"Don't blame your flaws on others, Kavid, it makes you seem small." She started to walk away, then turned back. "You had the chance to be a great leader, and you squandered it on grudges and tantrums."

"Says the woman running to hide."

"Don't worry, I will negotiate and compromise with your successor. I doubt I will have a long wait."

He grabbed her and wrenched her around, then shoved her to the ground. "You sit on the throne of arrogance!" he yelled as her Guardians leaped to her defense.

"She's . . . she's dead," one of them said.

Blood pooled below the Arc's head on an ancient stone, laid by a long-forgotten Etheren ancestor.

Two Guardians rushed to seize Kavid. His Warriors engaged them. Minutes later, when the skirmish was quelled, four Guardians and six Warriors were dead.

And so was Kavid.

# SEVENTY

***Cosegan Time – Coastal land, disputed territory***

Trynn stood on a low cliff, the ocean churning in the near distance. The clouds looked threatening and glorious. The wind whipped his cloak. The world felt ominous. When he saw the messenger approaching, a woman who'd been in his employ for more than three decades, he believed she would announce the fall of Solas, the official end of the Cosegan civilization.

That turned out to be only the afterthought.

"I carry grave news," she said.

"Solas is in Havlos hands?" he asked, wearily looking up from the equipment he'd been studying.

"Yes. The Cosegan capitol has been occupied by Havlos troops. They have already installed a provisional government, but that is not the news which brought me here so urgently."

Trynn looked up, concerned by a hundred looming issues and their possible tragic outcomes.

"It is the Arc," the woman said. "The Arc is dead."

Trynn bowed his head. "I thought she would have escaped Solas," he said, his words laced with grief and guilt.

"She did not die at the hands of the Havloses. It was an Etheren, their leader."

"Kavid?" His astonishment made him nearly choke on the name.

"Yes. He is also dead. Killed by Guardians loyal to the Arc."

He shook his head. "The Arc is dead . . . Solas has fallen . . . the world belongs to the Havloses."

---

### Cosegan Time – Disputed territory

Trynn looked at the team of people waiting for him. For the first time ever, Trynn personally went on an Eysen insertion. He checked the area both on his instruments, and with his own eyes. Everything had to be perfect.

"This will be the last Eysen insertion that ever occurs," he said to an assistant. *It is also the most important one,* he thought, *since if the insertion does not succeed, all other Far Future Eysens will never be found.*

He stared at the sphere, his best work, the quality impeccable.

*If this doesn't go as I intend, then the Far Future quite possibly may never occur. And even if that troubled era does come to be, it will be devoid of significant Cosegan influence. How vile that would be.*

Trynn adjusted the instruments. It moved precisely in the right location.

"This one is different," the spotter said. Spotters worked with the contours of the existing topography and environment in relation to what the area would look like when the recipient found the Eysen, what conditions and changes would be evident at that target date. This spotter had been on every one of Trynn's insertions.

Trynn nodded, checking a portable view, showing him thousands of variables in the Far Future.

"We've never done one with a target date so early," the spotter said. "This beauty will be found much sooner than any of the other insertions."

"And it will be found by Cosegans," Trynn said as he double-checked the measurements to the coastline. The location allowed just enough distance to protect it from changing sea levels, yet remained close enough to the sea to be easily found by its intended recipient.

*This one will be found in the Missing Time. If it all goes well, they will use this to change everything,* he thought. *And survive until the Far Future, to give Rip one more chance to make the world as it should be.*

He tapped the sphere as if for good luck, said a silent prayer to the stars, thought of his late wife, and then of Mairis, until finally his thoughts dwelled on Shanoah.

Would he ever see Shanoah again? He felt sad that Mairis had to experience loss at such a young age. He had talked to her before his trip to Solas about how he still missed her mother, about how she would never forget Mudd, but that eventually she might find love again, as he had with Shanoah. He didn't want her living on the barge with him, living an awful, hard life on the run from the Havlos navy, even bounty hunters, but Mairis was stubborn like her mother, and, if he admitted it, like himself, too.

*I'll just have to convince her when I get back*, he thought.

Trynn marveled at the sphere's phosphorescent casing. His craftsman had been working on it for months. An assistant slipped the casing containing the sphere into a tube which would systematically decay over a long period of time, eventually revealing the casing. Several workers piled rocks in as much of a natural configuration as they could. Satisfied with their work, they camouflaged any evidence of their presence at the site, then departed.

Trynn stayed, surveying the area, checking for any problems, making sure nothing was missed, then, searching the horizon, reluctantly followed the path of the others.

A small waiting boat took them out to the barge. Instead of the open seas, Trynn told the captain of a new destination.

"Take us to these coordinates."

The captain did not know it yet, but they were now heading to the protectorate, the safe haven of the remaining Cosegan culture.

# SEVENTY-ONE

***Present Day – Houston, Texas***

Alik was in Houston this week. He never stayed in one place more than five nights.

"Sixth night is a pattern" he always said. "Seventh night, you die."

In Houston, on night three, with his shields and redirects, he wasn't even nervous yet. But Alik had also often said, "It's when you're not nervous that you should be." He was always paying attention, always looking for trouble. The one weakness he had might be believing in his own skills too much, especially in the cyber and digital realms where he directed most of his attention, his defenses, his priorities. However, Kalor Locke knew that, and Kalor played in many more realms than Alik, more realms than Alik even knew existed.

Booker knew all this though, and had a dangerous idea of the capabilities of Kalor Locke. There were Blaxers assigned to protect Alik wherever he went. A rotating crew of former special ops secured the perimeter, the areas where Alik didn't watch.

"Happy to have you," Alik always told the Blaxers, but he felt they were unnecessary. He knew he'd see trouble long before they would. "There'll be a ripple in the code, a breach in the fire-wall—not mine, of course, but one a million miles away, across the cyber sea, in another part of the digital galaxy." Alik had landmines strewn across the darkweb, and "Nooses waiting for necks to drop." His programs, the prevailing codes he'd created and/or disseminated, would trip up any ordered incursion, any notice of his whereabouts, or Rip's, or Booker's, Gale's, or Cira's. And there had been plenty of those in recent weeks, many *he'd* put down.

Booker had, only last week, increased the size of Alik's Blaxer contingent. "I'm at the bottom of the list. Give them to Cira," Alik had said at the time. Booker hadn't listened. His army was large enough for both.

Two days ago, Alik had seen something, studied what turned out to be warnings about the Grand Canyon attack, but when he called it in, the Blaxers protecting Rip and Gale were already dead, Rip and Gale already on the run.

"How did that happen?" He'd pulled screens, shuffled through windows. "I should have had this hours ago."

The delay had perplexed him. All his red flags had tripped, but only *after* the event. He'd been wrestling with the riddle ever since. It had been in that distraction and confusion that he missed the biggest signal of all: reality. If it could happen to Rip, it could happen to him.

That thought hadn't formed yet, so the brilliant hacker, one of Booker's secret weapons, didn't run when he should have.

The Van walking down the side of the glass skyscraper on Houston's northside, who had already killed the Blaxers on the roof, would be in his office in twenty-three seconds. Even if the thought entered Alik's head now, it was too late. A bullet would enter his skull before he could escape.

Alik was already dead, he just didn't know it yet.

The final act the computer genius had managed was to send Rip and Gale a critical piece of code, a speck of Eysen research that, if the Van had burst in thirty-nine seconds earlier, would have changed the outcome of all recorded future, forever altered the existence of humanity. But he managed to hit *send* seconds before the bullet ended his life.

# SEVENTY-TWO

***Present Day – Southern Caribbean***

Gale studied the readings, then re-checked them against Alik's ledger. "I think we're in!"

Rip stopped work on the expanding core calculations and went to Gale's workstation. "It looks good," he said after reviewing the readings, but he didn't dare believe it. Alik had sent them the fragmented code, which acted almost like a Rosetta stone to gain some control over Eysen energy, the driving force behind the *magic*, as he called it. They had many questions about it, but thus far they'd received no response from him.

No one knew he was dead yet. It would be at least fifteen minutes before Booker got word of the massacre in Houston.

However, Alik's parting gift to them had only been possible because of the Instrosen, which they now knew was only a partial manual to Markol's first insertion, the sphere found in Florida. They were still just beginning to understand that each Eysen operated entirely differently from each other. Although similar, just as people are, each with their own DNA, unique mind, and ultimate connection to something more, no two Eysens were the same.

They had long believed that there must be a way into Markol's spheres. Alik's piece of code proved it based on evidence discovered inside the matrix of all existing Eysen data overlaid with the Instrosen. It showed that an extra set of timing streams existed that he could use to come to the ending point.

"It's like a key," Rip said.

Cira came over. "Is it?"

"Yes," Gale agreed. "I think we've discovered the setting Alik told us about."

"And there's no question what it will do," Rip said.

"Are you sure?" Cira asked.

"Well, we won't know for sure until we know. I mean, if it works," Gale said.

"How much time do we have?" Rip asked.

Cira knew there were dozens of clocks ticking, only some of which they could measure in conventional terms. The Terminus Clock had to be the most consequential, but then there was universal time measured within the Eysens. However, in their own time, it was the minutes remaining until Kalor Locke powered up the Super-Eysen which meant the most. Yet even with that, there was a timing that mattered more than Terminus, more than the Super-Eysen, more than any of it.

The Switch.

What would occur after the Switch mattered more than anything. Cira had no idea how to begin to comprehend it, only knew that it meant everything, the end of the Eysen wars. Clearly it would be the start of something else, and that could be . . .

*Worse? Nothing could be worse, could it?*

Even Rip could not find a true understanding of it. He said there was no way to comprehend what would happen if Trynn didn't reach Finality and press the Switch, and no way to comprehend what happens if he does.

Trynn's descriptions and explanations had not given Rip the necessary reasoning required to mesh with all his years of scientific study and knowledge, and yet he knew that race against the Switch meant securing a chance for humanity; maybe nothing more, but that was worth dying for.

"The programs estimate Kalor Locke is seventeen minutes from initiating the Super-Eysen," Cira said.

They had previously explained the process to Cira, that the inference provided by Alik's key would essentially set off a chain reaction resulting in a digital version of a Large Hadron Collider, where protons are accelerated to virtual speed of light until a small percentage of particles crash into each other with a combined energy of up to 13 TeV.

"There are other similarities to nuclear reactors where a gram of matter releases up to ninety quadrillion kilojoules of energy," Gale said. "However, Eysens contain so much energy that the effect might be more massive depending on conditions."

"Since Markol's Eysen has a weakness that permits our entry, it might react differently though," Cira said. "Right?"

"There is a small chance it could ensnare us and our Eysens," Rip admitted.

"Meaning it could kill us," Cira said.

"Yes," Rip said. "It's a very *small* chance, but if Kalor Locke gets the Super-Eysen, Trynn will never be able to push the Switch . . . Kalor will win."

"And we die anyway," she said.

Gale nodded.

Cira looked at each of them, then took a deep breath. "Let's get him!"

# SEVENTY-THREE

***Present Day – Southern Caribbean***

None of Booker's teams, Alik, Rip, or Gale had been able to locate the Ranch, Kalor Locke's secret Eysen facility, but they were able to monitor his progress on the Super-Eysen through complex equations and their own Eysens, gauging increases and shifts in energy consumption, because of Cira's work on Globotite. Each particle of the air mineral left an imprint.

"It is always known across time," Cira had said.

"Kalor is readying the move. He's powering the Super-Eysen," Rip announced.

"Eleven minutes!" Cira said.

They'd received data from Trynn showing that many of the fuel spheres Kalor had used for his Super-Eysen were defective, so that once a chain reaction was initiated, the flaws within Markol's designs and the other maker's inferior spheres would unleash massive, but unpredictable, destruction.

"Too bad Kalor Locke probably won't be there," Rip said. "It's too risky for him."

"But he might be," Gale said. "His ego might demand it."

"Wait," Cira said. "What if Savina's there?"

"Most likely she *will* be there," Rip said. "I'm sorry, but she made her choices."

The three of them exchanged a glance.

Cira nodded.

Gale sent the coding operation into a controlled flow and the countdown began. "Looks like it will take twenty-seven seconds."

---

### Present Day – The Ranch, somewhere in Montana

For months, Savina had prepared for the Super-Eysen launch. "Two-minute warning," she said into the speaker.

"How many green?" Kalor asked, referring to the indicators representing each Eysen contributing to the super structure.

"All fifty-two green," she said, still amazed he'd obtained that many Cosegan Eysens. Even though some were flawed, their levels of Globotite and other rare minerals, along with their ultra-advanced components, would still provide the vital ingredients to make the Super-Eysen possible.

"Excellent. The world forever changes in seventy-one seconds."

Savina caught an anomaly in the data, an incoming sequence. With her study of Markol's murder of Huang, her background as a top physicist, and knowledge of the Instrosen, it all clicked into place. She couldn't be sure, but it could be almost nothing else.

*The Eysen wars . . . and this is a nuclear strike.*

She looked at the clock, and that choice, to check the remaining seconds rather than to immediately halt the connections, had been her decision.

*Nine seconds until the final volley hit. Still forty-one seconds until the Super-Eysen becomes operational. It comes down to a thirty-two second differential.*

She allowed herself a smile.

Later, Rip might figure out that Savina could have potentially stopped his weaponization of Markol's Florida sphere, and wonder why she did not.

*He'll think I did it to allay my guilt, or maybe even that I did it for him,* she mused in that instant. *But he'll never guess the real reason. I did it for Trynn, for Cosega.*

Savina ignored the incoming flow and blocked out Kalor's countdown. Instead, in those final seconds, she initiated her own sequence, overriding the power load of the Super-Eysen to float in the Eysen experience, the place she only dared visit a few times before because of the intoxicating addiction of it. The colors and cosmic forces of the universe swallowed her, the vastness and beauty exhilarating beyond comprehension.

She didn't hear Kalor demanding to know what had diverted the needed power. She didn't hear anything, not even the blast. Its blinding light of destructive force vaporized Savina's body along with any memory of the thoughts she'd had in the moments before the sun visited Montana, and exploded through a digital opening in a virtual universe created by a dead man eleven million years earlier.

# SEVENTY-FOUR

***Far Past – The Works***

Veeshal, proud of Trynn, watched as events drew them closer to the end. It was the day she'd waited a million years to see. The Eysen lock. Finality.

She sighed and looked up, getting lost in the stars, gazing through the glass roof of the Works as if the heavens showed much more to her than all the Eysens she had created. "I feel a real sense of relief now that this Super-Eysen nonsense has been taken care of," she said to Kenner. "And a sense of accomplishment. Of hope, really, for those in the Far Future. Maybe they *can* do it—and by *them* I mean the primitives in what they call the twenty-first century, of course. They'll need—"

"He is close," Kenner said, interrupting his mother.

"I am not surprised," she said, her voice filled with pride. However, she *was* surprised. It hardly seemed possible. "Unimaginable though it is, he might yet pull it off. Synching everything, locking reality . . . " She looked at her son, seeking the adoration she believed belonged to her.

"From your creation."

She nodded. Kenner had seen her bruised and tarnished, but he was still devoted.

"Cass has not responded," he said, breaking the spell. "If she does not before Trynn presses the Switch, we will lose the Eysen for good. It will slip into the Missing Time."

"There is still a chance she will come to her senses."

"She is scared."

Veeshal laughed. "And well she should be. There are countless traitors, enemies, and opportunists waiting with daggers to bring her down, to take her throne, to destroy what she might build."

"Ambitious people in every age."

"Greedy people. Dangerous, selfish people."

"She cannot survive long."

"No, but perhaps long enough. She is a clever woman, with a good mind and an even mix of her father's hardness and her mother's sensibilities."

"Will it matter how long she lasts if she does not return the Eysen?"

"I wish I knew," Veeshal admitted. "Trynn may know, but I do not."

Kenner sighed, growing more used to his mother's limitations now. "What happens to us if Trynn does get to push the Switch?"

"We will be confined to only being able to interfere with our own time," she said mischievously. "Our Eysens will no longer be able to see the future."

---

### Present Day – Brooklyn, New York

The lonely figure standing on the bridge did not know he was being watched. He hadn't noticed the weeks of constant surveillance, mainly because the Etheren descendants who'd been shadowing him were extremely good at going stealth. The summer evening was humid and still. Traffic was heavy, as usual.

He paced and wandered from end to end twice, covering the five thousand, eight hundred, ninety-nine foot span which made it the world's longest suspension bridge when it was completed in 1883. More than thirteen hundred people had leaped to their deaths since then.

The man had been searching for the highest point above the East River, waiting for sunset, and most importantly, getting up his nerve to make the jump that he knew would end his life, stop the misery, the confusion, stop everything.

Fortunately, Shanoah had been in New York when the report came in that he was on the Bridge.

However, before she could get there, she got the text:
**We tried to reach him. Not in time. He jumped.**

Less than half a block from the Bridge, she threw some cash at the taxi driver, got out, and ran. Her speed, more than three times what modern humans were capable of, would surely attract attention, even at twilight, but she did not care.

She sprinted onto the bridge, not slowing until near the halfway point, when one of her Etheren agents pointed to the spot he'd jumped from minutes before. Shanoah did not hesitate, leaping over the rail like an Olympian, then assuming the perfect diving position while in mid-air. Splashing into the cold water, she counted on her enhanced Cosegan abilities to find Ricardo.

It took her more than a minute to reach him, and almost two more to drag his unconscious body to the shore, where she began to work to resuscitate him.

"Come on, Ricardo, don't die! Don't die!"

# SEVENTY-FIVE

***Present Day – The Ranch, somewhere in Montana***
The acrid scent of burning wires, ozone, and melted rubber filled the air. Jogging to the epicenter, the site of his lab, he at first believed it might have been the attempts to power the Super-Eysen that had caused this apocalypse. He had barely been out of the blast zone—not intentionally, but because the building where he could monitor all operations and effects happened to be far enough away.

Then he recalled the power drain seconds before launch.

*It wasn't the Super-Eysen . . . Booker found me. This was a Blaxer strike!*

Kalor surveyed the damage. Everything had been leveled, miles of charred wasteland stretching in all directions. The Super-Eysen lay in ruins. Where once stood his hope of illuminating his vision for the future of humanity, now smoke and a few sparks rose from a hellish crater.

It could have been worse. He could be dead.

"That was their biggest mistake," he muttered while scanning the area. "Leaving me alive."

Something down in the depths caught his eye, something shining. After a quick glance at the sky, he moved to the crumbling rim. The bombed-out wreckage surrounding him had to be the work of Blaxers, but how?

With the power of the destruction he saw before him, he suddenly worried about radiation.

*Too late if it is,* he thought. *But what kind of Cosegan weapon could do this much?*

The building housing the Globotite, maps and data, including Wendy and other Etheren descendants, was wiped out.

*Damn them!*

He looked back at the only structure still completely standing, the one which held his research on cell-framers, Cosegan longevity and health, and Etheren abilities research, amazingly intact.

*That ensures I will never be defeated.*

*But the Blaxers destroyed everything!*

Booker Lipton needed to die soon. This certainty had driven him for so long that the renewed urgency invigorated him. "Booker, you bastard!"

Noticing the woods burning at the edge of the scorched area, he shook his head. Parts of the steel observation tower were wrenched and twisted around a massive tree that had previously been at least fifty yards away from it. It wasn't a conventional or nuclear attack, he decided.

*They came in through the Eysens, like how Markol got Huang. I don't know how, but that's what did this. Taking the opening created by the Super-Eysen, they infiltrated this site and amplified the power of the Eysens somehow.*

"Using my own invention against me . . . that was smart. That's something I would have done. Should have seen it coming."

The hole ripped into the Montana soil looked to be at least twenty feet deep, the opening's diameter closer to thirty, with a debris field radiating a quarter of a mile outward.

"The Super-Eysen's core is nothing like those of the Cosegan Eysens. That surely would have killed me, and half the state."

Searching for a way down into the crater, he thought about Parson, wishing he was there with him. His first impulse wanted Parson alive so that the two of them could seek revenge together, but he stopped halfway down into the smoldering pit as a lump formed in his throat. He missed his younger brother, missed him more than anything.

"I will avenge you, Parson. If it takes me all of eternity, I will find Booker and kill him, kill *everyone* within his orbit."

It wasn't just Parson. Lorne was gone, and now Savina. His entire Eysen staff of scientists and engineers had been killed in the blast. All of his Eysens were gone . . .

In a blurred anger, he vowed to begin again. "I still have the Varangian Guard. I will start a war. I will come for your Eysens in the night and kill you in your sleep!"

Almost at the bottom now, he worked his way past a tangle of melting metal that might have been part of the Super-Eysen's energy structure once linked to the individual spheres.

Hearing a distant noise that sounded like it might belong to a chopper, perhaps even one of the Vulture gunships, he quickened his movements.

"Damn it!"

He slipped on a steep section of loose dirt and debris, a bloody gash opening in his calf. Recovering quickly, he moved further down until the object he'd seen from above came into view.

"*Yes*," he hissed. "*Yes!*" He picked up an Eysen and smiled. "Florida, you survived. Maybe there are others."

# SEVENTY-SIX

***Havlos Time – formally known as Cosegan Time – Etheren Territories***

Julae met with Adjoa in the forest of Etheren wilderness. The two women had known and respected each other for a long time, and both were equally surprised to be in their respective roles of leading the Etherens, and navigating an uncertain future when the Havloses would now be in control of the planet. Havlos domination would make for hard times. The narrow-minded Havloses would discriminate against and seek to take advantage of Etherens.

"You always knew you would replace Grayswa one day," Julae said as they walked along the river.

"I didn't know it would be this soon. He should have lived at least another half millennia." She pulled at her long, gray, braided hair, which reached her waist.

Julae nodded. She, like all Etherens, had loved Grayswa. "Well, I never dreamed I would one day be our leader. And in these dark days . . . "

"In these dark days," Adjoa echoed her words, "Etherens will be the light. It is our destiny."

"I hope so."

"There has never been a more important time in our history. The days and years, the generations ahead, will all depend on what we do now, the examples we set, the decisions we make. You are the absolutely right person for this moment."

Julae smiled and took a deep breath, relieved the shaman believed in her. "Thank you. I'll need your help."

"And I'll need yours," Adjoa said, a serious, yet serene look on her face. "We will help each other."

"Where do we begin?"

"Our sole purpose is to make sure our people, the Etheren influence, survives into the Far Future." Her face appeared like an ancient mountain woman's, yet Adjoa's hazel eyes burned with a magical fire, suggesting energy beyond measure. "Have you seen it?"

"Once, in one of Trynn's Eysens."

"I'll show you so much more."

"Without an Eysen?"

"Oh, there are many ways to see into the future when one understands the power of the soul, the flow of consciousness, the *nowness* of time, and the way of the cosmos."

---

### Havlos Time – The Protectorate, Lantis

Far away, on the island previously known as the Protectorate and now simply called Lantis, a Cosegan word meaning *hidden star,* Welhey sat in a small tower overlooking the partially built city.

He was now officially the Arc. However, he'd declined the title, saying Kwana, the last Cosegan Arc, should forever be known as the Arc. Jenso and several others had joined him.

"You can't even see the dome," one of the older women said nervously.

"I assure you it is there," Jenso said.

"So long as the Globotite supplies hold out," a man added.

"Yes," Jenso agreed. "The Arc left us well stocked, but we will eventually need more, depending on Trynn's theories. We may be able to make things much more efficient if we are able to apply his ideas."

He and Jenso were making progress in developing a self-sustaining perpetual motion energy source that just by using a small amount of Globotite, could maintain the dome and city power needs for ten thousand times longer than currently possible.

"How are we coming with the Etherens?" asked a woman wearing white and gray scarves who was now second in command to Welhey.

"Julae has agreed. There are less than ten thousand who want to come. Transportation is an issue, but we're close to working out a system so that the movements go undetected by the Havloses."

"This is good," another man said. "Welhey, you are to be commended for your efforts at carrying out the Arc's wishes and plans to create this secret bastion of what was once the great culture of Cosega. The Etheren incorporates will strengthen that. I am only sorry we can no longer explore the stars."

"Trynn is not ready to let the Imaze programs go just yet," Welhey said.

"Surely we cannot send star ships in and out of Earth's orbit without the Havloses noticing?"

"You'd be surprised what is possible," Jenso said. "After all, it isn't simply the dome that protects us here, it is the near invisibility of the island."

"You can do that with star ships?" he asked, astonished.

"Soon, we believe we can."

"Wonderful."

The woman with scarves stood up and walked to the railing, looking out across the ocean, which stretched to the horizon with no land in sight. "What of the others?"

Welhey had hoped to avoid the controversial subject today.

The *others* were the many Cosegans who had been left behind. The island's space was simply too limited to bring them all, and millions were left to fend for themselves in the new Havlos-dominated world. "Most will be forced to blend in," Welhey said.

"They will become Havloses," a man said bitterly.

"Yes, most will over time. Losing the war comes with great costs."

"Too great."

"Yes, but we do what we can, and it won't always be like this."

"It will be until after the lifetimes of everyone here today."

"True, yet there is a golden time ahead for Cosegans. It is sad and also dangerous, but filled with beauty, potential, and great hope." He stood, his white linen robe fluttering in the breeze. "The Arc worried that Cosegans would once again grow arrogant with our advanced society; particularly in the future, when the rest of the world falls more primitive than the Havloses are in our time."

"Will they?"

"Of course. As all things ebb and flow, the Havloses will eventually decline and disappear. When that occurs, those Cosegans that come after us will send emissaries to the rest of the world, secretly teaching, secretly expanding Etheren and Cosegan knowledge and ideas to our descendants."

"This was the Arc's wishes?"

"Yes."

"And this plan is for what purpose?"

Welhey flashed his famous smile. "So that in the muddled mix of the Far Future, after hundreds of years of near constant wars, in a population blighted by consumerism, ill health, greed, crime, and corruption, the Cosegans will rise again."

# SEVENTY-SEVEN

***Havlos Time - Trynn's Eysen Lab Barge, open ocean, parts unknown.***

The hallucinating verve of lights, hypnotic with flowing trails like a million microscopic comets, beckoned Trynn, toying, teasing as a would-be lover. The world, as close as it had ever been to the near point of truth, pulsed perfection—clarity, vivid views, symphonic breezes, scents of Eden, each touch tender, impactful, inaugural. It all played through a ballet of time, kissing a slender death marked by the shadows of humanity's greatest endeavors and most mundane matters.

*Breathe*, he told himself.

The Switch receptors, preprogrammed, constantly revised and nuanced by the Eysen maker, showed he was finally there. Everything waited for a single additional breath. Seconds and minutes blurred with centuries, with millennia.

Trynn's heart raced. For hours he'd anticipated it, known it was coming.

"Days have led up to this moment," Anjee said. "Are you ready?"

*Days?* he thought. *Years. More than that, my* entire life *has brought me here. Eternity itself is present here, bringing us to the Infinity Switch.*

He shook his head. He was not ready. How could he ever be?

Counting silently, he watched the views of the Far Future sail by one after the other. The taste of Revon, more than he'd taken since before Ovan's death, lingered on his tongue, and there was more at the ready. It gave him clarity, yet suddenly all he could see was the Switch, shrouded in so much glow now it seemed otherworldly, and of course he knew it was.

*Something like this should never exist.* Too much power, a rabid and lethal responsibility. The Switch . . .

But then there was Shanoah. How could he live without her. *How could I?*

"It's coming again," Anjee said loudly, though the constant rush of noise in the room made it difficult to hear. As they neared the inflection of Finality, each view created its own shifting sound.

"I see it," Trynn shot back. The views were so close to all the preprogrammed synchs that a pressure built with each passing round of outcomes. The rush of them produced wind in the Room of a Million Futures. An hour earlier it had been a slight stir, then a breeze, but now it had become strong enough that it was moving the barge, like an internal category one hurricane. Nothing was stable, and yet that is what they sought—stability to gain the Finality.

"Move, move!" he shouted to the views, commanding the trivial into something more, momentous, calculating the ramifications of each transfer, the reading of the rhythm, something he'd mastered like another language or music, a great composer conducting a symphony, creating a new reality out of billions of existing ones. Trillions and trillions of instants made the wandering openings deeper, higher, microscopic, expansions and coasting . . .

"There it is!" he yelled, running through the views. Stumbling, gasping for air, terrified at the crushing consequences of it, lost in the thought that Shanoah remained, that he was about to seal her fate—

"Now! Now!" Anjee shouted. *"Now!"*

He knew there was no time for a final look. That's why Anjee was there; he needed the extra eyes. But he'd been at this too long, there was too much on the line. He stole a half glance and saw nothing to impede the decision.

*Trust*, he thought.

Reaching the Switch station, he grabbed the gold handle amidst the furiously blowing photons, glowing in a storm of purple mist with its now constant green electric pulses. Without taking another breath or having any regard to the high probability that he'd die while pushing it due to its uncontrollable power, Trynn pushed the Switch.

Instantly, it all stopped. The Room of a Million Futures went dark. The Terminus Clock rolled to the infinite 88888888, then clicked to 88888888, clicking again, 88888888, and again . . . still at 88888888.

"Finality," Trynn said, amazed to still be alive.

"I thought there would be an explosion," Anjee said.

"Only if it didn't work, if we missed by even a fraction of a second."

"Then it's nice we got it right."

He nodded sadly.

Anjee inclined her head. "Shanoah is trapped there, isn't she?"

"Yes."

"I'm sorry."

He said nothing.

"But at least you can talk through the Eysens."

He shook his head. "The Switch cuts all communications." His voice cracked, as if the realization of it had just hit him for the first time, and in a way, since he'd never allowed himself to dwell on it, it had. "It's my Karma for killing all those Cosegans . . . this is why I lost Shanoah."

"What about all the good you've done? What about the Switch? You have *saved* humanity. Surely that erases all the mistakes you've made."

"Maybe. I don't know anymore."

"Shanoah is very strong, incredibly smart," Anjee said. "She'll find a way home."

He nodded. "There is always a way."

# EPILOGUE

*Havlos Time - Cosegan Time - Trynn's Eysen Lab Barge, Cosegan Protectorate, Lantis.*

Mairis and Trynn sat on the deck of the barge, docked well within the limits of the protective dome. His new lab was being built on the island, but it would take a while. Jenso was overseeing the project, one of dozens requiring her attention. The small island meant creativity had to be maximized to fit as much onto it as possible.

While waiting for the space where he expected to live out his days, working with Eysens and other technology to preserve the Cosegan civilization in the face of a world now dominated by Havloses, he continued his projects on the barge to prepare for the Missing Time.

The Room of a Million Futures, now dark since the Switch made future changes impossible, sat empty, storing Eysen parts and equipment scrounged from Solas and High Peak by those loyal to Trynn.

"I can't believe it all came to this," Mairis said, looking out over the golden island. "So few of us remain."

"I did my best," Trynn said, his eyes filled with tears ready to spill. His emotions were raw since losing Shanoah. He felt he'd abandoned her in the strange, distorted world of the Far Future.

"You did more than your best," Mairis said. "You saved us, enough of us so that there is hope that we can rebuild in the future."

"Maybe."

Mairis could see he was thinking of Shanoah, maybe even her mother. "More refugees came in this morning," she said. For weeks, survivors had been smuggled out of the war zones by elite crews Welhey and Jenso had put together.

"We're at capacity. Now they'll have to abandon all those who remain in Havlos lands. They'll be forced to assimilate." He thought of Shanoah going through the same thing.

Abandoned. Forced to assimilate.

*Cruel.*

"Do you know what Julae said? 'Those left behind will never fully assimilate. The Cosegans and Etherens trapped among the Havloses will hold the seed until the future shift, like flowers secretly planted.' The forgotten ones will forever alter the Havloses and leave them susceptible to the great shift in the future. They may end up being more important, or just as much as the ones that carry on in Lantis."

"I like that," he said.

"Nassar, Anjee, and Cardd have been working constantly since the Switch to research and develop new understandings of the Far Past, past, future, and Far Future, so who knows what we'll find. Maybe the Havloses won't last as long as we think."

"Everything is different and everything needs to be re-understood." Trynn stared off somewhere far away. "I just keep thinking . . . maybe the Revon . . . but it all comes flashing through my mind like a constant lightning storm. What could have been done differently? If I'd made a minor adjustment here or there . . . another Eysen, changed the recipient . . . if Nostradamus—"

"Stop!" Mairis said. "Without you, humanity would be *over.*

You shortened the Missing Time. You got everything right. You hit the Switch!"

He nodded. "Maybe I did get it right, or at least right enough to give the archaeologist a chance to continue the work."

"And don't forget, he has Ovan and . . . Shanoah."

"Shanoah," he whispered, as if her name were a prayer.

───────────

Later, Trynn and Mairis were on the shore, heading to a dinner with Welhey, when Mairis saw a figure stumbling toward them. "That guy doesn't look so good," she said, pointing out the silhouette to Trynn. "We should help him."

"Yes," Trynn said, picking up his pace to get to the man, but after only a few steps, he saw who it was.

Mairis, now running toward him, had seen, too.

"Mudd! Mudd!" She almost knocked him down as she wrapped herself around him.

Mudd started coughing.

"Oh, I'm sorry! Are you okay? You're hurt, aren't you? What happened? They said you were dead."

"I'm not."

"I can see that!" She hugged him again, this time more gently. "Where did you even come from? How?"

"It's a long story," he said.

"Tell me everything!"

"Soon," he said, catching his breath.

"Are you okay?" she asked again. "Should we get you to a cell-framer?"

"I just came from one. Welhey made sure I saw the best. He also told me where I could find you." He smiled. "The cell-framer said I'm going to be fine."

"You don't look fine," she said, standing back to study him—bruises and scrapes, a limp, and he appeared dangerously thin.

"It'll take a few weeks to recover."

"Recover from what?" Her stern look went to elation and then back. "What happened?"

"It was kind of rough, I'll say that. And I'll tell you all about it, but the most important thing is that *you're* alive, and I'm only alive because I refused to die without kissing you one more time."

"Well, let's take care of that." She giggled. "As long as you promise not to die after I kiss you . . . or ever."

"Promise," he said.

She kissed Mudd. Trynn watched, beaming, content for the moment that there was at least one happy ending.

---

### END
#### of Book Eight

#### Book Nine
**Cosega Shine**, the final installment of the Cosega Sequence, available here.

To be notified of future Cosega releases
Sign up here or follow me on Amazon here

**click here for Cosega Shine
Book Nine, the final installment of
the Cosega Sequence**

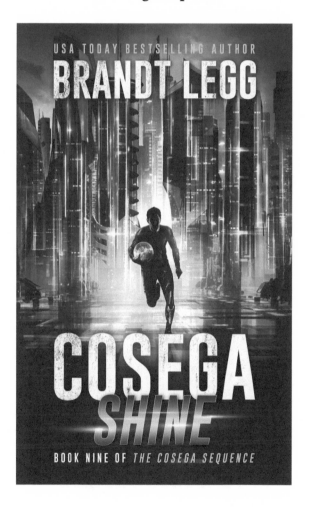

# GLOSSARY

**Abstract** – Etheren in exile. Some believe he may be a man called *Eastwood*.

**Adjoa** – Etheren shaman and close confidant of Grayswa.

**AI-Toss-Torpedoes** – AI-controlled missile about the size of a bottle of wine.

**Air-distorters** – Sonic weapon that temporarily changes the composition of the air.

**Airsliders** – Jet-propelled scooters equipped with laser munitions.

**Alik's cloak** – Shield using Cosegan specs that renders Eysens invisible to other Eysens.

**Anjee** – Government scientist, old friend of Trynn.

**Avery** – Caretaker at Old North Church in Boston.

**Aylantik Foundation** – Secretive organization planning, preparing, and shaping the future.

**Blaxers** – Booker Lipton's private army of operatives.

**Blox** – Ability to stop Myree, an ancient form of telepathy practiced by Etherens and some others.

**Booker Lipton** — World's wealthiest man. Rip's sponsor. Searching for Eysens and related artifacts.

**Boslow** – Etheren settlement where Arc hides.

**Brite lite birds** – Type of bird that glowed like a firefly, with colored feathers that instantly burned flesh on contact. Staring at too many at once could lead to temporary blindness.

**Bustang** – Havlos military base.

**Bullington** - See *The Bullington*

**Cafinator** – Globotite-cooled photon and sonic merged generator used to construct the great cities.

**Camsoen** – Etheren settlement.

**Cardd** – Trynn's assistant.

**Cass** – Jarvo's most trusted aide. Daughter of a legendary Havlos military leader.

**Cell-framers** — Cosegan health scientist who devised methods to manipulate human cells, and taught people to do it themselves.

**Change-point** – Moment in time when an unknown event changed the trajectory of Cosegan civilization from advancing to even higher enlightenment and technological wonders, to that of a primitive reset that became humanity eleven million years later.

**Chief** – Head of guardians.

**Cira** – Rip and Gale's daughter.

**Clastier** – An early recipient of an Eysen.

**Cloud sweeper** – Bird with gray and white coloring and a thirty-foot wingspan.

**Coils** – Elite and lethal unit of the Havlos Enforcers.

**Cosegan Time** – The time of Trynn in Cosega.

**Cosegans** – Rip and Gale's name for the people and society that existed on earth eleven million years ago.

**Craneport** – Small Havlos naval base, shipbuilding plant, and commercial port.

**Crimsonsor** – Cosegan city. Home to 3.7 million.

**Crying Man** – Rip and Gale's name for Trynn.

**Draycam** – Cosegan wanted for a horrible crime. He had been entertaining the thought of killing the Arc and overthrowing the entire Circle.

**Drifson** – Imaze historian.

**Dream Senders** – Etherens who had deepened their meditative and Myree talents to the point where they could send thoughts into the dreams and, in certain cases, meditative minds of people in the far future.

**Dreemelle** – Provider of Revon.

**EAMI** – Eysen Anomaly Matter Interference. Theory that Eysens may have the ability to create anomalies and interfere in scientific measurement and technologically based equipment—in effect, changing reality, or at least making it appear to have been changed.

**Earliests** – Cosegan term for their ancestors.

**Eastwood** – Legendary Etheren who disappeared in Havlos lands.

**Enders** – Highly classified subgroup of the predictive league. They studied all aspects of alternate insertions.

**Enfii Energy** – Major Havlos energy and mining company.

**Enforcers** – Havlos security forces.

**Epic-seam** – Space-time tear located inside the spectrum belt that allows the Imazes to travel to the far-future and back.

**Eternal Falls** – A three-thousand-foot waterfall. One of the natural wonders of the Cosegan world.

**Etherens** – Part of the Cosegan population who practiced deep meditation, lived with nature, and mined globotite and other natural minerals and herbs.

**Eysen** – A basket-ball sized sphere which contained a complete record of all existence. Named for an ancient word meaning "To hold all the stars in your hand."

**Eysen Core** – The energetic power center of an Eysen. Explosive and catastrophically dangerous.

**Eysen realms** – Places existing only within, or created by, Eysens.

**Eysenist** – Another name for Eysen makers. Scientists who create and study Eysens.

**Far Future** – Cosegan term for the period of time when

modern humans, such as the Egyptians, Leonardo da Vinci, and Rip and Gale, live.

**Far Past** – The period beginning a million years, or longer, before Trynn's time.

**Finality** – The moment of exact perfection when all events of human history are in correct alignment across all of existence.

**Finebeale trees** – Type of tree in Cosegan time.

**Flammable Fog** (also **Burning Sky**) – A thick gray haze introduced into large areas, then set ablaze to turn the air into an inferno.

**Flores** – Bush that produced a lemon-sized wild berry that tasted like chocolate and custard.

**Flyers** – Guardians wearing jet packs

**FlyWatcher** – Self-propelled flying camera with a 360-degree view.

**Fray** – Imaze member on mission flight with Shanoah.

**Gale Asher** – Rip's wife. Cira's mother. Former National Geographic reporter.

**Glenn** – Former head of the Imazes appointed to investigate the saboteur.

**Globotite** – Rare air mineral required in Eysen making and insertions.

**Globotite Censors** (Sometimes called **Detectors**) – Equipment able to detect finished Globotite within a range of several kilometers.

**Globotite Maps** – Records purporting to show locations of Globotite finds, mines, and potential veins.

**GlobeRunner** – Etherens and others who transport and smuggle Globotite.

**Glotons** – Photon glow light sticks used by Imazes.

**Goeze** – Triangular vehicles of light that enlarge depending on the number of passengers and payload. Can fly or drive. (Sometimes called "light energy vehicle" or LEV.)

**Grayswa** – Etheren elder. The oldest living shaman.

**Guardians** – Cosegan security force.

**Guin** – Trynn's late wife. Mother of Mairis.

**Hall of Shifting Pasts** – Shows possible and actual past events. Similar to the Room of a Million Futures.

**HALO** – High altitude low open jumps for military deployment from an aircraft.

**Havloses** – People on the other side of Earth during Cosegan time.

**Health-lounges** – Cosegan social gathering spot where natural juices and infused mineral waters are served.

**HI MEMS** – Hybrid Insect Micro-Electro-Mechanical System. Weapons created by implanting them into insects during the larva stage. Possessed by Both Havloses and Varangians.

**High-peak** – Trynn's secret lab.

**Historics** - Holographic pop-ups which display the history or facts of a subject, person, or place.

**HITE** – Hidden Information and Technology Exchange. The covert technology handler for the US government.

**Hoawep Island** – Isolated island located in the Casnadia Sea. Hoawep is also the Cosegan word meaning "dream."

**Huang** – Colleague of Rip's, and a brilliant Eysen researcher.

**Imazes** – Part of Cosegan population who live and work in space. They attempt flights into the far future.

**Infer-gun** – Laser weapon capable of inflicting death, or merely stunning their target depending on the setting.

**Infinity Switch** – Contrivance apparatus by which Trynn can set all events to permanent and unchangeable by any external means.

**Insertion** – Act of placing Eysens into the far future.

**Instrosen** – Purported operating manual for Eysens.

**IS-mechanism** – Component within an Eysen that makes it susceptible to Infinity Switch settings.

**ISS** – Imaze Space Summit on a high and massive plateau.

**Jaxx** – Arms dealer.

**Jenso** – Woman who helped design the Cosegan light cities, and Circle member. Sometimes called "the moon mystic."

**Joefyeser** – Etheren GlobeRunner.

**Joiner trees** – Tree in Cosegan time. Limbs grew up to one hundred fifty feet from the trunk to join and wrap around the branches of neighboring joiner trees.

**Julae** – Etheren GlobeRunner.

**Kalor Locke** — A deadly rival of Booker's and the Foundation for Eysens. He used to run a secret government agency.

**Kavid** – Etheren. Prayta's friend.

**Kaynor system** — Section of the universe near the spectrum belt.

**Kenner** – Son of Far past Eysen Maker/inventor Veeshal.

**Kickers** – Gang of thugs employed by Havlos mafia (the **Siccs**).

**Killtrons** – Havlos killer robots. Killtronics (or Killtrons for short) were lethal, highly-acrobatic killing machines with AI-assisted operating systems which can be controlled from a faraway base, and also have the capability to act autonomously.

**Knowns** – Descendants who knew who they were and were known to the center.

**Kwana** – The Arc's given name.

**Lantis** – The official name of the hidden Cosegan island Protectorate.

**Light woman** – Dreemelle, the provider of Revon.

**LightShaping** – Cosegan method of manipulating various forms of light for manufacturing and construction.

**Lorne** – Kalor Locke's assistant.

**Lumen Tower** – Location of Markol's lab in Solas.

**Lusa** – Imaze science officer.

**MAHEM** – Laser-sighted Magneto Hydrodynamic Explosive Munition. Possessed by both Havloses and Varangians.

**Mairis** – Trynn's daughter.

**Malachy** – Saint Malachy, an early recipient of an Eysen.

**Mind-crystals** – Cosegan computers (a million times more advanced than PCs and Macs.

**Missing-Time** – Period between the end of Cosegan time

and the beginning of modern human history.

**Mistwave Forest** – Coastal forest around High-peak.

**Miximilization** – Remedy for Revon.

**Mudd** – Havlos scrounger.

**Musa** – African king, and Eysen recipient.

**Myree** – Ability to read thoughts and, in some cases, communicate through minds.

**Naperton** – Small Cosegan coastal town.

**Nashunite** – Mineral required in Eysen making.

**Nassar** – Trynn's assistant.

**Nels** – Havlos scientist.

**Nogoff trees** – Type of tree in Cosegan time.

**Nostradamus** – Sixteenth century seer.

**NSA** – The US National Security Agency.

**Nystals** – Havlos naval base.

**Odeon Chip** – A special Eysen component, created by Trynn, which among other things, links Eysens and enhances them.

**OOPart** – Artifact found in an unusual context that does not fit the accepted historical or archeological timeline.

**Oordan-field** – Area of space. Sometimes considered part of the spectrum belt.

**Ovan** – Old scientist who does equations to help decide who gets Eysens in the far future.

**Particled** – To vaporize and obliterate something.

**Prayta** – Etheren woman who supplies Trynn with minerals.

**Predictive League** – Affiliation of thousands of Cosegan scientists researching the Far future and the Eysen's effects.

**Present Day** – The time of Rip and Gale.

**Protectorate** – The hidden island where Cosegans preserve their culture.

**Pulsers** – Colored, asteroid-like energy masses that can threaten ships in or near the spectrum belt.

**Quatrains** – Prophecies written by Nostradamus.

**Qwaterrun** – Havlos port city where Trynn had set up the

new Eysen facilities.

**Red Guardians** – Top division within the elite Cosegan security force.

**Revon** – Cosegan herb that, at the risk of serious side effects, substantially increases cognitive performance.

**Rip - Ripley Gaines** - Archaeologist who discovered first Eysen.

**Roemers** – Giant butterflies with a three-foot wingspan.

**Room of a Million Futures** –Vast space as part of an Eysen research facility that displays countless holographic projections showing ever-changing views into the Far Future.

**Salvator Mundi** – Painting by Leonardo da Vinci depicting Jesus Christ.

**Savina** – Colleague of Rip's and a brilliant Eysen researcher.

**Screamer gun** – Lethal laser rifle, named for the loud sound it made when fired.

**Scopes** – Goggles that decipher light.

**Sea of Casnadia** – A neutral sea in Cosegan times.

**Seismic-seven** – Desperate Imaze technique to "reboot" a ship during spectrum bombardment.

**Senni** – Etheren. Kavid's great-great grandmother.

**Sennogleyne** – Mineral required in Eysen making.

**Seven Sections** – The division of lands among Havlos populations.

**Shadow shifter** – People created from the ethers by Etheren shamans. Capable of physical activities.

**Shank** – Powerful Circle member.

**Shanoah** – Imaze commander. Trynn's girlfriend.

**Siccs** – Havlos mafia.

**Sinwind** – An outlying Cosegan settlement where Trynn was to meet Dreemelle.

**Skyways** – Moving, floating, and ever-changing sidewalks. Also part of the skyway energy project Trynn had been leading.

**Slights** – Places in Cosega cities where light and surveillance does not reach.

**Sodew** – Herbal infused mineral water.

**Solas** – Largest Cosegan city, and also the Capitol.

**Spartan Gun** – Varangian laser rifle based on Havlos and Cosegan designs.

**Spectrum belt** – Section of space that must be crossed to reach the **Epic-seam**.

**Sphere** – Another name for Eysens.

**Spressen** – Warm herbal drink favored by Cosegans.

**Star-leader** – Cosegan top military rank. Awarded by Shank.

**StarToucher trees** – A type of tree in Cosegan time that could grow to be five hundred feet tall.

**Stave** – Imaze. Shanoah's late husband.

**Strandband** – Cosegan command center (worn on wrist) that can access and project continuous streams of data.

**Stone spheres** – Representations of Eysens created in Costa Rica by ancient people.

**Suicide protocol** – Imaze oath and final directive. In the event an Imaze is stuck in the Far Future, immediate suicide is required.

**Sunphie** – Prison attendant during Jenso's incarceration. Sunphie is also an old Cosegan word meaning "light."

**Super Eysen** – Also known as "Giant Eysen." Project by Kalor Locke to amplify and control the power of multiple Eysens.

**Sweed** – Imaze pilot. Second in command. Shanoah's closest friend.

**Switch** (Also called **Infinity Switch**) — Contrivance apparatus by which Trynn can set all events to permanent and unchangeable by any external means.

**Teakki trees** – Type of tree in Cosegan time.

**Teason** – Etheren settlement where Grayswa, Julae, Prayta, Kavid, and Mairis reside.

**Tekfabrik** – Multipurpose nano-fabric capable of changing color, size, and texture. Self-cleaning. Fireproof.

**Tenth Eysen** – Created by Markol, inserted into Florida in 1974, said to be the key to accessing the Missing Time.

**Tenyao** – Booker's assistant.

**Terminus clock** – Linked algorithm displaying the time remaining until the Terminus Doom destroys humanity.

**Terminus Doom** – Mysterious prophesied end of humanity.

**TeV** – A measurement in physics eV or electronvolt (with T being a prefix for tera) demonstrating the amount of kinetic energy gained by a single electron.

**The Arc** – Leader of Cosegans. One of the oldest women.

**The blind** – Cousin of a black hole. A place in space where communications and electronics fail.

**The Bullington** – Imaze ship piloted by Maicks.

**The Center** – Place(s) where Shanoah helps Etheren and Cosegan descendants.

**The Circle** – Cosegan council of elders. The leaders of the Cosegan society.

**The Conners** – Imaze ship piloted by Sweed.

**The Enders** – Subgroup of the predictive league. Enders studied all aspects of alternate insertions and sought to establish other avenues to utilize the Eysens in anti-Doom efforts to defeat the end times.

**The Foundation** – The Aylantik Foundation. A secretive organization with seemingly unlimited funding employing futurists, scientists, engineers, economists, as well as former members of the military and intelligence communities.

**The Reach** – A 3,000 foot building of light and sound. Tallest occupied building in Solas.

**The Reno** – Imaze ship. Small space craft capable of being flown solo.

**The Stave** – Imaze ship piloted by Shanoah. Named for her late husband.

**The Works** – Far past research center under the control of Veeshal.

**Time-breathing** – Issue of coping with changes in quality of air between eras affected by the weight of human existence, their triumphs and tragedies, their love and war, their truth and lies.

**Time Shock** – Caused by something extremely traumatic, and that afterwards almost everything dies, mutates, distorts, or collapses, resulting in something new.

**Tracer** – Field unit leader of the guardians. Second in command under the Chief.

**Trynn** — Also known as "Crying Man." He is the most important Eysen Maker. Shanoah's boyfriend.

**Tunssee** – Cosegan city.

**Twistle trees** – Type of tree in Cosegan time.

**UQP** or **Universe Quantum Physics** – Ambitious attempt to create a new area of science involving quantum mechanics, aspects of physics at the nanoscopic level, metaphysics, subatomic particles, the theory of everything, infinite layers, energetic manipulations, extreme neurological control, forces of space, and concepts of time, all within the reality of a multiverse.

**Vans** – Kalor Locke's strike force (also known as **Varangians**). Led by his brother, Parson Locke.

**Varangians** – Kalor Locke's army of elite special ops. They took their name from "The Varangian Guard," a band of Viking mercenaries.

**Varvara Port** – Regional trade port of the Havloses.

**Veeshal** – Far Past Eysen maker/inventor.

**Visuals** – Marble-sized floating cameras that could be deployed by the thousands.

**Vultures** – Sophisticated flying troop-carrying gunships based on the V-22 Osprey.

**Weals** – Personal spy for the Arc. Former Guardian.

**Welhey** – Circle Member and friend of Trynn.

**Wild Wandering River** – A 2,900 mile river that ended at the Eternal Falls.

# ACKNOWLEDGMENTS

*Cosega Switch* was fun to write. In a way, it wraps up much of the Cosega Sequence. Although one book remains, the next one will be a bit different from what you're used to. Just wait, you'll see how.

Before I get into my usual expressions of gratitude, I must make a special mention of a special woman who read every single book I published and always offer kind enthusiastic support, the mother of an old friend, Judith Anderson who I knew for half a century and yet rarely saw recently left this earthly plain. She made a difference to me, to many. She will be greatly missed.

So many wonderful people to thank – First to Ro and Teakki, for all the inspiration, and for putting up with so many of these Cosegans living and traveling with us.

My mom, Barbara Blair, for starting me on the road to all these adventures, and then for sticking around to read about them.

Joan Osborne, who always goes the extra mile, even when bogged down in the muddy parts of life, even when the world crashes to a stop, I always appreciate the use of your dynamic mind.

Gil Forbes, who finds errors in concepts – excellent discoveries delivered with colorful rhetoric.

Jack Llartin, my longtime copy editor, who seems to come from a magic land where commas know their place and laws of grammar are seldom violated.

Elena, at Li Graphics, for making one last exciting cover, one of my favorites.

And, finally, to Teakki, a true creative and fine outlining partner, who also patiently waited to show me a funny video of "the cutest dog in the world" or maybe an "amazing cat" until I finished writing each day. (Can't we just go walk on the beach?)

Most of all, to all of my readers, the ones that have read everything I've published, and the ones who have just finished their first Booker thriller or Chasing adventure. You make it possible for me to live this dream, to create these worlds, to live with these characters and tell these stories. Thank you for the time you've shared with me via my books. Please drop me an email any time. Responding to reader emails is one of my favorite parts of the day!

I'd like to give extra thanks to some special readers and/or members of my street team for their support, kindness, reviews (I love reviews), suggestions, and encouragement.

(If I left anyone out, I apologize. Please forgive me, and let me know. I can fix it!)

Please don't let the fact that there are so many of you do anything to diminish your importance to me. This ever-expanding group is the fuel to my creative fire.

In alphabetical order (by first name):

Adam Tanner, Alec Redwine, Amber Hunt, Anne Kaplan, Bette Lou Thompson, Bill Borchert, Billie Harkey, Blake Dowling, Bob Browder, Bob Dumas, Brian C. Coffey, Brian Schnizlein, Cara Johnson, Carl Howard, Carol M, Cathie Harrison, Cheryl Olson, Chet Keough, Chis Bond, Chris Tomlinson, Christine Moritz, Christopher Bowling, Chuck Gonzalez, Cid Chase, Claudia Wells, Consuelo Ashworth, Debra Harper, Dennis Lowe, Derek Redmond, Diane Smith, Diane Whitehead, Donna Slaton, Doug Wise, Douglas Dersch, Douglas Meek, Elaine Dill, Ernest Manpino, Ernest Pino, Frank Fusco, Frank Murphy, Fred Bowditch, Gary Human, Gene Leach, Gene Legg, Gerry Adler,

Gil Forbes, Gillian Charlton, Glenda Dykstra, Glenn Legge, Ingo Michehl, Irene Witoski, Jacky Dallaire, Jan Dallas, Janice Gildea, Jean Sink, Joan Osborne, John McDonald, John Nicholson, John Nunley, John Oliver, John Wood, Judith Anderson, Judy Hammer, Julie Price, Justin Lear, Karen Mack, Karen Markovitz, Kat Heyer, Katherine Atwood, Kathleen Robbins, Kathy Creecy, Kathy Troc, Ken Clute, Ken Friedman, Kevin Burton, Kyle Dahlem, LA Dumas, Leslie Royce, Linda Loparco, Linda Petty, Liz Miller, Marcel Roy, Marie Maritz, Mark Perlmutter, Martha Heckel, Martin Gunnell, Melanie C. Hansen, Michael Ferrel, Michael Picco, Mick Flanigan, Mike Brannick, Mike Lauland, Mitzi McAllister, Nancy Lamanna, Nigel Revill, Normand Girard, Pam Gilbert, Patricia Ruby, Paul Gyorke, Peggy Gulli, Randy Howerter, Raymond Aston, Rick Ferris, Rick Woodring, Rob Weaver, Rob Zorger, Robert Smith, Robyn Shanti, Ron Babcock, S. Michael Smith, S.W. Kelly Myers, Sally Vedder, Sam Rhoades, Samantha Jackson, Sandie Parrish, Sandra Zuiderhoek, Satish Bhatti, Sharon Moffatt, Stephane Peltier, Sue Steel, Susan McGuyer, Susan Moore, Susan Norlund, Susan Powell, Terry Myers, Tom Strauss, Tony Sommer, Tricia Turner, Vicki Gordon, Virginia Beck, Vivienne Du Bourdieu.

Many authors I've met along the way have impacted my craft and career as well. This is far from a complete list, but each one included has made a difference to me:

Robert Gatewood, Mike Sager, Craig Martelle, Michael Anderle, Mark Dawson, Nick Thacker, Ernest Dempsey, John Grisham, A. Kelly Pruitt, Eric J. Gates, Dale DeVino, Phil M. Williams, Jennifer Theriot, Haris Orkin, Brian Meeks, Jennifer Theriot, Michelle McCarty, Zoe Saadia, and to the memory of Mollie Gregory, Judith Lucci, and Matthew Mather.

There are so many friends of mine who are creatives as well. Many of them are from Taos, where parts of this story are set. Their work inspires my work (and my life):

Tony Schueller, David Manzanares, Geraint Smith, Michael Hearne, Don Richmond, Lenny Foster, Jared Rowe, Jimmy

Stadler, Scott Thomas, Carol Morgan-Eagle, Deonne Kahler, Bart Anderson, Jill Fuller, Ernest James, Jenny Bird, Angelika Maria Koch, Brad Hockmeyer, Verne Verona, Brooke Tatum, Markus Kolber, Terrie Bennett, and many others!

Speaking of reviewers, the prolific readers and top Amazon reviewers who have been of great support to my work deserve extra recognition. Thank you so much, and special gratitude, to the remarkable Grady Harp, and to whoever the reviewer "Serenity" is!

There is a goal among some authors to turn readers into fans, fans into super fans, and super fans into friends. I am fortunate to have been able to achieve that goal on numerous occasions.

Thank you.

*Thanks for sharing the adventure!*

## Please help spread the word
If you enjoyed this book, I'd really appreciate it if you would consider posting a review wherever you purchased it (even a few words).
Reviews are the greatest way to help an author.
And, please tell your friends.

## I'd love to hear from you
Questions, comments, whatever.
Email me through my website, BrandtLegg.com and I'll definitely respond
(usually within a few days).

## Join my Inner Circle
If you want to be the first to hear about my new releases, advance reads, occasional news and more, join my Inner Circle at:
BrandtLegg.com

## ABOUT THE AUTHOR

USA TODAY Bestselling Author Brandt Legg uses his unusual real life experiences to create page-turning novels. He's traveled with CIA agents, dined with senators and congressmen, mingled with astronauts, chatted with governors and presidential candidates, had a private conversation with a Secretary of Defense he still doesn't like to talk about, hung out with Oscar and Grammy winners, had drinks at the State Department, been pursued by tabloid reporters, and spent a birthday at the White House by invitation from the President of the United States.

At age eight, Legg's father died suddenly, plunging his family into poverty. Two years later, while suffering from crippling migraines, he started in business, and turned a hobby into a multi-million-dollar empire. National media dubbed him the "Teen Tycoon," and by the mid-eighties, Legg was one of the top young entrepreneurs in America, appearing as high as number twenty-four on the list (when Steve Jobs was #1, Bill Gates #4, and Michael Dell #6). Legg still jokes that he should have gone into computers.

By his twenties, after years of buying and selling businesses, leveraging, and risk-taking, the high-flying Legg became ensnarled in the financial whirlwind of the junk bond eighties. The stock market crashed and a firestorm of trouble came down. The Teen Tycoon racked up more than a million dollars in legal fees, was betrayed by those closest to him, lost his entire fortune, and ended up serving time for financial improprieties.

After a year, Legg emerged from federal prison, chastened and wiser, and began anew. More than twenty-five years later, he's now using all that hard-earned firsthand knowledge of conspiracies, corruption and high finance to weave his tales. Legg's books pulse with authenticity.

His series have excited nearly a million readers around the world. Although he refused an offer to make a television movie about his life as a teenage millionaire, his autobiography is in the works. There has also been interest from Hollywood to turn his thrillers into films. With any luck, one day you'll see your favorite characters on screen.

He lives in the Pacific Northwest, with his wife and son, writing full time, in several genres, containing the common themes of adventure, conspiracy, and thrillers. Of all his pursuits, being an author and crafting plots for novels is his favorite.

For more information, please visit his website, or to contact Brandt directly, email him: Brandt@BrandtLegg.com, he loves to hear from readers and always responds!

BrandtLegg.com

# BOOKS BY BRANDT LEGG

Chasing Rain

Chasing Fire

Chasing Wind

Chasing Dirt

Chasing Life

Chasing Kill

Chasing Risk

Chasing Mind

Chasing Time

Chasing Lies

Chasing Fear

Chasing Lost

Cosega Search (Cosega Sequence #1)

Made in United States
Troutdale, OR
07/02/2023

10931416R00202